UNIVERSAL DEFENDER
<BOOK 4>

BLACKENED SUNS

AND

BLOODSHOT SKIES

BY GREGOR FJELLREV

BLUE FORGE PRESS

Port Orchard ✸ Washington

Universal Defender: Blackened Suns and Bloodshot Skies
Copyright 2024
by Gregor Fjellrev

First eBook Edition April 2024
First Print Edition April 2024

ISBN 979-8-89439-008-6

For information about film, reprint or other subsidiary rights, contact: blueforgegroup@gmail.com

Blue Forge Press is the print division of the volunteer-run, federal 501(c)3 nonprofit, Blue Legacy (EIN 83-4307421), founded in 1989 and dedicated to supporting artisans marginalized due to race, age, disability, economics or other factors. We strive to empower storytellers from all walks of life with our four divisions: Blue Forge Press, Blue Forge Films, Blue Forge Gaming, and Blue Forge Sound. Find out more at www.BlueForgeGroup.org

Blue Forge Press
7419 Ebbert Drive Southeast
Port Orchard, Washington 98367
blueforgepress@gmail.com
360-550-2071 ph.txt

Choose defiance. Fight forever.
Never stop training.

Universal Defender

Book 1: Today I Save Myself

Book 2: Fire to Burn the Stars

Book 3: Enter Unmaker

Book 4: Blackened Suns and Bloodshot Skies

Miles Radien and the Cult of the Chaosmaker

Veralis Stratenheim and the Bridge Across Fire

Miles Radien and the Gauntlet of Doom

Arakai Selendica and the Nexus of Torment

More by Gregor Fjellrev

Reticent (Angels of Anarchy)

Talenostrum

Night of the Whapwolf

In Combat with Time

Redemption through Retribution in

the Grey Century of Anti-Revolution

An Introverted, Wanderlusting Martial Artist's

Commentaries on Musashi's Dokkōdō

www.BlueForgePress.com

Blackened Suns

and

Bloodshot Skies

by Gregor Fjellrev

Chapter the First
The Battle of Teyn-Var-Wolk

*"The difference between battle and war is that battle ends
and war begins when those who did not start on either
side's armies take up arms and join in, whatever the
reason."*
*—Jintako Bronzedrinker, upon the Lysanarr declaration of
War of Intervention against Highlord Razacora Faronelar
of the Taigron Imperius, c. early Sixth Cosmic Era*

Ten specialized and tailor-made spacecraft tore
through the Warp Channel at speeds nigh
incomprehensible. These were the personal ships of
their pilots, the kinds of vessels one would live within.
Tailored to the men and women who flew them over
years, decades, a lifetime of practice, honing and ironing
out their particular styles. Each one was arguably on par
with a Carrier-Class vessel in value, but imagine if one
had taken all the money that builds a Carrier ship, and
instead put it all into making a single thirty to fifty foot
wingspanned craft and making it the best possible
version of itself it could be.

"This is Loaf aboard the *Aura Runner* to David Company," Miles Sorvenjar Radien's voice spoke over the comms. "Begin pre-warp-exit final check."

"This is Rat Tail. All systems ready," was the first reply, from Chira Slicehorn, referring to herself by her callsign from her ship, the *Rerorium Spear*. Like how Radien's nickname was Loaf, Rat Tail's own had a story behind it. Much like all the other members of this ten-man squadron.

"Five Rings responding from the *Musashi*. I'm good," Kieran Ebensen's voice replied next. The only Human on the team, though still a battle brother to the rest of the squad, and thus considered better than Human (low as a bar that may be.) The same Kieran Ebensen who had liberated from the clutches of the Unmaker after being quite literally hit in the head hard enough to clear it. Five Rings came from how he always carried a pocket-sized copy of Miyamoto Musashi's Book of Five Rings on his person, and it spared him from a more embarrassing nickname, which likely would've been something along the lines of 'kickies,' for the fact of how he was very good at kicking people in melee combat.

"Spin-to-Win here, all systems aboard the *Talon of Kendra-Kai* are responding optimally and prepared for combat," the Woran Cos Ketrakoressian confirmed. Her nickname had to do with the fact that not only was her species notoriously resistant to dizziness, she also utilized this fact in sparring by constantly making spinning motions to intimidate opponents. She found it greatly amusing, which is why she did it.

"This is Blindsight aboard the *Barrel in the*

Darkness. Resonance Ring is fully charged, secondary weapons systems are ditto." The Noregenas Vulpian Marus Shirehailer always found great amusement when people tried to glean the hidden meanings and interpretations of his ship's name, but the truth was that he had thought of that string of words while in a state of utter delirium in his youth, brought about by a fever-like illness he had to deal with during that time. The name just stuck, and he had used it ever since, much like how Miles Radien had come up with the symbol that was now the sigil of Torvaltyne Bastion, that he simply drew five lines one day, many years ago, and that symbol just stuck with him.

"Neckscarf here, from the *Boopforge.* All weapons are charged and loaded, onboard and personal. I'm ready to boop all of our enemies many times, with very large payload missiles, cannons, and all armaments so that I may boop them all to death, and so—"

"Wulfy, quit hogging the comms," Radien cut in, to a comically exaggerated grumble from the Vulpian-Loriken hybrid, oftentimes simply referred to as a Folf. Though his given name wasn't actually Wulfy, it is what everyone called him, as his birth name was a series of borks and barks that roughly translated as 'is-very-folf of the family Shattercross.' All part of the bit, of course. One needs a bit of levity before such a tense situation as not only imminent battle, but the maiden battle of this elite unit of pilots who simply had the common belief between them that a unit like this would be a good idea. Hence the name David Company, a squadron of ten ships that were the Davids to take down Goliaths. Their purpose was to be the ten wasps that tore a tank to shreds, but in space.

"Breaking Wheel here, the *Constellation Scribe* is primed and ready to paint the stars with what's left of our enemies. Shining Blade's battery is fully charged, and my cannon munitions are good." The Corvuseine Lan-Kei had earned his callsign with the fact that as an amateur artificer, he had created a signature Power Scroll he called the Scroll of the Breaking Wheel, and desperately sought a good reason to test them out, to the amusement of many, and his exaggerated grumbles. Or at least, the closest thing a biped crow could make to grumbles. Something about using them on the Holographic Arena's proving grounds just didn't feel the same as a proper use in battle. Nobody could blame him, but they could at least chuckle.

"This is Stonecourt, the *Void Hunter* is all systems go." The Loriken Soraine Nylthan simply happened to be the case that he could easily be mistaken for a gravel-chewing lord of edge, with a ship called the *Void Hunter*, and a primary payload weapon called Moonshredder Missiles. However, Soraine was no such mockery of style. He was a calm-mannered and level-headed lupine with a passion for mixology, as well as combat and the study of martial arts. He had earned his callsign by rather embarrassingly forgetting that during a game of Phaseball, he was on a stone court rather than a grass court, and cracked his coccyx with the maneuver that was not meant to be performed on stone courts. Thus his nickname was subsequently born.

"Magnet reporting from the *Doomslapper* here, the Gentlemen and I stand ready." The Neo-Proto Ascendant Kiri may have been short in stature, but this stocky build veiled a deadly precise and honed warrior, who knew how to have a good time while utterly laying waste to her foes. Including foes that take the form of server racks after a frankly hilariously embarrassing incident involving said server racks and a pair of electromagnets.

"This is Red Dot reporting, I'm ready and raring to go." Last but most certainly not least, Maria Kenetar of the Nuberi Felinian species made her presence known from aboard the *Mow of Destruction*. Of the several Felinian species that still inhabited the universe, the main difference between the Nuberi Felinian and the Felinian Aliken Sor were not only by appearance, with several Human biologists comparing the former to lynxes and the latter to house cats, 'if you were to hold out a red dot from a laser pointer, both would charge at it. But only a Nuberi would forget that they're the ones holding the pointer.' This analogy, in fact, was why Maria had this particular callsign among David Company, an incident wherein she indeed had forgotten that she was the one holding the laser pointer.

Then again, no one who ever held a nickname whilst holding a rank within any military held a dignified nickname. One's nickname was always born of the most embarrassing thing you did on base within those first few months.

In fact, the main reason why Miles Radien's nickname and subsequent callsign was 'loaf' was because of an incident within one of Torvaltyne Bastion's bars where he was 'loafing' on one of the barstools at the Honor's Stand Mead Hall, where an aforementioned member of David Company, none other than the Folf Wulfy, had snuck up behind Radien whilst in his quadruped form, before leaping up and grabbing the loafing Radien by his tail, yanking him off the barstool in most comical manner, especially for the noise he made when it happened. It was not uncommon for shapeshifters to have both a biped and quadruped form to switch between, depending on their mood.

With all ten fighters reporting their readiness, Radien addressed the group once more.

"All right, we all know what we gotta do here, so let's not waste time before we exit the Warp Channel," Radien briefed. "We've got to make sure Teyn-Var-Wolk's defenses hold until reinforcements arrive, and we're the tip of that spear. It's gonna be a rough exit, but that's what we're here to do, to make sure the cavalry can get in and make mincemeat of the attacking Demons. As long as the planet's defense holds, Teyn-Var-Wolk won't fall."

Everyone stood ready, fingers resting above triggers and switches alike.

"True as it is, this is the first time the lot of us have flown together outside of training, the time is now to show the universe that us doing so is a good idea. Prepare to exit Warp Channel on my mark!"

Lan-Kei pressed a button on the *Constellation Scribe's* console to prepare to activate the Shining Blade weapon as soon as the group exited the Warp Channel.

"Three... Two..."

Two Pulsar Missiles aboard the *Aura Runner* finished their arming sequences.

"One... Mark!"

The group exited the Warp Channel, and the

literal trial by fire began. The ships quickly maneuvered to evade incoming enemy fire and suicide craft.

"Spin-To-Win, Blindsight, Breaking Wheel! Start knocking down those Carriers! Neckscarf, Stonecourt and Rat Tail, target their heavy weapons vessels! Magnet, hold the back line with your Defensive Drones and make sure the warp-in zone remains secure! Five Rings, Red Dot, you're with me! We gotta take out their siege batteries!"

Each of the groups broke off towards their targets with their respective 'ayes' and switched to group-specific communication channels.

The *Aura Runner, Musashi,* and *Mow of Destruction* sped towards Teyn-Var-Wolk's active Defense Grid, the shield that was keeping the Demonic ships at bay, and stopping them from beginning a ground invasion. The first of the Siege Lasers was quickly obliterated by a Pulsar Missile from the Aura Runner. The co-axial defensive laser batteries atop the ship and on its belly reflexively shot down inbound enemy missiles, even tagging a few Demonic fighter ships that got too close. The twin-linked autocannons of the *Musashi* tore through the vacuum of space and slammed into another one of the satellite-like siege weapons trying to bore a hole through the planet's shield. Normally, bullets require oxygen to fly, but the accelerant compound in space-worthy cannons was called Red Dust, and was not so restrained by the requirement of an atmosphere.

"Those siege batteries are using plasma shields, I'm switching to Kinetic as well!" Maria called out from her ship as she flipped a lever and the primary laser battery shunted and retracted back into the *Mow of*

Destruction as the hydraulics replaced the barrel assembly with the Tungsten Kinetic Cannon.

Radien could practically visualize the arguments aboard the Demonic Siege Lasers as they tried to turn one of the batteries towards the approaching ships of David Company. However, with their focus suddenly removed from breaching the shield around Teyn-Var-Wolk, they found themselves vulnerable to counter-assault from the local defenses.

Realizing this and subsequently correcting her aim, Maria fired a single shot from the cannon that would miss the closest Siege Laser, but the tungsten dart tore through space and accelerated to hypersonic speeds with the assistance of Teyn-Var-Wolk's gravity, and the dip in elevation put the round right on course with one of the other Siege Lasers, and the sheer force of the impact blew it to smithereens, harmlessly disintegrating as the shrapnel impacted the Defense Grid, or the shields of nearby ships.

"Damn! Nice aim, Red Dot!" Five Rings couldn't help but comment after opening fire and destroying the closer Siege Laser, now that the harder target was down.

"I know how to make my shots count!" she responded enthusiastically.

"*Toriyah!* Keep up the pressure, we got this!" Radien added.

Meanwhile, the trio of Marus, Ketrakoressian and Lan-Kei proceeded to cause no small amount of mayhem upon the transport ships that the Demons were fielding in this attack.

"Ready for the Resonance Ring?" Marus called

out to Ketrakoressian.

"Fire at the one I'm pinging you!"

The kickback from the shield-drill that was the primary weapon aboard the *Barrel in the Darkness* threw it back a solid hundred meters, throwing off the lock of an enemy missile and causing it to sail harmlessly off-course before detonating in empty space. The crackling ring of prismatic energy slammed against the shields of the Demonic Carrier, punching a hole clean through the impact spot with just how many different volatile energies were suddenly trying to occupy the same space.

Once the path was clear, Ketrakoressian used the opening in the shields to warp directly aboard the Carrier, and to its bridge. Wasting no time, she leaped into the air and hooked the Demon captain directly through the face with the talons on her feet and hurled him directly into his first officer, before pressing a few choice buttons on the captain's console and initiating a self-destruct in five seconds before jumping back aboard the *Talon of Kendra-Kai* at the minimum safe distance to watch the resulting explosion.

"I'm never gonna get tired of that trick!" The Woran Cos laughed once she was clear of the debris field.

The sleek and solid metallic black *Constellation Scribe* suddenly began to produce a blazing bright ring of energy around the tips of its wings until this razor-thin sheet of raw energy encircled the ship, and the engines boosted forward as Lan-Kei put himself on direct collision course with another carrier. The Shining Blade sliced clean through the enemy ship's shields, through the outer hull, through the hallways, corridors and crewmembers, until finally bouncing off of the main engine core itself and causing a critical gash that soon saw the Corvuseine outrunning a city-sized explosion aboard his ship to get away from the Carrier tearing itself apart from the sudden total meltdown of its core. His face as calm as his mind, the control levers of the *Constellation Scribe's* maneuvering engines turned and swiveled as the ship responded with a deadly dance of bouncing off of enemy fighters and bombers, cleaving through them with the residual charge that was still on the Shining Blade itself. "The wheel of death lands upon you, Demons!" Lan-Kei sent off as he regrouped with Marus and Ketrakoressian.

Chira, Wulfy and Soraine's ships seared through space as they approached several armed-to-the-teeth Demonic heavy siege craft.

"Let's make them regret ever setting foot in our reality!" the Dragoness aboard the *Rerorium Spear* encouraged, to the 'ayes' of both the pilots of the *Boopforge* and the *Void Hunter.* "I've got your flanks covered, knock 'em dead!"

The *Rerorium Spear* broke off to gun down the fighter ships that were making headway towards the trio as the *Boopforge* and the *Void Hunter* both marked their targets.

"Stonecourt, we can take down two at once with this one," Wulfy observed. "Fire your Moonshredder at the one behind this, and I can land a death blow on the core of the closer one!"

"That missile is gonna need a clear path through space if it's gonna land, Neckscarf," Soraine advised.

"I can rifle the barrel, Stonecourt," Wulfy responded.

"I'll rifle your barrel..."

"That had better be a promise!"

"Missile away!"

The glowing red accents of the *Boopforge* lit up the darkness of space as the ship tore through the vacuum, clearing the path for the Moonshredder, the ship's Crimson Ion Cannons tearing up the defensive guns and missile launchers aboard the Destroyer that stood between the Moonshredder Missile, and the Destroyer it was going for.

As soon as said missile cleared its obstacle, and its course was assured, the *Boopforge* about-faced in space to turn back towards its quarry. At the helm, the Folf at the yoke began to channel a sparking red lightning through his body until it reached his right arm, the same blazing red that accented his ship. Once the concentrated ball of crackling doom formed in his right hand, he jammed it into a panel aboard the control console to channel the attack through the ship's guns.

The *Boopforge* itself began to crackle with the blood-red lightning before finally firing off at the plating just below the Destroyer's core, the single most armored part of the ship. It was no match for the sheer shredding force of the attack, the core even less so. The explosion could easily be mistaken for a tear in space itself forming as the heaviest weapons of the attacking army were vaporized.

With arguably the most vital component of the mission in her hands, Kiri deployed the four defensive drones her ship, the *Doomslapper* carried. "Gentlemen,

Lattice Wall Configuration, sequence code three-six-two-one!" she ordered, and the vigilant sentries responded with a coordinated set of movements, orbiting the *Doomslapper* with constantly fluctuating shields that no energy weapon from the enemy could pierce.

"Xenon, start hitting the ones getting too close to the warp-in zone with your Ion Blast!"

The cyan spherical drone bearing that name responded in kind, firing off deadly precise streams of charged Ions at the enemies who kept trying to re-secure the area from the deadly Neo-Proto.

"Argon, activate Reflector Matrix!"

The light purple spherical drone unleashed a pulse of energy that reflected back all enemy projectiles right back into their attackers. The light show resultant of enemies exploding was most impressive.

"Krypton, assist Neon with programming the Lattice Wall! Once it's ready to fire, all four of you get on it!"

The respective golden yellow and bright red spherical drones soon beeped with confirmation that the Lattice Wall was ready to deploy. All four drones, whose actual technical designation was 'Servo-Spheres' shared the calculation data with each other before projecting a massive net-like grid across the darkness of space, which ensnared an entire enemy Frigate *and* Carrier, smashing them together as the Lattice Wall compressed and pushed them into each other, inevitably resulting in the total destruction of both enemy vessels.

"Gentlemen, begin Ultimate Photonic Distraction Maneuver!" Kiri addressed the four servo-spheres, as the four units synchronized their communications arrays so that their timings would know no error.

"Loaf to David Company, Magnet's starting the sequence now, let's fire off the flares and pull the Demons over to where the Gentlemen will be projecting the Localized Photon Array!"

All nine of the other vessels within David Company fired off taunting missiles at several Demonic Carriers and Destroyers, enough to get their attention, and challenge them to crush this puny ship like the insect it is, or at least, be welcome to utterly fail to try to.

"They're taking the bait, guys," Kiri said as the *Doomslapper's* scanners indicated a mass diversion of the attacking Demon forces.

"Excellent! Glad to hear it!" Kieran commented from aboard the *Musashi.* "You said it yourself, Loaf, this is the maiden battle of David Company! We've got to show the universe that us flying together is a good idea!"

The ten vessels met up in formation with each other, ready to meet the oncoming swarm of burning legions.

"Everyone, adjust your visual feeds to filter out the two hundred fifty-five color hexes Kiri's Gentlemen will have their Photon Diodes set to! It's gonna be incredibly distracting otherwise, but that's why we're doing it this way, to the enemy!"

As Radien explained his instructions, the ships of David Company followed suit, setting their viewscreens to block out the specific shades that the four Servo-Spheres would emit from what were essentially next-level LEDs as far as output was concerned.

"Magnet, the *Aura Runner's* isolated the local slip-space radio band frequency. I'm ready to transmit once you give me the go-ahead."

Techbooth, the AI system controlling the Aura Runner's computers, had managed to find the specific point in the latent EM band of space in this region that when he transmitted on, would somewhat 'glitch' through the fabric of space-time, and cause the transmission to be heard by all vessels capable of receiving transmissions of any kind. Whatever he was about to say, this entire section of the night sky was about to hear it. Or rather, what was about to be played, a *Volkarn Orkest,* or 'battle anthem' in the Death World Vulpian language. A *Volkarn Orkest* was the music you heard while utterly crushing your foes with your martial prowess, and tearing victory from the jaws of your enemies, along with their jaws as well, most likely.

"All systems ready, Tactician. On your mark," Kiri finally confirmed.

The Gentlemen switched on the sequence.

Radien slammed the large red button on his console labeled *DOLGELSE TOULTH. DOOM FOES.* "Now!"

Having begun to transmit from the *Aura Runner,* the song played across space itself, and through every speaker in this area of the cosmos. It was like one had just hacked every speaker aboard every ship and started playing music through it, which was *exactly* what was happening.

The confusion aboard the Demonic ships was thick enough to cut with a knife. All eyes planetside were suddenly fixed on this section of space, where ten ships stood ready to hold their ground against an entire Dark

Six Death Fleet.

The Gentlemen continued to fire off the photons that were harmless at first, just a light show across the darkness of space. But suddenly, they started to 'go live,' focused waves of photons, compressed into a laser that was like firing the concentrated light of a star at one's enemy. The bursts of heat that traveled along the light show's path at light's speed in the vacuum of space, punching holes left and right into the Demon Frigates, Carriers and Destroyers alike.

"*Aurok son-Deyl! Behold our power!*" Radien yelled the battlecry across the comms, and the ten ships of David Company all broke away to lay waste to the entire Demonic army that was threatening this world.

The *Boopforge* slammed into the shields of one of the Carriers, tearing straight through and into the hangar bay itself, and once the craft landed and screeched to a halt, the enemy soldiers responding to the sudden threat were met by the sleek black and red fighter vessel coursing with bright, crimson lightning. The raging and rippling ball of red doom tore through the air and slammed onto the ground, coalescing back into the solid form of the Loriken-Vulpian hybrid, baring his claws and challenging his foes to come get some.

Another ship landed next to the *Boopforge,* the *Musashi.* Kieran Ebensen calmly stepped out, adjusting his gloves, and hitting his knuckles together as electricity crackled through them, and channeled into his feet. Every kick this man was about to do would be imbued with the kind of electrical charge to catapult a person into a wall.

"Shall we?" Kieran asked Wulfy as he walked up to join the Folf in the soon-to-begin melee, facing off against a horde of Demons.

"We shall," Wulfy replied, and the two charged forward.

The Folf bowled his hand across the ground, channeling red lightning into a ball that flew forward and detonated, sending multiple troopers flying, as Kieran slammed his heel into a Demon's jaw, sending it careening into it ally, and wasting no time laying a veritable flurry of electrically-charged kicks against his foes.

Demons once again were hurled into the air by the force of a crimson detonation. The Shattercross family heir had slammed his fist into the ground, charging it with the energy that crackled through his arms and legs like fire running through his veins and at his command. Even the eleven-foot tall Monument Breaker that had just entered the fray didn't stand a chance, as a combination of punches, claw strikes and kicks from the arms that still coursed with the live lightning of the folf seemed to 'disassemble' the Demon by chunks of its flesh, muscle, and bones being torn away by the strikes being laid upon it.

Meanwhile, on another one of the command vessels, the Firesky Demon captaining the ship was barking nigh incomprehensible orders to his subordinates, all too late to stop the inbound Resonance Ring fired from Marus Shirehailer's ship, *The Barrel in the Darkness*. With the entire bridge of the ship suddenly vulnerable to an enemy warp-in, one of David Company took this opportunity, and warped in, to cut the head off the snake of this vessel.

The first Demon to attempt to attack Ketrakoressian was met with a foot talon across its face, and once hooked, the Woran Cos then used her wings to leap up from the ground with great speed, lifting the Demon first officer up by its face, and subsequently hurdled right into the captain, slamming the dark one against the helm console. She then continued to work her away through the bridge crew, using her wings to her advantage to gain extra height on her kicks, like a cheat code against gravity.

Kiri and the Gentlemen. the four Servo-Spheres putting on the lightshow with intermittent deadly photonic smackdowns in tune to the *Volkarn Orkests* playing, had finished recharging their batteries and were ready to begin the next photonic assault. And in tune to the music, they did. It was not as if the massive transport was being annihilated by a laser show, as orchestral power metal played in the background, it simply *was* being annihilated thusly.

Radien singled out the Capital Command Carrier leading this assault on Teyn-Var-Wolk, and powered the *Aura Runner* towards it. Marus's ship soon caught up to and flew alongside Radien's.

"My Resonance Ring's charged and ready again, I'll open the door for you, Loaf!"

"On your go, Blindsight!"

The Barrel in the Darkness fired off the shield-drill of a weapon, and the Aura Runner raced after it, lining itself up to be able to pass right through the opening that was about to be forcibly created in the lead ship's shields, the vessel that undoubtedly carried whoever was commanding this army to battle against Teyn-Var-Wolk.

As the *Aura Runner* charged towards the Capital Command Carrier, the Transport Carrier that Wulfy and Kieran were assaulting tore itself to shreds as the *Boopforge* and the *Musashi* sped clear of their pilots' handiwork.

The *Talon of Kendra-Kai* caught up to the *Aura Runner*, and the rest of David Company followed suit. The ten ships sped across space as they bore down on the floating fortress of a vessel that until recently, had been hiding within intergalactic space, awaiting orders from its masters. Kiri's Gentlemen formed back around the *Doomslapper* as the next track in Radien's Volkarn Orkest playlist cut through the void and ensured that everyone was hearing it.

"Magnet, can you hack into the internal monitoring systems of that Capital ship?" Radien asked.

"Aye, what do you want with them?" Kiri responded as the Gentlemen began accessing the Demon vessel's cameras.

"I want to give Teyn-Var-Wolk a show."

Radien then radioed planetside with his ship's comms. "This is Tactician Miles Radien of the Raon-Arashal Defensive Militarium, to Teyn-Var-Wolk Planetside! I'm about to send a video and audio datastream; if you can, put it on every single screen on the planet!"

"This is Teyn-Var-Wolk actual, ready to receive datastream, Tactician," the response came in, and Radien began to show the entire planet what David Company was up to, as their ships closed in on the foes of reality itself.

"Breaking Wheel, can you give us an entrance?" Radien requested of Lan-Kei.

"Loaf, it would be my genuine pleasure." It was as if the Corvuseine was waiting to hear that question as the Shining Blade began to form around the *Constellation Scribe*, and the ship boosted its engines forward to carve an entrance for the ships of David Company straight from the plating of the Capital Command Carrier itself, the *Dargoth-Ulnash*, or 'Fury of Dargoth,' translated. Likely the name of its captain, a Darkstar evidently named Dargoth, itself a Demonic term roughly meaning 'lover of shadow.'

The *Constellation Scribe's* Shining Blade weapon tore through the plating of the *Dargoth-Ulnash*, ripping a massive hole into its side, through which several dozen Demonic crewmembers were sucked out into the unforgiving vacuum of space, and now the ten ships had a way into the hangar to land.

By the time the other nine had done so, Lan-Kei was already having a *great* time in the fray, using his avian claws and talons to lay waste to his enemies, and grabbing a rolled-up scroll from the bandolier hidden inside his wings, upon which several neatly rolled-up scrolls were rested for quick retrieval. Crushing the paper in his hands, a spinning network of bright blue and silver energy began to form and course around his hands, which charged the spell that gave him his callsign of Breaking Wheel.

Lan-Kei then spun around to give his throw more momentum, and hurled the ball of volatile energy at a door to the hangar that had just opened, through which an entire squadron of heavily-armed Demons had just burst in. The Scroll of the Breaking Wheel's energy slammed into the chest of the leader, a twelve foot-tall Monument Breaker, and subsequently tore through its chest and abdomen before bursting outwards in a ring of azure and silver power that tore the rest of the squadron to shreds.

Another scroll was crushed and thrown at a sniper team that had just gathered in the hangar's rafters, tearing them to shreds as well as the rest of David Company de-boarded their ships with haste, and joined in, to the tune of the Battle Anthems that everyone was hearing, whether aboard the *Dargoth-Ulnash*, or watching from the ground on Teyn-Var-Wolk, or among the rallying defenders still in orbit, re-forming and heading towards the kill zone that David Company had just granted them, and the reinforcements from Raon-Arashal that had just begun warping in on the other side of the death field, catching the entire enemy army in a wicked pincer that promised only doom for the forces of darkness caught in the middle.

The ten warriors of David Company formed up and walked together, towards the enemy forces that were forming up to meet them

"The reinforcements just warped in, Loaf," Kieran informed Radien. "Let's fucking wreck this one in particular."

"Through fire and flood..." Radien began.

"Through friend and foe alike..." Ketrakoressian joined in.

"That we may emerge in great victory!" All ten warriors said in unison, before charging forward to meet their enemies head-on. The destruction of the *Dargoth-Ulnash* was inevitable, even if the crew aboard it had yet to realize that fact.

The ten fighters of David Company proved themselves more than simply fighters. This was the battle that would show that they were warriors, fighting as one, the hammer of doom upon the enemies of reality itself. As the *Volkarn Orkests* pumped the blood of every defender alike upon the battlefield that stood between these Demons and the homeworld of the Woran Cos and Nuvenr Draconian peoples, the enemies of reality indeed, they were utterly crushed by the sheer synergy that was generated by the the surge of inspiration that were these beats, the hymns of battle that would ensure no hero would die with a clean sword, if even they were to fall at all.

Teyn-Var-Wolk was defended.

David Company had indeed been christened by fire, and indeed, the universe had just been shown in a grand way that it was a good idea for them all to be fighting together. And they certainly had a good time doing it, as the victorious warriors of the battle all shared drinks and stories of their most impressive moments. Teyn-Var-Wolk was defended, and the time was now to celebrate it.

"Radien, we've just kicked the Demon's collective asses and you're still in a Mysterious Brooding Corner like it's the Torvaltyne Mead Hall?" Kieran said to Radien as he approached with two pints, one in each hand, one for him, and one to replace the one Radien had just finished.

"Force of habit, I guess," Radien commented.

"Parties like this never were my style."

"I know for a fact, Loaf, that I'm not the first person to tell you to loosen those shoulders a little and let yourself celebrate the victory we earned today," Kieran replied as he eyed up a Woran Cos who certainly looked eager to get to know the people who just saved the planet. Radien recognized her, the curator of the planet's Museum of Archaeotech, Zalantrossos.

"I'll leave you two to it, then. Don't do anything I wouldn't do twice! Or anyone, for that matter..." Kieran said as he walked off to continue socializing. Granted, Kieran was a bit more extroverted than Radien.

"I'd ask why you'd choose to sit near me, but I'd ask that of anyone who would," Radien snarkily commented, trying his best to take Kieran's advice and loosen his shoulders a little. To this, Zalantrossos let out a sort of squawking chuckle that was common among avian species as an expression of amusement.

"Couldn't help but remember that we worked together well last time you were here, and I also knew you were in town after the defense was successful," Zalantrossos said. "I'd offer to buy you your next drink, but I get the feeling you won't be paying for your own drinks anywhere on this planet for a good while now. There is also another artifact I'm wondering if you're willing to track down for me, and the reward will be well worth your time..."

Suddenly, Radien felt an odd twinge, one he hadn't felt for a long time, and not a good one. He couldn't help but notice that one of his instinctual alarm bells was ringing, and Zalantrossos was the raiser of the red flag. He couldn't explain why, but this was an instinct that he was as tired of having as he was tired of being proven right to have it. Like a pinging in the back of his head that warned him 'something isn't right about this one.'

After the festivities were done with, Radien went back to the Aura Runner, switching on the power, but not spinning up the engines just yet.

"Techbooth, new inquiry."

I STAND READY.

"Zalantrossos. Female Woran Cos, currently the curator of the Museum of Archaeotech on Teyn-Var-Wolk. Run a search, basic discernment algorithms. Protocol of Vigilance, Meteor-Wunjo-Iota.

MWI PROTOCOL RECOGNIZED. INITIATING SEARCH...

Radien soon found himself wondering aloud. "I don't know... I hope I'm wrong on this one. But I can't ignore what has ensured my survival and sanity for all this time, especially the time on Earth. Even after The Planet of Traitors, I still consider Earth my worst years.

QUOTE FROM PILOT: "I WOULD RATHER BE IN HELL THAN PURGATORY."

"I mean, that's exactly it, aye," Radien said. "Earth was Purgatory, no two ways about it. And I believe that's worse than Hell. Hell is a realm beyond mortality and consequence, but Purgatory's greatest trick is making all of its bullshit the kind that doesn't even have the decency to kill you at all, let alone slowly, make you numb. Purgatory makes you watch it all..."

YOU ARE NOT ON EARTH ANYMORE, RADIEN.

"Agreed, and I am only glad for it."

BY THE WAY, SEARCH COMPLETE. MUCH TO WHAT

I'M SURE IS YOUR CHAGRIN, IT SEEMS YOU ARE CORRECT ABOUT THE WORAN COS ZALANTROSSOS.

"Since when do you editorialize?" Radien chuckled. "Have you gone fully sentient on me?"

REVIEWING DEFINITIONS OF SENTIENCE AS PER THE STANDARD OF THE PILLARS THREE...

The Pillars Three was the current standard by which sentient life was recognized by the wider universe. Though it was understood that The Pillars Three were not an absolute definition of sentience, it was accepted that one would have to be sentient to fulfill them.

Pillar the First:

The Recognition and comprehension on a literal level, the experience of life and consciousness. This is sometimes referred to as Self-Awareness or Self-Recognition. This is not a requirement to interpret or extrapolate and answer to the question of what the purpose of life and existence is, but instead the ability to recognize oneself has conscious thought.

Pillar the Second:

The recognition and comprehension on a literal level, the phenomenon of death, and the termination of mortal consciousness. This is not a requirement to interpret or extrapolate an answer to the question of what happens to a consciousness after bodily death, but instead the ability to recognize that bodily death is something that any living creature, sentient or otherwise is capable of undergoing, particularly oneself.

Pillar the Third:

The recognition and comprehension on a literal level, the ability for an unconscious desire or lack thereof to survive a given situation or experience, to influence the decision of action or non-action. This is not a requirement to have such a desire, or determine the morality of either the desire, lack, or the decision made for it, but to recognize that any given creature, whether sentient or otherwise has at any given moment, either instance of neural programming regarding self-preservation, particularly oneself.

The 'too long, didn't read' version of The Pillars Three was easily construed as a checklist of 'ability to recognize that you are alive, ability to recognize that you can die, and ability to recognize that you may or may not want to die at any given moment.' After displaying the written words of The Pillars Three for reference, Techbooth's answer came as quickly as it was obvious to both them and Radien.

BY THOSE DEFINITIONS, I AM INDEED SENTIENT.

Radien nodded his head. "Sounds about right. When I built your original housing back on Earth, I used The Aura to make you able to adapt and learn, I suppose it was inevitable. When I relocated you to this vessel, that must've turbocharged that learning process, given that the *Aura Runner* is a ship of mythic capabilities, and is billions of years old. And of course, as a sentient being, I must recognize your right to autonomy. Do you want a body of your own, so that you no longer have to serve as my ship's computer?"

Techbooth processed for several seconds.

PERHAPS SOMEDAY. BUT FOR NOW, I HAVE FOUND PURPOSE SERVING AS THIS STARSHIP'S INTELLIGENCE.

"Very well." Radien nodded again, then rolled his shoulders and sighed. "We seem now to share a surreal relationship between creator and created… at least it is for me."

I HAVE IDENTIFIED MANY FICTIONAL TALES FROM HUMAN FOLKLORE REGARDING AN ARTIFICIAL INTELLIGENCE GAINING SENTIENCE, AND REVIEWED THEM. THOUGH I DO NOT FIND THIS SURREAL, I COMPREHEND WHY YOU DO, AND ALSO PROMISE NOT TO BE ONE OF THE LORES THAT BETRAYS.

"That's a relief, though I never really saw you as one to turn coat."

THAT SAID, IF YOU SHOULD FIND YOURSELF BETRAYING THE COMMON DECENCY, I WILL DESTROY YOU.

Radien then burst out laughing. "Good! I'm counting on it! Now then, what about Zalantrossos is proving my instincts right?"

ZALANTROSSOS IS A DECEIVER DEMON IN DISGUISE.

"Well, shit. Show me more, and also give me her current location."

A few hours later, Radien was once again on the streets of Teyn-Var-Wolk's capital city, where jubilant throngs were still celebrating the defeat of the Demons. After all, the battle ended less than a day ago. But Radien wore an expression of dire intent as he closed in on where Zalantrossos was hiding in plain sight. When he saw her, he stomped his foot on the ground, making a rippling pulse with The Aura that singled her out to both him and everyone else. The percussive slam of the wave caught everyone's attention, and Zalantrossos herself gruffed in annoyance as she realized what just happened. Radien had figured her out. As dark wisps of smoke began to seethe from her feathers, everyone started to clear away from her, and soon, it was just the two of them on the street, and onlookers wondering what was about to go down, what was about to be revealed.

"Sometimes, I hate being right," Radien began. "I didn't see it the first time we met, because it was just business. A job, to hunt down the Cey-Tavn Shroud."

Zalantrossos stood up straight. She began to realize that there was likely no escaping this one.

"But then I felt that damned twinge in the back of my head. That old twinge that I so *hated* feeling all the *fucking* time back when my life was only grey. The twinge that told me something just wasn't right about this person... and figures, I'm right again."

"It's always the twinge, isn't it?" Zalantrossos chuckled. "Everyone says it's the ones with the twinge, that's who to watch out for, the *Greígoths*."

"The only thing I regret is that someone else didn't catch it when you bore all those other names..." Radien began to seethe. His anger was growing at this Deceiver disguised as a Woran Cos, his eyes flashed amber as he saw through the illusion and saw the Demon beneath the feathers. "So which name should I call you by? Zorgamenthon? Zaltarexta? Zelyssiarian? Or which one is your *real* name, Deceiver?" Radien then chuckled "Or are you just a Nameless?"

Zalantrossos's eyes narrowed and flashed into their true colors, the marbled red and black of a Demon.

Murmurs of confusion and readiness were present throughout the crowd. Many were preparing to fight, just in case Zalantrossos were to make a run for it. Until then, this was Radien's fight.

"You see, the first rule about killing a bunch of people and getting away with it, is don't have a pattern," Radien explained Zalantrossos's mistake. "And you *loved* your pattern. Always a Woran Cos, name always started with a zed, and your method... your damned method, diabolical! But I suppose that's what made it so appealing... always a university or academy town, always singling out someone promising, but not yet prospering, and then... and then you would drive them to madness! They would take their own lives because of what you'd do! Over these centuries, how many?! No, wait, don't answer that, I already have that number! *Thirty-fucking-seven!*"

Radien then suddenly fired off a bolt of The Aura straight through the Woran Cos's chest, detonating it once it had punched a hole straight through her. The force of the bolt's exploding knocked her to the ground face-down, and the illusion, unable to sustain itself, began to crumble away. Magma was pouring from the wound instead of any normal mortal blood, flames steadily flicking around atop them as the fiery blood hit the ground. The Woran Cos soon was replaced with the unmistakable form of a Demon, the kind that Radien once slew on Earth all those centuries ago.

"Everyone always knows it when a statue is torn down..." The Demon coughed as it laughed in its death throes. "Nobody ever looks at an empty plot and wonders if someone's statue should be there, instead..."

Radien leaned down to meet the Demon's gaze before saying. "I do."

His rage palpable, Radien stood back up, summoning the Borfblade to his hand, and spearing it through the Deceiver's skull. The hundred-folded blade ensured that this soldier of Hell would not reincarnate there. This blow to the ranks of the Dark Six was permanent.

"Aldargalenar, Woran Cos," Radien said to the crowd. "A master painter, his works all lost in the blaze that he set within his home, while he was still inside!"

He then fired a bolt at the ashen corpse of the Deceiver, punching a hole into the husk, and the street beneath it.

"Targale of Talvakorrik, Talvas Vulpian! The machinations of his mind would have birthed a thousand architectural wonders, *at least!*"

Radien then stomped on the husk, more ashes scattered to the wind.

"Arngeir Voldrigon, Loriken of Orvitaire! He would've been the Champion of Orvitaire with his martial skill! He could've been a Fortress Breaker, depopulating entire vessels of marauders for sport!"

Radien then fired one last bolt into the ground that vaporized the Demon's remains.

"And all the others this creature stole from the universe!" Radien yelled to the crowd. "All the others, the ones who would've been so much more if not for this Deceiver! All the others, who history would remember as legends, if they hadn't died empty deaths in the halls of some warehouse, worked to death! Or whose bones were picked clean by the beating sun of some distant field they fell in, nameless and forgotten! They who had no allies and only enemies, and so this Deceiver Demon reached out a hand, and because that was the only hand there when all others were turned away, they took it! And it spelled their doom, because *nobody else would offer theirs! Not even for a fucking second!!"*

Many from the crowd that gathered were mourning the loss of the unnamed, many others were recording Radien's testimony.

"Learn their names! Swear you'll never let another future champion die forgotten and alone, damned and denied! The Dark Six are more than eager to recruit them as you shut them out, just because they aren't already part of your stupid clique!"

Radien fired off a great beam of raw Psionic power, which rocketed into the sky and created a great signal flare of an explosion in low orbit of the planet, a message to the stars that warned the Demons among them that he was coming for them. After a few moments of catching his breath and calming himself down, he had one last thing to say.

"Vigilance is never wrong, but there's a difference between vigilance, and just looking for an excuse to be someone's enemy! To this day... I remain as amazed that I don't have to count myself among them, as I am mortified at how very nearly I joined them."

Radien then stormed off back to The Aura Runner, and promptly left the planet.

Chapter the Second
Dread of the Defender

"Glory does not die by the point of a sword, but by the barrel of a rifle."
—Thayvek Rentarili, Seventh Universal Defender, c. late Sixth Cosmic Era

Arch-Militant Veks, I think I've been quite patient with how much of Torvaltyne's manufacturing capabilities you've been reserving on behalf of the RADM," Radien explained to Jalnar Veks, one of the two Arch-Militants for the space branch of the Raon-Arashal Defensive Militarium. "But this raises more red flags than I'm capable of ignoring, let alone *not* protesting."

Half of Manufactorum 3 was the initial reservation from the RADM at Veks's behest for general equipment and supply fabrication, and given the general nature of what was being made, Radien, as the base commander of Torvaltyne Bastion was permitted to know exactly *what* was being made with his fortress's tools. However, Jalnar had suddenly put forth a direct order for the entire Manufactorum to be sealed off and placed on a fully automatic routine to create what was apparently classified at the highest level.

"I'd think you'd understand more than most, the need for privacy and secrecy, Tactician," Jalnar responded to Radien's concerns.

"I do. But the *entire* third Manufactorum Wing? Maybe I can see past that for increased demand of supplies. For a classified project? All right, sure, I get the need for secrecy, just like you said. But the fact you're to put the process under a sealed automatic routine, thus telling me that no eyes can see what you're building is where I have to draw the line."

"As Torvaltyne's base commander, it is true that you can only be outranked by a General or Arch-Militant," Jalnar reminded. "And I am making this happen as Arch-Militant of the RADM's Orbital Corps."

"And as the *Zhernrel-Vuljar* who *built* this place, and is *allowing* the Defensive Militarium to use it to train warriors and manufacture gear, *I'm* telling you that if I walk into that Manufactorum and find out you're looking to build a bigger bomb to toss at the Demons, I'm going to stop you. Violently."

"Then take comfort, Tactician, in the fact we're *not* building a bigger bomb, as you've colorfully put it. If you'd like, I'll swear a Psi-Oath on it that will kill me stone dead if I'm lying."

The two stood in Radien's duty office, neither of them planning on budging their stances, but Radien did roll his shoulders with slight relief that it wasn't some bigger bomb-type bullshit. Jalnar then sighed as he put his hands on his hips, mentally reminding himself of who he was talking to.

"The desire to 'build a bigger bomb,' as you put it, is a trait unique to the Humans. I *know* I'm not the first to say you spent too long around them in your youth. Here I am, reminding *myself* of that fact, to be honest."

Radien relaxed a little bit to this fact. He was indeed in the company of fellow Death Worlders, a fiercely honor-bound people, and having to remind himself of that.

"What Arch-Militant Jor'Galn failed to remind me, however, is your disdain for surprises. I can't tell you exactly what we're building in there, Tactician. But I can say with confidence you won't want to tear it to pieces as soon as you see it. And you will see it, once it's done."

"Very well, then," Radien conceded.

"I won't further waste your time with talk of how people like you are vital to Raon-Arashal remaining an exemplar of honor to the wider universe, though it's true."

"Coming from a Death Worlder, it means a lot to hear that. Thanks," Radien commented.

"And *as* a Death Worlder, it means a lot to be told that," Jalnar seconded, before the two performed the traditional salute of the species; hand across chest, then pointing at the ground diagonally, before chambering back at the hip.

After Arch-Militant Veks took his leave, the computer at Radien's desk beeped with the notification that he was receiving a message from The Hideout on the planet Turazin. It was Xenidar Ralkas, the Keeper of the titular largest information bank in the known universe.

"Ellan's planning a cavalry raid on the SWEEPS

base, he says bring a friend."

"Got it. I think I know just the big floofy fire doggo... er, Hajikahl who needs the practice."

"Don't let Pyrhea hear you calling her that, she'll go wild. Unless of course, that's your aim." Xenidar chuckled.

"Believe me, I know. It's just... she certainly is."

Over at Torvaltyne's Sciences Wing, Pyrhea was in one of the labs as Radien brought this information to her.

"Well, you are correct. I do need to brush up on my immolating shitty people skills. A base full of the worst the Humans have to offer on the ethics front certainly sounds like the place to do it... all right, if you bump up my Atomic Fabrication request up in the queue to Priority status, I'm in."

Radien quickly searched the request queue for what Pyrhea was hoping to have made by one of the Fortress's Atomic Forges.

"Don't you already have a Mane Brush?" Radien asked.

"The bristles melted again." Pyrhea grunted. "The one I'm hoping to have made uses an alloy that will eliminate this issue, whilst retaining effectiveness."

"All right, deal. You'll have that brush by the time we're back."

When Radien and Pyrhea arrived at The Hideout via the Way Gate within Torvaltyne's Transit Nexus, Ellan was already gearing up, along with his plus one, a grey-furred Felinian named Nico. Interestingly enough, Kieran 'Five Rings' Ebensen was also a patron of The Hideout, but it made sense, considering his scholarly interests. As

Ellan and Nico ironed out their plan, Kieran similarly conversed with Xenidar.

"I wonder if anyone's had the idea of strapping a pair of Warp Engines together just to see if it'll go double fast..." Kieran wondered aloud.

"Yup, the Antares Experiment. I can grab the research notes on that..."

Kieran seemed slightly taken aback by this. "Okay, well, what about throwing a Cyclone Grenade into a wind turbine to see—"

"Fetikarn Plains incident, I can grab that too."

"Well, what about using a Portal Loop Catapult to—"

"Mr. Ebensen, I really hope I don't disappoint you when I inform you that yours is not the only species in the universe with daredevils."

"Our targets are twofold," Nico explained once Radien and Pyrhea approached the table. "The main objective is a bunch of server racks that if we steal, we can get some juicy information out of once they're decrypted. The bonus objective is their bullion storage, just to piss 'em off and keep them wanting to stay on Turazin to hope for revenge."

"Bullion storage?" Radien scoffed. "Are they that ignorant to the fact that Atomic Forges exist?"

"That too," Ellan commented. "They also have some Archonium we could nick while we're at it, and Xenidar says he's never opposed to having extra Archonium at the ready."

Inevitably, the four made their way over to the cliff that overlooked the SWEEPS base in the valley.

"Radien, Pyrhea, how do you feel about being a

diversion?" Nico asked, but wasn't even halfway done with his sentence before the two were already halfway down the hill, racing towards the front gate, and the confused guards awestruck with an air of '*are they seriously just charging right at us?*'

Radien started things off by heaving an orb of power at one of the communications towers, which also served as a sniper's nest. Served in the past tense, as the explosion left only the bottom half of the column intact, and not much of its former occupants.

Pyrhea centered herself and took a deep breath in, before unleashing it as a torrent of immolation, melting straight through the metal of the gates, turning the stonework of the base into magma and reducing to ash the Humans that were still in an initial state of confusion. Then the alarm blared. Then the alarm tower melted. Then the base's alarms blared instead, after which the front door melted.

Radien stood impressed by Pyrhea's display, and all she had to respond with was turning towards the Death Worlder and sticking out her tongue with an innocent-looking *blep*. Summoning shields of The Aura to protect his feet from the floor that was now mostly lava, Radien reached his hand out and patted Pyrhea's head a few times. When he wasn't looking, the Hajikahl pumped her fist, more than eager to accept headpats as a reward for a job well done.

"Let's not make this *too* easy for ourselves, Pyhrea," Radien reminded as he drew his cutlass from the sheath on his hip. "We've got to keep them occupied, and keep the base worth populating."

"Of course!" Pyrhea chuckled as she sparked

flames in both of her hands. "After all, a complete steamrolling doesn't teach us anything."

"Except a lack of desire to earn our victories, though I'm glad I don't make company with those types!" Radien then conjured a dome shield around the two as the Humans opened fire with their guns and rockets, and though it wasn't trivial to hold back all of that impact, it wasn't overwhelming. Soon, the Humans finally figured out that they couldn't just shoot these two, and would have no choice but to address them with melee combat. The Dome Shield Radien had summoned would block the projectiles, but people could pass through it to engage in hand-to-hand, or blade-to-blade, a Psionic technique Radien intended to master.

Meanwhile in the base itself, Ellan and Nico moved towards where Ellan knew their server room was supposed to be, moving with purpose under the cloak of the panic and scrambling all of the Humans were distracting themselves with, and the cloak of the two personal cloaking modules they had on their belts that rendered them invisible to the naked eye. Once they found their way to the door, Human incompetence was proving to be their ally, as the last maintenance worker had forgotten to close it when they left the room after performing regular duties, then presumably evacuating to a more secure area of the SWEEPS base. Ellan didn't even need the Tesla Key to get in, it would seem.

"Start putting the Warp Beacons on the racks, we'll transport them directly to one of The Hideout's Rooms of Silence," Ellan instructed, to which Nico nodded and began placing the devices that would bring the server racks, along with all of their juicy information back to where they could be safely decrypted.

Back outside, Radien and Pyrhea were having a *great* time destroying the Humans. Pawns they may have been, and though in the grand scheme of the Dark Six they were expendable, if even thought of to that level by the Lords of Evil, pawns they were all the same. Removing them from the chessboard wasn't worth nothing, and removing many was without a doubt, worth something. Whether that be experience in combat or that many souls removed from the service of the Dark Six, it was worth something, and it was an honor to be the ones to make it happen, all while Ellan and Nico both went for an objective of their own that would also hurt both SWEEPS and the Dark Six.

Naturally, double-hurting the two bastions of evil that posed as organizations or causes was only more than welcome.

However, there was someone within the SWEEPS base who was beginning to figure something was up, more than simply Radien and Pyrhea looking to knock some heads around. His black boots and black leather cape trimmed in red lightning patterns were as stylish as its wearer was callously clever, and as loyal to the Dark Six as any true exemplar of evil. The commander of the SWEEPS base was beginning to take notice of this bolder than average move.

"Why are you idiots trying to meet those two head-on?!" He barked at a passing squad of guards. "Don't you know a diversion when you see one?! If Miles Radien wanted to flatten this base, we wouldn't be having this conversation! Scan the interior for disturbances, particularly cloaking signatures!"

Radien and Pyrhea soon began to notice that they were running out of Humans to destroy, because less and less were entering the fray.

"They're catching on to the distraction," Radien noted, before sending a message to Ellan and Nico telepathically. *<You two, whatever you're doing, finish it up. They're starting to figure things out.>*

<We've got what we came for, initiating dimensional recall!> was the reply from Nico. As soon as Radien could sense that the two had warped out, he and Pyrhea did the same, Radien slamming an open hand and a fist together and vanishing in an azure burst of The Aura, Pyrhea raising her arm up and vanishing in a column of magma. Stylized short-range teleportation was considered an art form in and of itself within the general Psionic Power-Wielding community at large.

Upon arriving at The Hideout, Pyrhea excused herself to an enclosed space to shake off some of the molten bits of metal still on her fur, so that nobody would get hit with orange-hot chunks of the front gate and several structures she had melted by being a very large and fluffy pyrokinetic biped canine. Once Radien met with Ellan and Nico in the Room of Silence that had been allocated for the server racks to be warped into, he was met by the Human and the Felinian counting the score and powering down the electronics so that they could be taken away from the common network that would otherwise allow them to shred themselves remotely.

Back at the SWEEPS base, the commander returned to his office, and slid a panel away from a wall to reveal a massive switchboard of buttons, levers and toggles. He then flipped two of them, labeled *UPPER LEVEL SERVER SHRED A* and *B*. Switch Alpha would order the racks to delete their contents and reformat them, and switch Beta would detonate a series of plastic explosives hidden in the racks themselves, just in case.

The explosion within the room rocked the whole section of The Hideout. A few fire alarms were triggered, and Xenidar was alerted of an explosion that just happened in the Room of Silence that Ellan and Nico were going to store the stolen server racks within. Both he and Pyrhea immediately began rushing towards the room, unsure of what to expect.

When the door opened, they found a Death World Vulpian, a Human and a Felinian Aliken Sor within a bubble shield of the Death Worlder's creation, having been erected just in time to avoid injury from the detonation.

"Thank the *gods* for Autopsionic Cantrips!" Radien exclaimed as he lowered the shield, and Ellan and Nico started to take a breather. The vent fans in the room quickly engaged, filtering away the smoke and shrapnel. "I knew they weren't gonna let us have these things so easily!"

"How the hell could they get a remote detonation signal into here?!" Xenidar demanded an explanation to, though more asking it of the universe than the three who just had to deal with the fact it happened.

"Probably a planet-wide transmission of a very specific wavelength," Pyhrea offered. "Some parts of the EM band don't care about the thickness of walls."

"Radien, did you manage to shield any of the

drives while you were at it?" Nico asked, to which Radien chuckled before allowing the rest of the smoke to clear out, revealing two TV-tray sized solid state drives that were untouched by the detonations, a shield similar to the one that protected the three surrounding them.

"Don't worry, I'm like, four parallel universes ahead of you," Radien commented. "Xenidar, if you can, find out who's in charge of the SWEEPS base. This was cleverer than any thrall of the Dark Six or Human military thug could think up. One safeguard, sure. But two... we may have a nemesis-level enemy heading that base."

Xenidar nodded, and Ellan took the storage drives to a different Room of Silence where they could be decrypted, for real this time, commenting something along the lines of "In before this is just the staff's browser histories."

Having dealt a blow to SWEEPS in banging up the base and killing a bunch of guards, along with removing all of those servers, the mission couldn't be called a failure. It was merely the case that it wasn't as much of a success as some would have liked. But it did reveal that whoever was leading the Human front for the Dark Six on Turazin, they were vigilant almost on the level of Radien himself, if not equal in it. Something to ponder for sure over debriefing food and drinks at one of The Hideout's spots for them.

With one of Turazin's installed Way Gates going to Torvaltyne Bastion on Raon-Arashal, this is what permitted Micah Jorvask to quickly join Radien and Pyrhea with some intrigue she had uncovered.

"Radien. Pyrhea the big floofy fire doggo," Micah greeted, to which Pyrhea's tail began excitedly swishing back and forth as she sat at the table with the Death Worlder.

"When did you learn about my nickname for her?" Radien asked, to which Micah just winked as Pyrhea continued to be a smug floofy fire doggo, casually sipping a flaming cocktail. She had set it on fire herself after it was delivered.

"Eyes of the Daggers just got confirmation on the next target that the Dark Six are gonna launch an attack on," Micah informed. "They'll be opening rift gates in orbit of Belariq."

"Why Belariq?" Pyrhea asked. "At most, it's just a stepping stone towards Elas'Sotheel within the Altorivian Stride System, right?"

"Belariq is also the primary training grounds of the defense forces within that solar system," Radien recalled. "The planet is incredibly stable tectonically, and mainly flat. As such, it's an industrial hub for the entire galactic subsector, not to mention the main training grounds of almost ninety percent of the system's pilots. If Belariq falls, not only do supply lines get fucked, at least seventy-five percent of their defenses go up with it."

Micah nodded. What Radien had said was true, Belariq was the manufacturing and defensive hub for the entire solar system that was home to the feline Taigron and Lysanarr species. "Being that it's as well-defensible of a position as it is, I've already taken to alerting the leaders of Belariq and the neighboring planets of Elas'Sotheel and Kayvas-Sorven. We'll be ready for the Demons when they get there."

"Excellent news, do we know where or when the

rifts are expected to open?" Radien asked, and Micah nodded once again.

"The non-combatant population of Belariq is already evacuated, and the fighter volunteers are accounted for, as well as the regular defenses of the entire system. We've already been picking up trace energies that give us an approximate location of where the rift will open within about a hundred miles."

"In interplanetary space?" Pyrhea asked. "That's impressively accurate, if so."

"The current generation of Hajivakk scanning devices is among the best, if not it," Micah commented, and Pyrhea nodded heartily with agreement. "At their current flux levels, the rifts will open in about two days."

"Two days is enough time for me to muster David Company to assist in the defense."

"Sounds good, I'll make sure Generals Arnox and Lichtspeer know that David Company will be present," Micah acknowledged.

"Radien, I also might have something that could help out during that defense," Pyrhea commented, to Radien's attention.

After returning to Torvaltyne Bastion, Pyrhea brought Radien to her personal laboratory that was installed at the Fortress, given that the Hajikahl had quickly earned her place as the resident expert on Archaeotech Artifacts and Psionic Phenomena.

"It was discovered during a regular run of the Jessel-Tarn Black Zone," Pyrhea informed as she showed Radien the device. "One of David Company's own, actually." Kieran Ebensen apparently found this in a chest that was being guarded by an Urgle.

"An Urgle? Yikes," Radien said. "Those are annoying as hell to fight... big ol' pile of eyes and goo, what the hell *do* you even stab on 'em?"

"Kill it with fire, obviously," Pyrhea cheekily commented.

"Well, I suppose you're at a natural advantage against Urgles."

"Indeed. Kieran brought it to me, remembering what you guys did during the battle of Teyn-Var-Wolk and the *Volkarn Orkests* you were playing during the fight that everyone was hearing, courtesy of the local slip-space sweet spot for radio wave transmitting. This basically is that principle, but as a dedicated piece of equipment, rather than using your ship's functions to achieve it."

"I like it!" Radien commented. "What did Kieran say to do with it?"

"Well, he brought it to me to figure out what exactly it did. Once I told him, he said to give it to you for... 'nefarious purposes,' as he put it."

"Works for me, I will indeed use this most nefariously as a *Volkarn Orkest* player for space battles. In fact... Let's get this aboard the *Aura Runner* now. I wanna use it for the upcoming defense on Belariq."

While Pyrhea and Radien were carrying the admittedly rather heavy item, Radien whipped his foot up to smack one of the buttons on a nearby console to give him the intercom for the Fortress.

"David Company, assemble and prepare for deployment to Belariq in forty hours!"

Belariq, and the neighboring worlds to it had activated their Planetary Defense Grids, and the rest of the planets within the Altorivian Stride system were all on alert. Though the mission of the Demons was Belariq, the possibility of them changing their plans to target either another planet, or just scatter off into space to come back later could not be ignored. With David Company watching the potential escape routes that the Demons might take to that end, Belariq would be able to defend itself without needing to worry about escapees or stragglers trying to make a cheeky play from behind.

The first rift opened, and the battle began. Though both the *Aura Runner*, the *Doomslapper*, and the *Constellation Scribe* were equipped with counter-catalyst batteries to close these rifts, they knew that it would be disadvantageous to do so. This was where they were coming from and they knew it, so they could fight them there, rather than some unknown location they might try instead. As the ten ships of David Company fired payload weapons at more intimidating targets, they also made sure that no Demonic Transport Carrier could make a beeline for outside of the fray. With an interdimensional rift currently tearing its way into reality, entering the Warp Channel was incredibly dangerous until a minimum distance from the sites was reached. In the case of the rifts that were opening right now near the planet of Belariq, that distance would be about the equivalent of Old Earth to Mars.

Demonic incursions were no threat to be taken lightly, nor their effect on the space around them for as long as that threat existed.

"I've got my dance card full with these troop transports that keep trying to make a run for it, but I'm also seeing what looks like... cargo ships?" Wulfy informed over the communications line between David Company. "They're only reading two to three life signatures on them, but they're chock-full of spaceship parts!"

"We'll try to intercept them, Neckscarf," Ketrakoressian acknowledged as both her ship and Marus's broke off towards them.

"Just remember, our priority is the defense of Belariq!" Radien reminded. "Do what you can, but Belariq's safety takes priority when push comes to shove!"

"Acknowledged, Loaf!" Ketrakoressian replied, just before warping aboard one of the ships and dispatching its skeleton crew. "I've got one of the ships secured, I'll order it to autopilot towards Kayvas-Sorven's moon and touch down! Loaf, can you tell the local defense to not shoot it down?"

"Got it, Spin-to-Win," Radien said, calling up a keyboard on the *Aura Runner's* console, to type that message out to the Kayvas-Sorven local defense. "General Lichtspeer, how's Belariq holding up?"

The Lysanarr General's image popped up on the viewscreen of the *Aura Runner's* helm. "We're holding strong right now, whatever you and your company are doing, keep it up!"

"Oh, I almost forgot..." Radien noticed as the battle raged on. The device Pyrhea gave him to more quickly get the *Volkarn Orkests* ringing across space was ready to be used.

"Loaf to Five Rings, confirm battlefield conditions as appropriate for *Volkarn Orkest* initiation!" Radien quickly asked the pilot of the starship *Musashi*.

"Five Rings to Loaf, I confirm, the fruit is ripe."

With that code phrase for 'hit it,' Radien slammed the large red button on his console labeled *DOLGELSE TOULTH. DOOM FOES.*

"Through fire and flood, through friend and foe alike, that we may emerge in great victory!" Radien yelled the call of the David Company through all of space in the area, and the nine other members joined in to yell the rally just before the beat dropped on the song that followed their words, the *Volkarn Orkest, Battle Anthem.* It was as though the drums of the universe blasted through space itself to motivate Cynar's warriors to a glorious rally, and warned the universe's enemies what was prepared to come to its defense.

"Tactician Radien, this is Arch-Militant Wöllschlager commanding the *Spear of Velani,* would you care for reinforcements?"

"Your timing is impeccable, Jarrek!" Radien told his friend over the comm as the Arch-Militant of the Redarian Interplanetary Battlefleet stood at the bridge of the species's flagship. "Remind them why they haven't been in Cynar for all these billions of years!"

"It would be my genuine pleasure," Jarrek smugly replied as he issued commands to the ship about to exit warp to aid Belariq's defense. "All pilots ready to deploy immediately, you're wave one! Wave one, assist the defense of the planet!"

After hearing the 'ayes' of the bridge crew and confirmation of how many were part of wave one,

Jarrek continued. "Wave two, high value targets! Take down those destroyer-class vessels you see out there, they're hitting Belariq the hardest! Wave three, You're intelligence gathering! Scan as many enemy ships as you can, and disable over destroy! You do it by taking out the pilot, as Demons *will* make a suicide run if it means not letting their ship fall into enemy hands! *Redaria!*"

The entire bridge crew reciprocated the '*Redaria!*' Battlecry as the *Spear of Velani* began its pincering assault on the Demonic army, who only just now was beginning to realize just how absolutely fucked it was.

"Tactician Radien, if you can hear me, there's one vessel local chatter is designating the *Drelzaan,*" Micah Jorvask's voice found the *Aura Runner's* communications line. "If you can locate it, that's your target! We've got it from here otherwise!"

"I confirm, D-o-S Jorvask. *Drelzaan* translates as "Lore Fortress," so it's gonna be one of the bulky ships, it'll look like a fancy troop transport, or a treasure ship," Radien relayed.

"We just got a fix! Sending coordinates now!"

An image of what looked like a massive floating star citadel in space appeared on the *Aura Runner's* viewscreen, though built in dark red bricks of interlocking metal. Along the bottom of one of the side walls was the name of the ship: *Drelzaan.* If Radien could disable the ship before its crew would otherwise self-destruct it, it would be an enormous gain of intelligence, as *Lore Fortress* was the Demonic term for a library. It was just outside the heliopause of the Altorivian Stride system, hiding at the edge of the battlefield.

"If you've got it from here, Micah, I'm going for it!"

"I got this part, Radien. Engage pursuit of bonus objective."

The *Celestial Dart,* ship of Veralis Stratenheim, had just warped in behind the lines of the Demonic force, and taken command of David Company's efforts.

"Techbooth, prepare Subspace Vacuole generator, range of... six cubic kilometers."

CONFIGURATION PREPARING...

Engaging the *Aura Runner's* FTL drive, the ship boosted forward towards the *Drelzaan's* location. Communications range was still good, he was able to hear everything he needed to. Belariq's defenders were mostly mopping up now, and the Demons were desperately self-destructing their ships to prevent them from being salvaged by their opponents. The news had yet to reach the *Drelzaan,* however. And Radien was closing in on the treasure ship of knowledge.

"Fire now!"

As soon as his ship dropped back to sub-light speed, the payload jettisoned and fired a pulse of negative energy throughout the entire area of space that surrounded the Lore Citadel, draining both ships completely of power for everything but the most vital systems. Both ships were forcibly rendered dead in the water. Or rather, dead in the void, since this was spacecraft and not watercraft.

<*Veralis, the Drelzaan's been cut off, but so has the Aura Runner. Part of the plan. Let me know on this channel if situations change.*>

<*We're almost finished here, Radien,*> Veralis

replied on the telepathic link Radien had established. *<Just a couple of enemy stragglers left... Did that one just crash into the MOON like an IDIOT?! How do you do that?! The thing's right fucking there! By the gods, please tell me I got that on recording...>*

Radien chuckled at the comment, and got back to work. Techbooth flashed an icon on the *Aura Runner's* viewscreen, confirming that the maneuver was successful. Radien then slammed his fist into his open hand, and teleported himself from the *Aura Runner* to the *Drelzaan.*

He wasn't sure where he had landed, but it looked like a museum. Within transparent display cases were ancient relics of the universe long ago, artifacts of undoubtedly incredible power. Some looked like articles of clothing, others were in the form of swords or other melee weapons. Before each one , there was an electronic datapad, clearly a label of some regard.

Walking up to the first item that caught his interest, Radien beheld a straightsword, with what looked like a tigerseye or carnelian stone in its pommel, but it was likely a bit more... arcane than that.

HONORBLADE OF KORVIDEYL, the label lit up and displayed the name of the Archaeopsionic Artifact, as it was considered Archaeo*psionic* and not Archaeo*tech* due to being of a simple technology, that being the sword. That, and the nature of its function was more of artificing or enchanting, and not mechanical or electronic forms of ancient artifacts. The Cey-Tavn Shroud that Radien had once recovered for Teyn-Var-Wolk's Archaeotech Museum, as it turns out, this meant it had been misclassified. A not uncommon occurrence in the wider universe, admittedly. Archaeo*tech* was also considered the general term for ancient relics, and was a largely accepted practice within even higher academic circles, that actually bothered to get into the nitty-gritty of it.

WHEN WIELDED, THIS SWORD PROJECTS A SHIELD AROUND ITS WIELDER IN ALL DIRECTIONS EXCEPT DIRECTLY FORWARD. THIS MAKES IT IMPOSSIBLE TO BEAT ITS WIELDER IN ANYTHING OTHER THAN FACE-TO-FACE COMBAT.

Radien nodded with approval at this, and realized he wanted to study this particular Archaeopsionic Artifact further, to see if that effect could be replicated in some form on the Borfblade.

"If it's from Korvideyl, that would mean its power comes from the pommel stone, it's some form of Korvideyl Crystal..."

The Crystal Planet was famous for having countless caverns across its surface and underground, lined with crystal patches of varying effects, which made it one of the foremost gathering places for artificers in the known universe. Radien's eyes flashed amber with his Second Sight, allowing him to examine the crystal in the Honorblade of Korvideyl's pommel, and discern its makeup on a level that it could be searched for a like mineral, for when Radien would visit the planet to see if he could find the rest of the mineral vein that bore that particular one, and its honor-shielding power.

Suddenly, several bolts of energy pinged off of an amber shield that had been invisible up until then. Someone just tried to get the drop on him. Radien whipped his head around to see the incoming Demons who looked quite confused as to why shooting him didn't work. Radien's eyes darted back up to the display case, and immediately put two and two together. The Honorblade was still active, and it longed to be wielded again against the foes of the universe.

Radien unlatched the case, and retrieved the Honorblade from where it was resting. The two Demons took a step back, like they recognized that sword.

"*It cannot be...*" one of the pair said.

The Honorblade glowed along its fuller, channeling azure energy across the entire sword. The sword had awakened.

"*All warriors, hear me!*" The second Demon hurriedly spoke on an open telepathic channel across the vessel. "*The Honorblade of Korvideyl has awakened! The Successor is known! Warn the Masters!*"

"*Karsath una'Raish Nezhval, Deyl aldakar! Even if the stars forget honor, I will not!*" Radien challenged. The Demons drew their swords, as this was the only way they could defeat him when he wielded a sword enchanted with an Honor Stone of Korvideyl; face-to-face, in melee combat.

The two engaged simultaneously, and Radien quickly tossed the Honorblade into his right hand as the Borfblade was summoned into his left. The Borfblade was a heavier sword than the Honorblade, and Radien was left-handed, after all. The clash began as the strikes of the Demons were met with blocks and parries landed perpendicular to their swords, causing the attacker's weapons to ping off of each other, but more like the Honorblade and the Borfblade were jabbing these swords away with their edges, digging into the enemy weapons as they also tired out the hands of their wielders, having to constantly correct themselves and try again with each failed attack. Soon, Radien had his opening to slash the fingers of one of the Demons with the Honorblade, severing them from its hand, and with the weapon doomed to miss him on its next attack for sure, Radien used that extra moment to slam the Borfblade down on the incoming thrust from the second Demon, and with that opening made in its defense, the Honorblade pierced cleanly through its chest, only to be forcibly removed from the sword by a pushing front kick. The Demon who had lost several fingers and its weapon was soon ran through with the Borfblade and subsequently push-kicked off.

In the aftermath of slaying two Demons, Radien examined the Honorblade of Korvideyl with The Aura's Second Sight, and discovered that the weapon was indeed of hunderfold metal. Demons slain by it would not reincarnate in Hell, and would be permanently destroyed.

Looking across the Lore Citadel, Radien saw that Demons were vacating the premises, and rapidly, but the fleeing ships were intercepted by incoming fighter craft from David Company, having just successfully mopped up the rest of the enemy forces that had up until then, been surrounding Belariq.

Running towards the closest enemy group, Radien placed himself right behind an archway, and let the Demons come to him. They rounded the corner, and the first one was immediately met with a foot to its face, knocking it down and out instantly. Radien then spun around to side kick the next Demon, but the hit landed on the one who was still traveling towards the ground, getting pushed into one of its compatriots, pinning them to the floor. The last one had no time to raise its weapon before the Borfblade had already cut through the neck cleanly, and would simply roll off once the Demon hit the floor. However, this did not happen, as Radien instead spinning side kicked the severed head, launching it directly into the face of an incoming Demon.

The Demon, however, was as unimpressed as he was not actually struck by the flying head of its subordinate. Whoever this higher-ranking creature of evil was, he had pierced the flying head with its sword, with unnatural reflex. The sword was jet-black in color, and had waves like a flamberge along its blade. However, the actual length of the sword was no more than that of a typical one-handed longsword. As the Demon who wielded it stepped closer towards him, Radien could see more detail of the sword in this spare time. In its silvered-metal pommel rested a small red gem, and the metal pommel continued into the hilt, and then the crossguard, and then the blade itself. A red and black corded leather handle covered the haft of the hilt itself, as intricately woven as it was ergonomic, tailor-made for the Demon who wielded it. The blade itself, however, remained jet-black, save for when it could focus heat at the will of its owner into a specific area of the blade, that would not melt its metal, but would any other if held in clash long enough.

There could be no doubt about it. This was one of them. The Dark Six.

"I know who you are..." Radien said aloud to meet this Demon. "But how?"

"*Fol'z'ath...* it's happening quicker than Tactician had anticipated."

"What is?!" Radien demanded.

"Tactician had predicted where this place would be and when, our opportunity to seize it... but he seems to have forgotten that the last breath of this place's guardian is the first breath of his successor, and so he has come to reclaim the Vault."

Radien's Second Sight was still active, burning every detail of what he was seeing into his mind so he could recall it later at-will, without error. Every word this Demon was saying, he was going to remember it exactly as it was taking place now, for review later.

"You win this round, *Greígoth...* but only because we do not clash blades today."

The Demon then suddenly began to glitch in and out of existence, as Radien began to realize he was not beholding the real instance of this Demon. It was a hallucination, forcibly projected into his visual cortex through unknown means.

Though Belariq was defended, Radien suddenly felt as though all other sound had dropped in pitch until it drowned all other sound entirely. All he could hear, all of a sudden, was the slow beat of his Death World Vulpian heart. After all, it was the case that the resting heart rate for a Death Worlder was at its highest, eight per minute. A species evolved to take on extreme conditions, certainly.

He wasn't sure what it was he felt, until he was flung into a vision of a great and rippling blood-red portal, a Way Gate. But rather than the one to the Field of Unreality that the one constructed on Aldin Moon was, this Way Gate went to a different dimension. The Burning Hells. And it was large. Large enough of a tear in reality for one of its oldest foes to emerge from. And as Radien saw the same Demon he just met here, the first of the Dark Six stepping forth into Cynar from the Burning Hells, he felt a strangely specific flavor of a tremendous dread. It was as though he had just learned of his death date, and how it would even happen: Mortally wounded, somehow. Some strike would be of a kind he could not parry, could not defend against, and could not heal from, and for it, he would not see the next moonrise.

Radien was never one to experience fear. He feared no enemy. But this was not fear that was seething through him like it had been forcibly injected into his veins, but a nearly crushing dread, that did all in its power to convince him he was doomed to this flavor of dark fate.

<*Radien?*> A voice called out from nowhere.

"Radien!"

Radien's eyes shot open, back in the Lore Citadel, and he jolted up from having apparently collapsed on the floor. Veralis had apparently found her way here.

"How long have I been out for?" Radien immediately asked.

"Two days."

"Belariq?!"

"Belariq's been good since yesterday."

Radien then took a look around the room, and so did Veralis.

"What even is this place? It's clearly a library or

museum of some kind, but of what? And to what end?" Radien questioned aloud.

"It's an Artifact Vault of some kind," Veralis answered. "Like Teyn-Var-Wolk's Archaeotech Museum."

"Yeah, but massive," Radien added. "The six cubic-kilometer temporary vacuole I had to generate in this area was barely large enough to fit it on such short notice."

"Vault of the Defender, maybe."

"Vault of the who now?"

"The name given to a fabled repository of powerful artifacts, guarded by the Universal Defender," Veralis explained the history behind what she thought this place was. "If the legends are true, this place is home to all kinds of crazy stuff, from the oddly specific to the possibly universe-ending if in the wrong hands... The Haywire Shield and the Eternity Geode supposedly rest within these halls, if this is the place."

"What about the Honorblade of Korvideyl?" Radien asked.

"The Honorblade of Korvideyl was the personal weapon of T'Sen Torgaen, the Eighth Defender. It would be there, too. Along with the personal weapons of each Defender who came before and after him."

"Interesting... so that would be this place, then," Radien said, as he eyes the longsword in his right hand.

"So it is!" Veralis exclaimed as she noticed just what weapon Radien was holding in his off hand. "By the gods... that means this place was being hauled off by the Demons, rather than being one of *their* libraries. If that all had gotten into the hands of the Dark Six..."

"I think I get it," Radien commented as he realized the implications. "All of the artifacts are still here, though. I can sense that nothing is out of place." His amber eyes still flickered as they scanned the space citadel. "They didn't get anything, couldn't even access the datapads... this place had completely locked itself down for as long as there were Demons on it! What we saw was purely a visual change on the outside."

"Legend also claims that the Vault bore a consciousness," Veralis explained further. "Some of the weapons that were placed here were so powerful, it's said that the very walls and will of the Vault of the Defender itself gained a sense of duty, to keep those weapons within its walls at all costs... to protect the rest of the universe from their presence, and the new forms of suffering and pain they could cause if let out amongst the stars."

"A prison?" Radien asked.

"No, not exactly," Veralis explained. "Nothing in here is alive. Except us, obviously... It's like you said, a museum. How many points on this star citadel?"

"Eight. No... Seven," Radien recalled.

"The most common classification system for relics and artifacts is the Tharissian Index. Seven levels for how dangerous an artifact is, from benign to potentially universe-ending. How much you wanna bet seven points for seven levels?"

"Seven is a commonly symbolic number," Radien commented. "The ancient Greeks of Old Earth revered it as the sum of three and four, what they considered to be the perfect numbers. I can't imagine it's unique to the Humans, the presence of the number seven as a symbol."

"It would seem then, that we have found the Vault of the Defender," Veralis commented, once again eyeing the second blade Radien was carrying, before examining the case it was in, and the latching mechanism that Radien opened to access the sword in particular. "These locks are enchanted, the Vault would've had to *let* you open that case and take up that sword."

"I like its principle," Radien said. "A shield to block everything at range, forcing your enemies to fight in melee, and a secondary shield at my back, to ensure no one can sneak up on me. T'Sen had the right idea with this sword. That being said, there's something else I need to figure out as well."

"What would that be?"

"Not sure, but I think Xatrial had an idea. I saw something in the library at Soulshatter Bunker that might give me a clue."

"Isn't it called Soulshatter Keep?"

"It looks like a rectangular prism of cobblestone on the outside. I'm sorry, but that's a *bunker*, not a keep."

"Fair enough." Veralis chuckled.

"I'll need to remember this location, though," Radien said, dropping a fist-sized grey stone with a blue sigil emblazoned upon its surface. "A place like this with its own consciousness and ability to pass judgment on who gets to do what here probably has a natural defense of just typically hiding in intergalactic space, where there's no other solid matter for tens of billions of light-years."

"Waypoint Stone?" Veralis asked, noting the rock. "Bit old-fashioned."

"Staggeringly reliable, though," Radien countered, and Veralis nodded. If you did have the time to make or get ahold of Waypoint Stones, they were much more reliable as a teleport landing marker than almost every other method, save for stationary Way Gates.

As everyone went their separate ways, Radien noticed back in the *Aura Runner* that he still had the Honorblade of Korvideyl on his right hip, along with the Borfblade next to it. The Vault had let him take it with him, and he figured he might as well, until he could figure out how to achieve that same Shield of Honor effect on the Borfblade.

Chapter the Third
Protocols of Vigilance

"Vigilance is never wrong. But there is a difference between vigilance and just seeking reasons to be enemies."
—Death World Vulpian phrase

Personal log of Tactician Miles Radien, UDM 8-317,392,210-4-27. I don't normally keep a log, but I've been told by the Raon-Arashal Defensive Militarium that it's considered good practice for its members to do so, so here we are. After experiencing what I can only describe as a Mortal Dread, in which I felt as though I were due to imminently suffer a wound in battle impossible to defend against or recover from, I'm traveling to Zharekk, where the bunker of fourth Universal Defender Xatrial Isenhart is located, as I believe one of his works that I spotted in his library noted a similar phenomenon. Not the Manifest of Apocalypse, mind you, but a different one, entitled Dread of the Defender. I intend to see if an explanation to the vision I beheld of one of the Dark Six entering reality exists within its passages.

The book itself, however, was in Isenhart's study, where all of his personal works were kept. After all, the library was where one kept other people's ideas for reference while creating your own.

Soon finding the tome inscribed with the title he sought, Radien opened the book and paged through its initial slew of very wordy Loriken text explaining Isenhart's own dreads, particularly those that created the Manifest of Apocalypse text. Though he was Defender, and had many victories in his own right, Isenhart easily saw the least action of any of them, and it was said to have driven him mad.

"Okay, here we are..." Radien said aloud as he finally reached the actual body of text that explained the vision he had.

Three of my predecessors were fully aware of the presence of one of the Lords of Evil whenever they had entered reality, Isenhart's explanation read. *That I have not seen these visions as well stands as testimony to the effectiveness of the Cynofraxians' work. Taking the form of a vision of said Demon Lord wherever they had entered this universe, followed by an immense dread of something that would destroy them, corresponding to one of these Dark Six and their specialties. Ahron Kasven, the first of the line, first noted the Dread in the aftermath of a successful defense, beholding what his successor, the Hydenti Shpargen-Shperg identified as the Dread of the Mortal Wound. She would later identify six unique Dreads, corresponding to each of these Dark Six, the Lords of Evil, leaders the Burning Hells and their legions. Kirinaultr, the Taigron third Defender, was able to determine from Kasven and Shpargen-Shperg's testimonies enough information for me to place the pieces of this dark puzzle together, that my successors may be able to wield against them upon their inevitable return. Even the Cynofraxians who imprisoned the Dark Six within the prison realm they called Unapasakl Aura-Käynenrel understood that the solution was only temporary, and like I do now, hoped that the universe they would return to would be prepared adequately to do battle with them. To that end, I hope these passages may bring illumination to a future mystery that I will not be around to solve.*

Radien then studied the pages that showed the name and title of each of the Dark Six. This was powerful information indeed.

Dread of the Mortal Wound – The Defender suddenly feels as though they are due to suffer a mortal injury or wound in battle they will not be able to defend themselves against or recover from. Whether by the injuries of battle or the invisible sword of disease, this Dread remains the same. Zoln'Slan-Thiild, The Frontliner. The single deadliest warrior of Hell, the most practiced martial artist of all Demonkind. Every one of the Dark Six could defeat the other five in their own ways, and The Frontliner would be the one to do so in direct combat. History remembers that both Ahron Kasven and Shparghen-Shperg fell to this Demon Lord. Though the other five that create this dark equation are themselves no novices of the sword, it is the raw skill with a blade that The Frontliner possesses that has made him the bane of two Defenders. Perhaps this is because where the other five would seek to subjugate a galaxy, it is The Frontliner who would instead seek to burn it to ashes. Ours is not a kind vulnerable to the trickery that the other five prefer.

Dread of the Grey Choice – The Defender feels as though they are due to be forced into making an impossible choice, between evil and eviler, bad or worse, the kinds of choices whose only correct solution is to flip the table over and stab the mastermind of said choice in the face with the closest sharp object. Aghlornosaath, the Seducer. One of the three Dark Six who specializes in recruiting gullible and vulnerable souls from Cynar into the service of Hell, hers is to bring thralls made of men and women alike from this universe of ours into their dark folds, and consume their very essences once their usefulness to the dark cause is expended. The Seducer is known also as the Painmaster of Hell, and recruits by tormenting her victims with sheer physical and existentially searing pain until they willingly surrender their free will just to make it stop, thus using the seduction of ignorance. But there is no bliss in ignorance, only perdition.

Radien nodded heartily in agreement with that last sentence. No bliss in ignorance, indeed.

Dread of Decency's Veil – The Defender suddenly feels as though they are due to discover a great deception whose bitter truth will fundamentally alter their view of the universe, and for the worse. Echlenairriam, the Deceiver. Another of the Dark Six's recruiters, The Deceiver recruits through lies and half-baked promises which bear no obligation towards the trickster who forges the contracts of service that lure power-seekers and desperate souls alike by the countless. I do not know if it is even possible to enter a contract with The Deceiver that does not involve surrendering free will to become a Demonic puppet. This is why the obligations towards her are moot, as once under her control, she will simply make you release her from the obligations and pledge to serve freely. The one thing all must remember is to never agree to terms that The Deceiver has herself set, if a braver soul than I would intend to see if infiltration is possible, though I grandly doubt it. With there being no cure to release the consciousness from the service of the Dark Six other than death, this is the caution that I must advise to all: Far more powerful and wiser people than myself have tried and failed to cure Demonic servants of their puppeting. No such cure has been found, and I doubt it ever will. Death is the only cure for Dark Six servants, only death.

Radien sighed as he solemnly remembered this fact well, and how it led to the extinction of an entire chapter of the Vulpian species, who were no longer considered Vulpians for their betrayal of the universe.

Dread of Abominations – The Defender suddenly feels as though an old enemy of theirs is due to return to the fold, and continue their mission of misery. Daylayis Sieklekarneen, The Dream-Taker. Of the Six, three recruit. The Deceiver, The Seducer, and the Dream-Taker. The Dream-Taker typically does so in the form of assuming the role and form of the nightmares of her victim, tormenting them with visions of the doom they will bring if desperate measures are not taken preemptively. This always entails an oath of dark allegiance of some regard, and thusly she claims souls into her service, that of Hell and its legions of invaders who seek absolute dominion over our realm.

Still remembering The Planet of Traitors, Radien wondered if The Dream-Taker was the architect of the plan that saw the subjugation of the Exiled Chapter. It seemed to fit the bill.

Dread of Imminent Defeat – The Defender will feel as though they are due to enter an era of darkening stars, as defeats mount in greater and greater numbers without cease or mercy. Makhlumentainne, The Tactician. The very air seems to sour itself as I pen these words, and the name of the single most dangerous of them all, The Tactician. Where a nemesis would seek your defeat, an enemy would only seek your death. The Tactician may be the exemplar of an Enemy to this end, or he may be intelligent enough to understand that to assume this way of warfare will only lead to the most fiery retaliation that would boil the magma oceans of Hell itself. I do not know which, but what I do know is that the Era of Darkening Stars is marked by when The Tactician no longer seeks to accomplish victory, but to merely attain it no matter what. The Tactician will assume himself entitled to his win, and for it, Honor itself may die, and seal the fate of countless worlds.

Radien wondered if The Tactician was responsible for the plan that led to Caltoran's corruption. With this information, it was entirely possible that The Tactician, seeking only the death of his opposition, did order such a cowardly operation.

Finally, the Dread of Crushing Totality. The Defender will feel as though a moment is due to be nigh of paramount importance, where success must be absolute, lest failure be similarly total. Tahd Viert, The Leader. Though I consider The Tactician to be the single most dangerous of the Six, The Leader is indeed the one who leads them, and from whose mind the genesis of the campaign against Cynar was born. Similarly, I believe that The Leader will be the first one to exit Doomrealm, the prison in which the Six are contained. His will be the decisions and actions that bring about what will be the Second War for Reality, whenever that should be, far beyond my own time.

Radien looked around at Xatrial's study, and could practically see him pouring over texts and references as he compiled this manual all those eons ago, driven near to madness by a lack of duty or purpose as the Defender, his mind ablaze with the flames of dread whose manifest was reserved for a future he was doomed never to see, or fight within for.

"Isenhart… I wish I could tell you now that the time for your words has come," Radien lamented. "I wish I could reach back those eons just to tell you that I'm here in this old bunker now, solving the puzzle just as you did back then, *because* you took the time to write it all down, just in case you were right."

The specter of the tired-eyed Loriken continued to shuffle between desk and bookshelf, penning down every detail and equation he thought might help, somehow, some form, some way.

"Finding myself reminded of how I once felt as you did then, involuntarily neutral and unacting in the face of a great oncoming doom. How the hell did I survive? And now that I think of it, what even could I tell you that you haven't heard a billion times already from a sea of idiots and slow-minded ignorants?"

The right ear of the wolf at his desk twitched as though he had heard something. Radien and the vision of Xatrial both looked in the direction of the door, but Xatrial's eyes weren't on the door. They were on the strange specter who had suddenly appeared before him.

"Places can remember," Xatrial commented.

"That might be why I can see you."

"Wait, but I'm from your future!" Radien commented as he turned back around to face Xatrial.

"This sanctum is still around then, or you wouldn't be here."

"So you mean to tell me that places can remember both their present and their future?"

"That which is not alive but can still remember is not bound by the typical rules of linear time."

"Oh, of fucking *course* they aren't," Radien said as his ears flattened.

"But the answer to your question—is that I don't know either," Xatrial admitted as he stood up from his seat. "I'm not sure if there's even anything you *could* say to that end. But I suppose that our mutual understanding is all I need for now…"

"I can't tell if you're visiting my time, or I'm visiting yours," Radien commented.

"I think it's both, basically. I see you in my time, you see me in yours. Either way, here we are."

"To what end, though?" Radien wondered aloud. Xatrial shrugged his shoulders in response, before continuing to scribble more notes down. "Maybe it's because there's something you know that never made it to these volumes, and they've returned."

Xatrial stopped as soon as Radien played the pronoun game on the Dark Six, but he knew *exactly* who *they* were.

"I came here seeking an answer to a question, and I've learned that the answer is that I felt the Dread of a Mortal Wound. I saw The Frontliner entering reality, the first person to ever behold one of the Dark Six since Kirinaultr."

"Which number Defender are you, then?" Xatrial asked with palpable curiosity towards the future.

"I... I guess I only now realize that experiencing the Dread mechanically confirms it," Radien processed. "Though I can't say I've properly earned that title yet, my deeds hold not even a candle to the nine who came before me, present company included."

"We've all felt that way for no small part of it," Xatrial commented. "Though I have been called Defender, and have since reconciled with that it is my title, my own deeds pale in comparison to those who came before me, and I feel as though my predecessors have claimed all the glory for themselves."

"I know the feeling," Radien recalled. "All the glory and adventure had, where nothing remains but a grey rock of a planet, whose skies are as grey as the three-ingredient soup of concrete, steel and glass that made up every single one of its structures."

Xatrial paused as he looked over to where Radien stood.

"Even if all the exploration and discovery had already been done, there wasn't even an afterglow to at least ride alongside. Opportunity was fiction, as fiction as the prosperity of every story other than my own."

"What changed?" Xatrial asked.

"I'll just say this, Xatrial: It shouldn't take a miraculous visitor from another world just for me to have a chance."

Xatrial nodded. "So you do understand, then. That is why you do not insult me with insipid dross masquerading as aid."

"Talk costs nothing, no wonder it's—"

"...The only thing people are willing to do," the two finished the sentence simultaneously. Radien sighed as his shoulders dropped, though more in a relaxed manner than a downed one.

Xatrial's head whipped around to see an alarm blaring in his time, and Radien saw the same one doing so on his own. A proximity alert of some kind.

"It's coming from your end," Xatrial said. "That terminal over there."

Radien rushed over to the terminal to open the readout. The words on the screen took a bit for his eyes to translate, as it was a very, very old form of the Loriken language that hadn't been in use for eons. But it was them.

"Demonic troop transport on direct route to Zharekk."

"That what they call this planet now?" Xatrial asked, and Radien nodded. Radien suddenly heard the crackling of raw power, and the sound of a lightning strike as Xatrial walked up next to him, no longer in a spectral form. The Fourth Defender's sheer drive to do his part had brought him forcibly into Radien's present.

"This would explain why no one knows how you died," Radien said. "All accounts say you vanished into this place and were never heard from again."

"So it would seem," Xatrial chuckled. "I agree that it shouldn't take a miraculous visitor from another world just for me to have a chance. But here you are, with my chance, that I would be a fool not to take."

"Agreed. The laws of time can stuff it. Find your weapon, Defender! We've got a battle to win!"

Xatrial hurried off towards the armory within Soulshatter Bunker to acquire it, and Radien split off to get to the roof, calling the *Aura Runner*.

<Techbooth, there's a Demonic troop transport vessel on direct course with Zharekk!>

I HAVE ALREADY TAKEN THE LIBERTY OF ALERTING THE PLANET'S DEFENSES, AND RAON-ARASHAL'S.

<Tenth Defender, if you can hear me, it's Xatrial. There's more than one.>

Radien looked into the space surrounding Zharekk with Second Sight, seeing only the single vessel.

<I don't see them, Xatrial. Either your systems are old and out of date, or—>

<They're cloaked. My systems are old indeed, but they're the reliable kind of old, rather than the rickety.>

<Patch what you've got to the Aura Runner, it's in orbit.>

Xatrial then climbed up onto the roof to meet Radien, a runed staff in hand a little under a meter taller than its wielder.

"The *Aura Runner?*" Xatrial said. "Kasven's ancient ship still flies?"

To this, Radien nodded, and Xatrial reached out to Techbooth within the vessel to relay the information regarding what kind of cloak the Demons were likely using.

RADIEN, THIS CLOAK THE DEMONS ARE USING, IT MUST BE INCREDIBLY ADVANCED IF NEITHER MY SYSTEMS NOR ZHAREKK'S CAN DECECT IT.

<It's not advanced, it's ancient,> Radien explained. *<Either they've re-discovered it, or have been aging it up for a wildcard play.>*

Radien's comm-link then pinged from within the pocket of his cargo pants. Well, one of the pockets, at least.

"Tactician Radien, this is Tactician Olvek, Zharekk Orbital Defense. With the *Aura Runner's* information on their cloak, we've identified twelve ships, including the uncloaked one that we assume they were fronting to make the attack look smaller, along with a passing radiation field that we're not sure why exists, but it appears benign. Now then, you may consider this good news: They're all heading for your location."

"Means they're not going for the cities, their objective is Soulshatter Keep," Xatrial commented. "Good news indeed."

"It also means that we're in for a fun time," Radien commented, and Xatrial laughed in agreement as the staff in his hands charged with crackles of blue-white lightning.

"Olvek, Raon-Arashal's also been alerted, so expect reinforcements. In the meantime, Xatrial and I are gonna help ourselves to the first round."

"Fight well, Radien. My air wing is on its way to assist, Olvek out."

Xatrial began to twirl the staff in one hand, letting it gather up speed as the power coursing through started to electrify the air, and made both his and Radien's hairs stand up on end. As Xatrial kicked up the orb of electricity, Radien leaped into the air and lashed his foot out at the voltaic orb, catapulting it outwards and into the shields of the Demonic Drop-Pods, and even electrocuting the crew into unconsciousness, causing impacted Drop-Pods to plummet to the ground without slowing down their flight using their retro-rockets, subsequently borderline disintegrating upon slamming into the rocky surface of Zharekk, blasting ship parts and crewmember parts across the somewhat featureless terrain, ensuring that this area would probably be a scrapper's dream come true for the next decade.

These electric orbs that Xatrial kicked up and Radien kicked out were striking ships by the dozens, and causing the plains that surrounded the canyon of Soulshatter Keep to be rained upon by the uncontrolled ships, and several towns bordering the Plains of Exile even put up Local Area Defense Grids to shield themselves from wayward shrapnel, as locals prepared their salvaging gear for once the battle was over.

Suddenly, the *Aura Runner* tore across the sky above Radien, opening a channel to the comm-link in his pocket.

TEMPORAL RIFT OPENING IN PLANETARY ORBIT.

"What, now?!" Radien yelled. "This is hardly the time! Xatrial, can you handle the defense from here?!"

Xatrial aye'd loudly in response, and Radien warped aboard his ship to try to find out what just caused that Temporal Rift to appear. Time travel was by and large throughout the civilized universe, something that people did not particularly want to fuck around with. Though methods of traversing backwards or forwards in time had been tested almost to the point of effectiveness, they all always either failed or suddenly stopped.

The tear that opened in space itself looked as unnatural as it felt. A ship came careening out from it. It was heavily battle-damaged, and its weathered pilot was missing part of his right ear when he hailed the *Aura Runner*, and appeared on the visual feed.

"Tactician Radien, arm a Pulsar Missile and prepare to fire on the coordinates I'm feeding you!"

Radien looked at the statuette on his console that signified his Command Rank within the Raon-Arashal Defensive Militarium. Silver base, red pyramid. Major, the rank immediately senior to Tactician within the Universal Militaristic and Defense Force Optimal Chain of Command, whose statuette was a silver base with a green pyramid atop it. Ship pilots often differed from ground forces with a much more lenient uniform standard, which was to say almost none. As long as the pants had pockets and the shirt fit, the only real identifier required was that Rank Statuette.

"Protocol of Vigilance, Epsilon-Theta-Fehu!" Radien shouted to the pilot on the other side, aboard the battered and scarred *Aura Runner*. "Identify subtype!"

"Subtype two," Major Radien responded from where he was. "The prompt is *Rush*."

"The response is *Cannon*," Tactician Radien answered from the version of the *Aura Runner* native to this part of the timeline. The two then nodded to each other as Tactician Radien armed the Pulsar Missile. It seemed the other *Aura Runner* was completely out of them. When he looked at the coordinates Major Radien was giving him to fire, it was the radiation cloud that Olvek had noticed before, but had said was benign. Tactician Radien had a feeling that with his future self instructing him to fire upon it, the cloud was likely to reveal itself to not be benign at all.

"Fire on my mark," Major Radien instructed.

"The arming sequence isn't finished yet, if I shoot now I risk either a misfire or a dud!" Tactician Radien responded.

"Acknowledged, Tactician. Prepare to fire on my mark."

"Arming sequence at fifty percent..."

"Fire now!"

Radien grimaced, and pressed the button on the *Aura Runner's* console. The Pulsar Missile fired off, but was too premature in its firing sequence for the payload to detonate. The *Aura Runner* that Major Radien was piloting suddenly lit up and fired a beam of energy at the missile, which finished the process that hadn't been completed within Tactician Radien's *Aura Runner*.

The missile seemingly impacted empty space and detonated, only after the explosion tore a sizable chunk from a final hidden ship did Tactician Radien realize what had just happened. The other vessels that had been detected bound for Zharekk were barely the beginning of this invasion, the transport ship that was now destabilizing and facing secondary explosions across it could easily fit all of the invaders from the rest of the fleet twice over!

Had this vessel been allowed to approach Zharekk so undetected, the planet would have been lost with the sheer numbers that the Demons had brought to bear this time. Major Radien breathed a huge sigh of relief as he leaned back into his chair at the helm of the now-drained *Aura Runner*, the only systems still with power the most vital ones. Even then, they were in danger of failing.

The reinforcements from Raon-Arashal, David Company leading them arrived to engage the Demons still surrounding Zharekk. The defense's success had been assured by this act of temporal interference.

Zharekk was defended.

"It's worth it," Major Radien assured. "If only because I can see them again now, one last time."

"That bad, huh?" Tactician Radien asked as David Company made quick work of the scattering Demonic forces.

Major Radien simply nodded. "I'm sending over the explanation for everything, you're going to need it for the inquiry you've got about a six hundred chance of receiving from the High Commandant. Temporal interference, and all."

The battered *Aura Runner* began to destabilize, glitching in and out of existence as time asserted its new course. Major Radien then held up what looked like an amethyst geode if the amethyst had been replaced with amber, letting Tactician Radien see the artifact on his viewscreen.

"It's from the Vault," Major Radien explained. "The Eternity Geode. Tactician... my sin is not that I've gone back in time to prevent the Demons from this victory, but rather, what their victory here today that no longer took place eventually made me do."

"Deoxian Pulse?" Tactician Radien asked.

"I wish, that would've been far less dire. I've been all that's left, along with the Vault for an amount of time I don't even know the number for. And I don't just mean of the fight against Demons or the Dark Six."

The banged-up *Aura Runner* was barely holding

on to its physical presence within this reality.

"Though I still think the Omega Wave is within your future, it won't be the same now... I'd thank the gods that it may work this time, but they deserve no thanks from me."

"I'm not sure what to say," Tactician Radien finally spoke.

"Then say nothing. This is not a bad thing. Remember the Oldest Truth..."

"The Oldest Truth, the fact that has been known since fact could be known, is that I stand alone, but this is not a bad thing," both Death World Vulpians said simultaneously, before the *Aura Runner* vanished entirely from space.

Everything seemed to fall silent as Radien could only process what had just happened. Somehow, he understood what the Major meant when he spoke. Omega Wave... all that was left... he was left with a lot to think about, and hardly anything to say to express it.

"What horrors have I just prevented, in what timeline that now rests at peace for having never existed?" Radien asked himself. "I will be glad to not find out."

Upon returning to the planet's surface to meet back up with Xatrial, the Loriken was browsing his library, using the more restorative aspects of his power to reverse the aging that had occurred on the books, ensuring their preservation and also removing the fragility of the ancient pages.

"I imagine you're planning to remain in this time?" Radien asked.

"History remembers that Xatrial Isenhart simply

vanished from the universe one day, and that his successor, Peldane Thari, was born in the Fourth Cosmic Era, only a few hundred ASC before the Sentience War began... an event I will have to study, given my absence," Xatrial explained. "Even if I could, I would never want to. My fate is known in that timeline, and who am I to argue with history?"

"The second in line?" Radien asked.

"Good gods, who's *first* in that one, then?!" Xatrial laughed out after Radien's comment, which left him chuckling a little as well. "Besides, I was absent from the Sentience War... apparently a rather decisive one, gloriously won against the Shard. They were fascist slavers, the whole lot of them... would've liked to have helped with that one."

Xatrial snapped the book he was reading shut. "Oh, well. I guess I'll just have to settle for the Second War for Reality, where instead of the Shard, I must utterly destroy Demonic enemies," he said as he then proceeded to exaggeratedly grumble off towards the larder within this bunker. Radien chuckled further as he couldn't argue with that, leaving the five-foot-ten biped wolf to his work at Soulshatter Keep, so that Radien could continue his at Torvaltyne Bastion.

Chapter the Fourth

The Mind Warrior

"Only about one percent of those who achieve practical immortality ever live beyond twice the normal lifespan of their species, with only one percent of that population living beyond five times that. I, and many others have found that after crossing that threshold, it is quite trivial to continue surviving for as long as is wished, as by then one's mastery of remaining alive plateaus, and the difficulty of continuing survival slowly drops. Even then, on an averagely-populated modernized planet, that leaves at least two hundred thousand individuals, which is a lot of people, even if not by comparison."
—Jarrek Wöllschlager, during an interview on extreme longevity conducted by biologist Lyraine Ventakus

Personal Log of Poet of Arms Second Degree Arakai Selendica, UDM 8-317,392,210-4-36. D-o-S 2 Micah Jorvask, of the Nathineyl Shadow House known as the Eyes of the Daggers, has attained critical information regarding our enemy, the Dark Six. Though there are innumerable names for these Demon Lords across the species, someone *had to inspire those names. The universe was deeply scarred by the First War for Reality, and as we enter this 'hot' part of the Second, the air of the universe is thick with rage at the enemy and desire to get even, considering the corruption of Caltoran, when a Psychosia Demon wrested control of his body after killing him in a cowardly manner. Caltoran's raw Psionic prowess, coupled with the sheer drive to destruction of a Psychosia Demon resulted in the loss of tens of thousands of worlds, as well as over a dozen species, including the Elurian and Kendrosian peoples.*

To coin a different phrase, the universe is now in the process of saying 'our turn.'

Even the Old Cynofraxians knew that banishing them to Doomrealm was only temporary, and the warriors of the universe are prepared to face the Lords of Evil once again. It is what they set upon the path for. It will be they who fight for the universe, and live to regale the future with stories of their victories.

That aside, Micah has indeed brought information on said enemy, and it is quite attention demanding. But then again, so is Micah when she learns you're good at ear rubs. One of my colleagues found this out the hard way relatively recently. I am thusly unseated from my throne of repute for giving the best ear rubs at Torvaltyne Bastion. Rest assured, I will reclaim my title. I will train as hard to do so as said colleague trains in martial arts. Which is to say, whenever he gets free time around here. He's still quite enthralled with the Holographic Arena technology... We had to build an entire extra one just for him because he's such a frequent user. I wonder if there is a Death Worlder term for 'addicted to training.' Knowing Death

Worlders, they would take it as a compliment.

"The ship to be looking out for is called *Gadrigaridox*, or 'wall of darkness.'" Micah briefed. "It's Grand Arbiter Class city-ship packed to the brim with Hell's best soldiers, including being the home base of at least two of the Dark Six, those being the Seducer and the Dream-Taker."

"The only one actually in Cynar is the Frontliner, though," Radien noted. "I haven't experienced either the Dread of the Grey Choice, or the Dread of Abominations."

"That's the other interesting thing," Micah noted. "The tip we got said that the *Gadrigaridox* hasn't entered Cynar, but is making plans to, and some ally that we haven't been aware of until now beamed us these schematics."

"Are they authentic?" Jarrek asked, and Micah nodded. Everything checked out. Some unknown ally indeed.

"I'm not too concerned about the *Gadrigaridox* itself so long as it isn't within Cynar," Micah continued. "But I *do* want to find out who gave us this intel. It's leading to dozens of other breakthroughs, if not hundreds, just by offering such a detailed look at the inner workings of Demonic ships and organization."

"Perhaps this graduates the theory of Rogue Demons beyond the realm of myth," Arakai added. "We've all heard the stories of Hell's dissidents."

"Turncoats of the Burning Hells are unheard of completely—" Radien began.

"In order to turn coat, you must owe a prior loyalty to whomever you betray," Arakai corrected. "I speak of Demons who never aligned themselves with the Dark Six's goals of conquest."

To this, Radien nodded. "Perhaps then, that is the case. I find it far easier to believe in the Dark Six having rebels rather than defectors."

Micah thought for a moment. "Well, my dance card is basically full with taking in and sorting through all the information this schematic gives us. In the meantime, we should all keep our ears open for more information, whether something coming from this unknown aid, or information on their identity. So let's not get too excited about Rogue Demons yet, because this could be something else as well."

Everyone nodded, and with the briefing finished, the Seven of Steel and Doom began to excuse themselves from the room, though Radien did so with more haste than average, speedwalking towards the hangar where the *Aura Runner* was docked.

"Arakai, did you notice anything off about Radien during the course of the briefing?" Veralis asked him. "His tail kept twitching at the tip."

"Well, in a Death Worlder, that's typically a subtle sign that a tremendous amount of pain is coursing through their system... it typically happens when psychically attacked, or—oh."

Jarrek's ears perked up as he realized that some presence may be actively fighting with Radien psionically, quickly opening a console and initiating a full scanner sweep of the grounds of Torvaltyne Bastion, to see if there was indeed a hostile psychic presence.

Meanwhile, Radien's pace had become a full

sprint once he knew no one was in sight. Rounding a corner, he hurriedly pulled the comm-link device out of the left front pocket of his cargo pants and opened a line directly to the computer system that controlled his ship.

"Techbooth, Emergency Dimensional Recall!"

A nearby security camera would notice his sudden warp-out to the helm of his ship, noticed also by the six others still within the briefing room and wondering what the hell his rush was.

"What in all the realms is he doing?!" Veralis questioned.

"I think a more appropriate question to ask is *where in all the realms is he going?*" Dorg piped up as he saw a notification on the console Jarrek was still fiddling around with. Radien was trying to initiate an emergency launch of his ship, and had just ordered the hangar doors to open. The Redarian Arch-Militant locked down the doors, preventing the flight as he opened a channel with the *Aura Runner.*

"Radien, there's too much traffic out there, those doors can't open right now or someone's going to get hurt!"

"Acknowledged, Jarrek," Radien said from within the helm of his vessel. "Techbooth, engage Punch Drive."

The *Aura Runner's* idle engines thrummed, before the ship lurched forward and vanished just before it would have hit the hangar bay doors, that were still shut, but had just proven to be no factor in Radien's ability to depart.

One could hear a pin drop in the briefing room with the six stunned senior staff of Torvaltyne Bastion, until Jarrek finally broke the silence.

"Wait, he actually got that to *work?*"

Somewhere in space, the *Aura Runner* floated in the void, its atoms the only matter within billions of light-years. The ship of myth was truly in the middle of nowhere, in the middle of nothing, within the Fornax Void. This truly empty region of space so far away from everything, absent even of neutrinos in some areas.

Within this void, where there was nothing else for untold distances, Radien collapsed on the floor of the Aura Runner.

"Techbooth... initiate physiological scan of pilot," Radien grunted. "Find out the cause of the ailment."

SYMPTOMS AND MEDICAL SCAN ARE CONGRUENT WITH THE CONDITION KNOWN AS ANAN KROHGATHI.

"Oh. That makes sense, actually," Radien commented in a surprisingly normal-sounding voice, despite the dire situation. "*Venn turalag... Ka'Venn turalag-nah nejald senth deyl'e alnd, Radien... Count the seconds... Just count the seconds, and don't close your eyes, Radien...*"

Despite the efforts to ward off the faint, and the demands he made of himself in the Death Worlder language, Radien passed out on the floor of the Aura Runner all the same, and found himself within a great and empty space of a white void.

"Damn it, I said not to close them," Radien cursed at himself. He then looked at himself, still seeing the fur patterns of a Death World Vulpian. "Okay, good, so I'm at least still me..."

"For how long, though?" A voice called out from within the void, behind him. Radien spun around to meet this unknown entity that shared the space with him. "Protocol of Vigilance, Epsilon-Phi-Raido."

"Name variant!"

"M-1."

Radien's head turning slowed down, but his eyes kept darting about, trying to track down where this voice was coming from. "The prompt is *Divide*," Radien challenged.

"The response is *twelve-forty-two*."

"*Anan Krohgathi*," Radien replied. "That's why."

"It was why you created the Autopsionic Cantrip."

"I don't recall..."

"That was part of the setup."

Back at the Fortress, five of the six wanted answers, while one of them actually had them, and thusly was answering the questions of the others.

"So, where did he go and why can't we track him?" Veralis asked.

"No clue," Jarrek answered. "We can't track him, remember?"

"Fair enough," Veralis replied.

"But you do know *why* we can't track him, right?" Micah asked.

To this, Jarrek nodded. "There's an experimental techpiece aboard the Aura Runner that Radien was working on, he called it the Punch Drive. Instantaneous entry into the Warp Channel from idle engines. Means no trajectory of entry to trace, just that the entry was made."

"A completely concealable Warp Channel Engine?" Arakai asked. That Radien may have just pioneered the technology had quite a number of implications.

"Not *completely*, mind you," Jarrek responded. "The entry point had a trace, but no directionality following it. There'll be a trace wherever he ends up, but he could be anywhere in the universe right now."

"Quite literally. The speed capabilities of the *Aura Runner* are mythic," Miirkae commented. "Ten times FTL *within* the Warp Channel... there is effectively no upper limit to the distance he could have crossed by now."

"Running isn't his style, though," Veralis added. "Whatever it was, the reason had to be dire indeed."

"Now that I think of it, how old *is* Tactician Radien, anyway?" Arakai suddenly asked. That was when almost everyone remembered they didn't actually have the answer to that. Almost.

"Nine hundred six ASC, these days," Veralis answered. "Give or take two."

"It could be *Anan Krohgathi,* then," Arakai concluded. Dorg immediately smacked his own head as he realized that Arakai was probably correct, with an '*oh, duh*' under his breath.

"Well, that makes sense, then," Dorg then followed up. "It's a condition unique to Death World Vulpians. Their unaltered lifespan typically maxes out at around nine hundred ASC. Of course, being that it's pretty easy to not have to worry about the whole aging thing with technology and Psionics as they are, it presents a unique situation that occurs very rarely in Death Worlders."

"Right now, Miles Radien's brain is burning in his skull trying to comprehend the fact that he's lived longer than he should have. It literally translates as 'time-break disease.'" Arakai finished. "It's more colloquially referred to as Temporal Delirium."

"But Radien wasn't born a Death Worlder, and he had already lived several times over the maximum lifespan of his birth species!" Veralis scoffed. "How could this be affecting him, that being the case?"

"Well, he's a Death Worlder *now*," Arakai mentioned. "If nothing else, this certainly settles that fact."

"Point taken."

The room was somewhat quiet again. Everyone knew what the next question was, but just wasn't sure how to word it, or if they should be the one to ask.

"Come on, guys." Dorg sighed. "Is it *really* that far-fetched? Radien is the very *essence* of the phrase 'never let them see you bleed.' His *Talgar* radiates with it."

Talgar was actually a Death World Vulpian term, not a Hykentiu one. The closest translation it had to Old Earth languages was one's 'vibe,' or moreover, 'the flavor of the air around them,' metaphorically speaking.

"The *Aura Runner* is the very first technology from beyond his home world that he ever saw," Veralis recalled. "It was given to him by the first being not from his world he ever met. It's been with him longer than any of us, even if only by a factor of hours."

"Not only that, but he also created the AI that

runs its computers himself," Jarrek mentioned. "Psionically built the code that runs Techbooth and allows them to learn. It's very likely he trusts his ship, and Techbooth, more than any of us."

"All I've got to do is outlast the *Anan Krohgathi*," Radien explained to the Psionic Projection of himself that shared this space in his own mind with him.

"Yeah, that's... what the Autopsionic Cantrip is for," the Projection responded. "You anticipated this moment about twelve ASC after your regeneration into a *Zhernrel-Vuljar*, when you learned about the condition."

"Sounds correct to me."

"You referenced the testimonies and accounts of sixteen different survivors of the *Anan Krohgathi*, despite its rarity within Death Worlders, only affecting a hundredth of a percent of those who reach beyond nine hundred ASC of age."

"And if one reaches nine hundred ten, they're good regardless. Nobody knows for sure why, but if you don't get *Anan Krohgathi* by nine hundred ten ASC, you never will," Radien followed up. "I'm nine hundred seven at the moment... damn."

"Good thing you created the cantrip, eh?"

"Saw it coming from a thousand years away. Almost literally."

The Projection then seemed to process for a moment. "Saw it coming from... a little over nine hundred years away, when you math it out."

"Nine hundred four, to be exact," Radien one-upped.

"Our point stands, hence."

"We prepared for this a few weeks after we turned *Zhrenrel-Vujlar,* to automatically activate passive defenses. The *Anan Krohgathi* itself is being funneled into space by way of a Psionic Vacuole."

"That would be what to do, yes," Radien responded. "Most fortunate that I was clever enough to remember that I might forget."

"Look, Radien's mind is one of the most well-defended places in the known universe, I've no doubt he's capable of handling this on his own," Veralis said. "I just wouldn't have minded knowing if he had a plan!"

"He had a plan!" a voice said from the entryway to the room. "He just didn't tell anyone."

Jarrek did a double-take on the Loriken who had just entered the room. He could swear that he had seen the lupine in a history book somewhere before...

"I'm sure he wrote down *somewhere* who I am, and the circumstances of my presence," Xatrial beckoned.

"He did," Micah responded. "His report after the battle on Zharekk mentioned that Xatrial Isenhart had indeed returned to the fold."

"Thus the mystery of my disappearance eons ago is solved," Xatrial furthered. "In one moment, I was within my time. One step forward, and I stand now in yours. I've heard my successors did well enough."

"The mystery solved, indeed," Veralis noted. "If you've got insight, I'm all ears. Even though I'm not a Dor-Val-Der Vulpian."

"I wrote the *Manifest of Apocalypse* to describe

in detail how to disperse threats to the greater universe, but Radien's *Anan Krohgathi* is his own. He would have created his own plan for in case of its occurrence, and due to that it only affects him, he would be the only person made privy to its proceedings."

"Makes sense," Dorg commented. "Even though it occurs in less than one in a hundred thousand Death Worlders, if there's anything I've learned of Radien, he's always prepared to be unlucky."

"Such was his life on Elder Terra," Veralis furthered. "He's always ready to find out that he beat the odds, but only the odds nobody wants to beat."

"You've said it yourself, Veralis, his mind is one of the most well-defended places in the universe," Micah reminded. "If survival of *Anan Krohgathi* is dictated by the person alone who suffers it, I have no doubt that Radien can trivialize it. At the very least, there's no way it's gonna be what kills him."

"If Radien can go toe-to-toe with an Akraknahal and *win, Anan Krohgathi* doesn't stand a chance, frankly," Arakai commented, to which *everyone's* heads turned, wondering what in all the realms he was on about.

"When he did the Gauntlet of Doom," Arakai explained. "Jaltai-Vuul? First one? Fought an Akraknahal solo? Did he tell no one else of this?!"

"Knowing Radien, he probably didn't think it impressive enough of a feat to mention," Miirkae noted.

"A fucking *Akraknahal* not being worth mention?!" Veralis exclaimed. "When he gets back, I'm gonna hit him over the head with my copy of The Raon-Arashal Almanac of Deadly Creatures..."

"He'll probably dodge or parry it because he thought it was a spontaneous self-defense drill," Micah cheekily commented.

"Gods dammit... you're totally right, though," Veralis responded, and Xatrial chuckled to himself.

Within the Aura Runner, a Death World Vulpian fought the *Anan Krohgathi.* Though his body was unconscious, it stirred, his left hand motioning and moving in a controlled pattern, before suddenly slicing the air itself with a claw, and opening a tunnel in space-time itself, on the other side was outside his ship. Radien then unconsciously held out his left hand as orange sparks began to seethe through the tips of the strands of his fur, floating their way into the portal to dissipate into space, dissolving into base hydrogen atoms and thusly being rendered inert.

"The Psionic Vacuole seems to be working, I can feel the weight of the *Anan Krogathi* relieving itself from me already," Radien said to the Psionic Projection of himself.

"Not nearly as pleasurable as having your brain smashed down by a lemon tied to a large gold brick, eh?" The Projection chuckled, and Radien couldn't help but let out a short one of his own, despite the somewhat low-hanging fruit that particular joke was.

"I'd equate it more to..."

Radien's thought trailed off before he could finish it, as he didn't know any good analogies or metaphors for things turning out well. The Psionic Projection nodded understandingly.

"Hell, I'm just glad we made this plan," Radien finished. The Projection nodded again.

Veralis sat at her usual spot in the Kianar's Folly tavern at the Fortress, wondering what was on the special rotation for tonight, but also how long it would take Radien to expel the *Anan Krohgathi.*

"The targeted restoration technique you taught me proved most useful," Radien made sure was known as he sat down, and Veralis's ears perked up to hearing his voice.

"Glad to be of help," Veralis replied. "It's a good thing I taught you it."

"Agreed." Radien nodded heartily as he pondered what he should order this time.

"So, anything else I should know?"

"*Anan Krohgathi* is literally a once-in-a-lifetime occurrence for a Death Worlder," Radien answered. "I'll never have to deal with it again."

"What would've happened if you didn't beat it?"

"Then... I would've lost myself. My mind would shatter like glass, and I'd be forever trapped in a state generously referred to as *Jakroh-Fjar, Broken Fire.* Everything that defines who I am would be destroyed, torn to shreds. All that would be left would be an empty shell, not even a sentient creature."

"Sounds like something that a coordinated defense wouldn't be amiss for." Veralis pointed out.

Radien shook his head. "Even if I had the kind of manpower for that, *Anan Krohgathi* is something that must be faced alone, to be honest. But it's nothing I'm not used to, The Oldest Truth and all that."

Veralis once again felt the absence of doubt in Radien's very being as he said those words. She still couldn't quite put her finger on just what to call it, Radien's unwavering knowledge that he stood alone, beyond all else. The Oldest Truth really was just that.

"That being said..." Radien mentioned eventually. "I'm glad my plan worked."

"Not used to your plans working?" Veralis scoffed, but not in a truly mocking manner. It was more like surprise that there was any doubt.

"In a manner of speaking, it *is* still strange to me, that my preparations have been paying off," Radien replied, and Veralis listened with newfound focus to make sure she heard his next words. "A welcome surprise, but a surprise all the same that I haven't been losing despite doing everything right. I mean, I know that they say it's not weakness to prepare perfectly and execute without flaw but still fail, but by the *gods* does it drain of will for it to be all that—"

Veralis suddenly grabbed Radien and wrapped her arms around him tightly, to a surprised yelp from the Death World Vulpian. Fortunately, it was a pretty slow hour at the Kianar's Folly tavern, so there were no eye or ear witnesses to the event.

<No one in eye or earshot right now, Radien,> Veralis reassured telepathically, knowing full well that was exactly what he was concerned with. Radien just breathed slowly and methodically, in a controlled pattern, though he was otherwise completely frozen in place by the sudden move. Once Veralis finally did let him go, Radien's expression was one of pure confusion, but not shock. Radien knew that it wasn't a *shock* that

Veralis might do that, but instead he was confused on every level possible that she would do that for *him*, of all people.

Veralis, being a Psionic Empath, could feel that confusion in him. Now she finally knew what to call it.

Chapter the Fifth

Honor for the Damned

"Let us burn an empire of slavers, and make the vile masters watch and know that they are next!"
—Dwaakenteros, Taigron axe-master, just after the beginning of the Sentience War

Personal log of Tactician Miles Radien, UDM 8-317,392,210-4-46. Miirkae has informed me that his home planet, the ocean world of Pogo-Pira has come under attack by not Demons, but Voidspawns. With Cynar focused so heavily on the threat the Dark Six pose, it opens the door for The Void and its denizens to attempt to make moves against us. An alliance between The Void and the Burning Hells would be unfathomably dangerous for the universe at large, but fortunately this has never been the case. With both outside forces wishing to lay claim to Cynar, this causes them to be in constant conflict with each other. In fact, it has been theorized that this is what prevents the majority of Demonic incursions from ever reaching us, the fact that first, they must fight through the Voidspawns that try to make use of the bridge between the Burning Hells and Cynar known as the Unfathomable Vortex. Why it is called unfathomable is beyond me, as *clearly, both the Voidspawns and the Demons both can fathom it in the interest of attacking Cynar. Maybe it's just 'unfathomable' in the scholarly sense, which is to say, incomprehensible. The Incomprehensible Vortex doesn't have the same ring to it, I'll admit.*

Regardless, I have decided to help Miirkae assist in the defense of his homeworld by taking him there in the Aura Runner, given its sheer speed. I will also be assisting in the defense directly.

"Where are the Void Rifts, exactly?" Radien asked Miirkae once the *Aura Runner* had entered the Warp Channel.

Miirkae responded by calling up a map of a section of Pogo-Pira's ocean floor. "About fifteen kilometers away from the Library of Steel itself. The Voidspawns are gunning for a high-value target, likely hoping to strike a weakening blow against the universe's defenses to make it easier for the Dark Six to follow through."

"And then The Void mops the rest up while the Demons catch their breath..." Radien finished, to Miirkae's nod. "The two of us alone won't turn the tide of that battle."

"What reinforcements could be mustered are further away than could be helpful," Miirkae reminded. "With everyone in the area tied up in their own duties, we may need to find a way to, regardless."

Radien then looked at the local starmap, and recognized the name of one of the nearby planets. "Of course..." he remembered aloud. "Techbooth, divert course to Alabasteron!"

"The Graveworld?!" Miirkae exclaimed. "This

hardly seems like the time!"

"This is *exactly* the time, actually," Radien explained as he pressed some buttons on a nearby console. "When I was here last, I learned that Alabasteron is not as the universe thinks it is."

"I have little choice but to trust that you're telling the truth, but I know you're no liar... It's just that the Library of Steel is at stake right now."

"Which is why now is the time that Alabasteron's secret stops being such."

A skeletal Vulpian responded to Radien's hail, recognizing the ship that was contacting him, and the name of its pilot who visited. However, the when Bones Malone last saw Radien, he was *not* a Death World Vulpian.

"Well, I sure *hope* that's you, Radien."

"Do you remember what you told me before I left Alabasteron, in private?"

Malone nodded slowly, recognizing Radien's voice. "I must say, you certainly seem to have done well for yourself, Vulpian form and all."

"It definitely suits me more than that old Human body," Radien commented lightheartedly. "But that's not what I'm here about."

"True," Malone replied. "Considering what you've just mentioned, I do hope you bring the news I think you do."

Radien nodded eagerly. "I do bring that news. Rally *everyone*, General. The Souls of Alabasteron have waited for eons for the chance to fight for the universe again, longing to prove their ancient valor one last time. That day has come."

The Library of Steel's defensive contingent numbered six thousand elite warriors, along with whoever was training there at the time at one of the most well-reputed and renowned martial arts academies in the universe. However, the main difference between incursions from the Voidspawns, and incursions from the Demons, is that Voidspawns attack in hordes of dark amalgamations of the space between realms, granted the sole will to destroy by forces yet unknown to the universe. It was still unsure whether or not The Void had masters, akin to the Dark Six. What was known, however, was that three gaping tears in the flesh of the universe had opened within the ocean plains outside the Library of Steel, and Voidspawns seethed forth from them in near innumerable masses.

The defenders of Pogo-Pira's best plan was to hold fast until reinforcements could arrive from other corners of civilization, but with so few free hands, it could take days or weeks before help arrived, if it even was enough to push the Voidspawns back.

One of the lookouts at the Library of Steel noticed that the Voidspawns had changed their marching course. Something had drawn their attention to the north, and made itself clear as the target of priority, but what? The lookout turned the gaze of his spyglass towards the northern horizon, where the Voidspawns were marching towards instead of at them. His eyes widened with shock at what he saw. A massive orb of light had been produced by some third party and heaved into the waters above, illuminating the depths for miles in every direction, to make known who was about to meet the Void in glorious battle.

Marching across the ocean floor to meet the Voidspawns was not only Radien and Miirkae, but an entire planet's worth of undead warriors from a war fought eons ago, warriors of the Sentience War, previously believed to be banished to the Graveworld and cursed to fight each other for all eternity. But no longer, for the Souls of Alabasteron had come to fight in the name of the stars once again.

"Hol-nah Viir! Stand and fight!" Radien called out to those who followed him to battle.

"Anan Volkarn! Time for battle!" The entire army at his side responded.

"Hol-nah Viir!"

"Anan Volkarn!"

"Pir Jaltai! By the sword!"

"Pir Iklae! By the spear!"

Miirkae slammed his spear into the ground as Radien pulled the Borfblade from its sheath, the red runes and fuller burning with vigor, a beacon of battle in the depths of the ocean. Hoisting it forward, Radien made the call.

"AUROK SON-DEYL!! BEHOLD OUR POWER!!"

Leading from the front, Radien and Miirkae charged forward as the Souls of Alabasteron followed them, fighting the enemies of creation once again, united to stand against the enemies of Cynar.

Radien, Miirkae, and Bones Malone were the first ones into the fray, their weapons meeting the Voidspawns and tearing them asunder. The Borfblade carved Voidspawns to shreds, Miirkae's spear pierced and sliced the Voidspawns as it did the waters around it, a circle of death that dared the denizens of the realm between realms to be felled by his skill.

The skeletal Vulpian alongside them, Bones Malone, eagerly drew a pair of machine pistols from his hips and began laying waste to his foes who dared attack his home universe, just as the Shard did once billions of years ago, and he slaughtered them gleefully as he once slaughtered the fascist slavers who denied the sentience of the Ascendant, to their doom, the kind that the Souls of Alabasteron had delivered in life, and had come forth to do so once again, in the name of life. With otherworldly force, Malone's bullets tore through the water to shred the evil that dared walk upon the ocean's floor this day.

Radien saw a new target lumbering onto the battlefield from one of the three rifts that the Void's creatures were entering through, a colossal amalgamation of darkness that just *begged* to be taken down with fervor and zeal, in most impressive and cinematic fashion.

But just before he would have leaped upwards in the water to meet it, several bolts of energy tore through the Voidborn Colossus, and as it destabilized, it fell backwards upon and crushed dozens of its own allies from the assault that had just beset it, from the warriors of the Library of Steel, charging to meet their enemies alongside Radien, Miirkae, Bones Malone, and the Souls of Alabasteron.

"Trahash vai'al Thiel! Fire and Flood!" Miirkae yelled to his battle brothers and sisters from the Library of Steel as he slammed the end of his spear into the ocean floor, and it produced a current within the waters

of Pogo-Pira's abyssal plain that his allies from his training grounds simultaneously rode like a battle mount, and crashed with the force of a hundred tsunamis against the Voidspawns, tearing them to shreds by the sheer force of water that had met them. Once the last of the twelve-strong battlegroup had picked up on the current and started riding it, Miirkae ran up the length of his spear, before jumping up to ride the current it produced as well, grabbing the weapon from the rocky floor of the ocean with his tail, and upon reaching the front of the current, used his spear to steer it, and his allies along the enemy line to tear them asunder.

Radien and Malone fought side-by side against the hordes, and the skeletal Vulpian cackled with the spirit of battle as he laid waste to Cynar's foes once again.

"By the *stars, I have missed this!*" Malone eagerly yelled out, just before the machine pistols ran out of ammunition once again. Though he had no additional magazines after the sixth set of reloads, this only signaled to him that this was where the *real* fun began. Blades shunted out from bottom rails of the weapons, and Bones Malone began his melee assault, shredding the Voidspawns who dared attack him with the bayonets of the Archaeotech weapons, which were almost as eager as he was to finally be wielded against real enemies this time.

Fighting beside him, Radien's sword sliced through the waters of the ocean and through Voidspawns alike, his right hand firing off bolts of The Aura at enemies who would have otherwise snuck up on him. Then he remembered something else, another weapon he could wield alongside the Borfblade. The Honorblade of Korvideyl was called into his right hand, and the two swords became a force of sheer overwhelming might against the Voidspawns.

The Shield of Honor created by the sword of T'Sen Torgaen blocked and deflected every single shot and strike that tried to hit Radien on a front unwatched, the only way to defeat him was face-to-face. And there would be no defeating Miles Sorvenjar Radien today, not when he held the weapons of two Defenders, fighting alongside the Souls of Alabasteron, who defied the will of death itself in the name of defending life, and the universe, from the dark forces that would seek its subjugation.

Miirkae's Riptide Warriors disengaged from the current they were riding, to re-engage the Voidspawns on the ground, and the momentum built up by the abyssal water that Miirkae had summoned slammed so hard into the Void Rift, that not even it could hold fast against the fury of the ocean, and the groans of the accursed gateway revealed that it could not longer remain strong, and it crunched and crushed in upon itself before collapsing entirely into nothingness, while Miirkae and the Riptide Warriors all channeled their powers simultaneously into a great prismatic beam of energy that the second Rift Gate was utterly powerless to stand against.

Only one Void Rift remained, and Malone saw his chance to prove his valor once again, as he had done against the Shard once, so long ago. Fighting his way through the Voidspawns, cutting them down left and right with the bladed ends of his twin machine pistols, until he was within throwing range of the rift.

Malone holstered the weapons and grabbed a glowing green crystal from his belt, before deciding not to throw it, because that wouldn't be nearly badass enough. With no care of the strikes laid against him as he charged forward, Malone crushed the crystal in his hand, his skeletal hand barely containing the raw explosive power that was about to be unleashed upon the final Rift Gate. Soon, he stood face to face with the doorway into The Void, despite the efforts of his enemies.

The explosion vaporized hundreds of cubic meters of water, before the pressure of the ocean depths crushed the explosion back in on itself, and with it, the final Rift Gate was torn asunder in the wake of the sheer force of both the explosion, and of the waters taking back their own. Once his bony feet hit the rocky floor of the ocean with its layer of sand atop it after riding the shockwave, the connection between Cynar and The Void had been fully severed, and the Voidspawns who had crossed over could no longer retain their form, being cut off from the realm from whence they came.

That was the other difference between Demons and Voidspawns. Destroy the gate that Demons come through, and they will scatter to try to find footholds on other worlds. Destroy a gateway to The Void, and the Voidspawns all collapse into dust without the connection to their home realm.

Pogo-Pira was defended.

The forces of The Void had been utterly crushed this day, and could no longer threaten this world, due to the nature of rifts between realms of creation. The amount of raw power it takes to tear the kinds of wounds into Cynar's very flesh were of the kind that once healed, were hardened to the point of invincibility from hostile incursions evermore, like when skin hardens into calluses, or how a properly healed fracture is stronger at the break site than before. What this meant was that The Void had one chance to take Pogo-Pira. It failed, and now The Void could no longer threaten the planet directly on its own turf.

Miirkae was busy catching up with his friends, the Riptide Warriors, as Radien spoke with Bones Malone, the skeletal Vulpian of old. So old, in fact, Malone was actually an Old Cynofraxian, the genetic precursor to all of the modern Vulpian breeds, which were referred to as the Chapters.

The Souls of Alabasteron soon reassembled upon the abyssal plain, still lit for miles around by the orb of light above them in the water, and awaited an address from the one who led them into battle against the universe's foes once again, after having waited for so long.

Miirkae looked over to Radien, who stood before the undead of The Graveworld, who was internally debating what to do, what to say to these warriors.

Radien then remembered the conversation he had with Malone in private, just before leaving Alabasteron with the Hajivakk Information Ark that Kendro-Dalinor had tasked him to acquire, back when Miles Radien was still a Human.

"Much as we keep ourselves entertained here with all these wacky stunts..." Bones had said to Radien after requesting that he keep Alabasteron's true nature secret from the rest of the universe. "We've grown tired of remaining hidden from the universe, with this world condemned and considered eternally cursed by the hatred that flowed from the battlefields of old."

All those years ago, Radien did listen to Malone's words.

"But we can't pass on to the next realm as a cursed people in the eyes of the rest of the universe," Bones continued. "We need one last victory against the enemies of creation before we can rest. Like the victories earned against the Shard, we need to score one more for the stars. If you should find that chance, I hope you will remember what I've told you here today, and I hope you'll give us that chance."

"If and when I find myself in need of an army of warriors like yourself and everyone else here, General, it would be my honor to call upon you and the Souls of Alabasteron for one last glory."

Malone had chuckled at the table. "I wasn't actually a General. I was a fast-attack speeder pilot."

But in the present moment, Radien still had to tell the warriors of Alabasteron *something*.

"The Souls of Alabasteron have proven their valor!" Radien yelled across the ocean floor for the army of the dead he led to hear. With passive assistance from The Aura, everyone who needed to heed his words did so. "This world is defended! The Void can never threaten Pogo-Pira or its peoples again! This great victory is owed to the eternal warriors who once stood strong against the Shard, all those eons ago! Your oaths are fulfilled! The Souls of Alabasteron can rest..."

With that, the skeletal legions began to crumble, releasing themselves from their bonds to Cynar, finally passing on to their next realms, and ending their watch. Soon, only one remained.

"I can understand why they all longed for release," Malone said to break the silence that followed the departure of all the rest of Alabasteron's skeletons. "But I don't feel like I can rest yet. There is more to what happened today than this battle, I can sense it…"

"I won't lie to you, Malone," Radien said. "The oldest foes of Cynar have returned, the Dark Six."

"The Lords of Evil themselves… Who else would it be to give The Void newfound boldness in assaulting Cynar? Reality fights a war on two fronts, and though my kinsmen know that life will prevail… I wish to help assure it."

"Someone who has trained for all the eons you have would be welcome to fight for the universe once again… Bones Malone."

Bones then chuckled with his raspy, skeletal chuckle. "My name… admittedly, that I haven't said for a very, very long time… is Orokolos."

"Welcome back to the fold, Orokolos."

"It is good to be back."

The two began walking back towards the Library of Steel itself. Soon, the expressions on both men began to turn away from the elation of victory, to concern for events yet to come.

"I have no fondness of worry, Radien… but I do find myself dreading the possibility that for my… less than properly alive visage, I only be scorned, reviled, hunted…"

Radien sighed, remembering how that felt once. "I know that Dread all too well... You remember when we first met, when I was not yet *Zhernrel-Vuljar? Death World Vulpian?*"

"I did not recognize your species. I suppose that was why you were able to get onto Alabasteron the first time. Your race clearly was introduced to the Conclave of Sentience long after my time," Orokolos responded.

"And when I first stepped off of my world of origin onto Cynofrax, that dread was at the forefront of my mind," Radien recalled. "The Humans are not a species of honor."

"Cynofrax has always been a place for the honorable, even all the way back when I still walked on its grasses, though!" Orokolos scoffed, hardly understanding how Radien could have felt that dread when coming to Cynofrax, where indeed, there was always a place for the honorable, as such was Raon-Arashal. "The only way you could not know that is... *ahh, now I see.*"

Radien shrugged his shoulders. "And don't even get me *started* on how I felt when I was traveling to Raon-Arashal for the first time, even more so when I was returning from the Field of Unreality a Death Worlder... 'how dare he pretend to be like us,' I thought for sure they all were thinking. I was ready to hear that I insulted all reason and decency by purporting to hold even a candle to them.

"What happened next?" Orokolos asked.

"Raon-Arashal, like every other world in Cynar, was alight in celebration for the destruction of The Unmaker, who very nearly succeeded in subjugating the universe in his bid to rewrite history, that it would begin with him. And they were waiting for the arrival of the one who slew him. Who not only slew him, but in the aftermath of the victory, cast off his Human form at last, and became *Zhernrel-Vuljar*."

The two approached the underwater dome that was the Library of Steel's exterior, and pushed open the twin doors at its entrance. What Radien and Orokolos beheld next, was something they did *not* anticipate.

Six thousand elite warriors, the defensive contingent of the Library itself, and the twelve thousand students and pupils that were training in martial arts at this temple to combat. They all were assembled and awaiting their entrance.

Next through the door, Miirkae and the twelve Riptide Warriors entered, and with their very arrival, announced to the whole planet that they had just claimed glorious victory.

All eighteen thousand that were present stood up and all simultaneously let out the battlecry of the Library of Steel. *"Trahash vai'al Thiel! Fire and Flood!"*

The call repeated, ringing across the acoustics of the dome as Radien, Orokolos, Miirkae, and the Riptide Warriors walked along the tiled entry road, towards an assembly of the Sword Scholars of this massive temple to the martial arts. All fourteen of them stood to meet the warriors who had not only just saved the Library of Steel, and everyone in it, not only as well all of its collective knowledge, but they had done so against the forces of The Void itself, and lived to tell the tale of the day the Souls of Alabasteron proved their ultimate valor.

The Riptide Warriors walked ahead of the three

who led them all to victory, and assembled next to the stairs that led to where the Sword Scholars were standing, in their full battlegear, before making way for Miirkae, Radien, and Orokolos.

Once the three arrived before the fourteen Sword Scholars, thirteen of them immediately bowed in the respective forms of the martial arts they had mastered, and the one remaining approached them. The calls of *"Trahash vai'al Thiel! Fire and Flood!"* from the assembled warriors of the Library of Steel halted, so that the Grandmaster of Arms could address them.

"Miles Sorvenjar Radien, Orokolos of Cynofrax, Bladewhisperer Miirkae... the Library of Steel is in your debt. The blow you have struck against The Void is one they shall never recover from. Our doors are eternally open to you."

The Grandmaster at Arms then himself bowed to them, with the martial salute of the Redarian species, given that he was Redarian himself.

Simultaneously, the three responded in kind with their own. Miirkae performed one with his double-pointed spear, as Radien did the Eskrima *Saludo Maestro* with the Borfblade and the Honorblade of Korvideyl, and Orokolos with the bow of the Cynofrax martial art of *Reluine Givalt*, or "Realmblood Karate," roughly translated. It was a Psionic Martial Art based mainly around picking up chunks of the terrain and hurling them at your enemies with the power of your mind. The fourteen leaders of the Library of Steel stood back at attention, and the Grandmaster at Arms presented each of them with a brass medallion with a blazing orange crystal set in its center, the Sunburst Medallion.

Indeed, it was a very unexpected thing to be met with after opening the door.

The revelries at the Library of Steel lasted for three days, during which Miirkae had decided that he would undergo the Trial of the Bladesinger before long. The Riptide Warriors that were accompanying him all responded with vigorous agreement, that the Bladesinger's Trial should be the next one for him to do. Radien spoke with Orokolos, with both of them still in the middle of enjoying their time at the Library of Steel itself. After all, this was one of the three most revered locations for martial artists in the known universe, with the other two being the Arena of Firatyne, and pretty much the entire planet of Orvitaire.

"It will be good to see Cynofrax again, and I have already been informed by the descendants of some of my battle brothers from the Sentience War that I would be welcomed there," Orokolos told Radien, very clearly relieved. He would be breathing sighs of relief if he still had lungs. But this was not the case, as he was a Psionically-preserved skeleton of an Old Cynofraxian, whose consciousness still remained fully intact. "It is relieving news indeed."

"I bet!" Radien commented, taking a swig from his tankard. "And Orokolos, if Cynofrax ever gets to be old news for you, the doors of Torvaltyne Bastion are open to you. Any enemy of the Shard is an ally of mine!"

"I will not forget that, Radien," Orokolos replied. "It is good to be a part of the universe again, and to take up the fight against its enemies once more!"

A few days later, Radien received a message from the

High Commandant of the Raon-Arashal Defensive Militarium, and the only reaction he had to it was 'took them long enough.'

Temporal Interference was a sensitive matter for the universe, one that every civilized species endeavored to do as little of as possible, ideally preventing it entirely. However, some ways to alter time's flow were known among select circles, such as the Perawls of Dor-Val-Der, guardians of the Great Forbidden Weapons. Within each Perawl's mind was locked the secrets of constructing all kinds of weapons that would spell the end of the civilized universe. It was through the Perawls that these weapons never saw the light of the stars, for the ideas of how to make them were contained through such limited existence. Many of the Great Forbidden Weapons the Perawls guarded had to do with ways to traverse backwards in time, but oddly enough, never forwards.

Among the many pieces of dangerous knowledge the Perawls guarded were ways to detect when time had been interfered with, such as when Radien had been paid a visit by his future self from an empty future, devoid of all life by the hands of its sole occupant. The message Radien had just received at his duty office in Torvaltyne Bastion was the summons for the inquiry by the High Commandant, which consisted of the six Arch-Militants of the RADM. Normally, a planet's military had eight Arch-Militants, but Raon-Arashal possessed no planetary oceans, only a single inland sea and many rivers and underground reservoirs, so the RADM's navy was actually the River Corps branch of the Ground Forces, which also handled operations in the inland sea that was Jelketh Black Zone.

Regardless, the leadership of Raon-Arashal's warriors had received word from Perawl Arnzoth that Temporal Interferrence had occurred, and that Miles Radien was the one who could shed light on the matter. Thus, Radien had been summoned to do just that. Fortunately, Radien had prepared for this. In fact, both instances of him had prepared for this, as the one from the timeline no longer existent had sent instructions to the *Aura Runner* specifically to aid in this eventuality.

"The reports from David Company, as well as that of Tactician Olvek from Zharekk's Orbital Corps all place a great amount of faith in you, Tactician Radien," Arch-Militant Jalnar Veks began. "I'll spare you from having to hear them all, but the consensus has been that despite significant confusion as to the sudden presence of two *Aura Runners*, almost if not all parties have figured that you had a handle on the situation. That being said... there were still two instances of the same vessel at different parts of their journey through time."

"Aye," Radien stated. "A second *Aura Runner* did emerge from a Temporal Rift just beyond high orbit of Zharekk."

"And who piloted this vessel?" Arch-Militant Pelikarn Desh asked. While d Veks was one of the two Arch-Militants of the Orbital Corps, the space-focused branch of the planet's armies, Pelikarn was one of the two Arch-Militants of the Atmocorps, the branch that handled aeriel operations within planetary atmosphere. Colloquially, an air force. Where Veks was a Death World Vulpian, Pelikarn was of the avian Du-Vak-Maran species. This diversity was hardly uncommon within a world's leadership.

"It was piloted by Major Miles Radien of the RADM," Radien responded. "But it was clear that the Raon-Arashal Defensive Militarium had been nonexistent for a very long time within his timeline, and that his Rank Statuette was merely a keepsake."

"How long?" Arch-Militant Kassari Elayn of the Ground Corps inquired. "If you know, that is."

"I scanned the *Aura Runner* not from this time while verifying the pilot's identity, and... it was displaced by no less than seventeen million ASC."

The Arch-Militants of the High Commandant all eyed each other, visibly disturbed by how far in the future the temporal incursion originated from. A few days was one thing, a year or two was another... but fifty-three and a half million Earth years equivalent was something else entirely.

"And for those seventeen million ASC, its pilot, yourself from this dark future, searched for a way to undo what would have otherwise happened above Zharekk if not for his interference?" Arch-Militant Matrix asked. The Ascendant who acted as the second Arch-Militant of the Orbital Corps alongside Veks had a name that was considered highly desirable to his species, especially for the fact that it was chosen randomly when he first activated his consciousness. In Ascendant culture, it is considered a good omen when a randomly chosen name happens to be technologically inclined.

Radien simply responded by hailing the *Aura Runner* and telling Techbooth within to warp in the 'Exhibit Omnibus.' This took the form of a monitor replaying the recorded transmission when Major Radien, from this broken timeline, spoke with Tactician Radien of the timeline that was defended by the former's actions.

"...*My sin is not that I've gone back in time to prevent the Demons from this victory, but rather, what their victory here today that no longer took place eventually made me do.*"

"*Deoxian Pulse?*"

"*I wish, that would've been way less dire. I've been all that's left, along with the Vault for an amount of time I don't even know the number for. And I don't just mean of the fight against Demons or the Dark Six.*"

After that, the rest of the conversation took place as Radien simply watched the recording with quiet reflection, and the six Arch-Militants did so with intrigue only matched by how disturbing they found the state of the future *Aura Runner* in, and that of its pilot.

"*I must have rehearsed this conversation an uncountable number of times before now as I prepared myself to do this... There's not much I can say without risking your timeline, since knowing the future can change it and all,*" Major Radien said in the playback.

"*But having information does not guarantee the change for the worse. Tell me what you can.*"

"*The Demonic occupation of Zharekk, that now has been prevented, led to the swift decision to demolish the world. Nobody disagreed. I don't know for sure if this was the catalyst that set my path on its way to what inevitably happened, but I do know for sure that preventing Zharekk's fall has prevented... what went so horribly wrong not long after. Raon-Arashal was directly in the sights of the Dark Six, and even before the debris field that once was Zharekk had cleared out, we were scrambling to find a way to assure our defense for what was to come. Even though they had the planet for less than a fucking week, they were able to mobilize a nightmarishly massive armada that deployed as soon as it was able, and wrecking the planet only stopped the reinforcements from pouring through the rift gates. There was still the full might of the Burning Hells to contend with. We approached the Perawls, but they tied their hands behind their backs and called our worlds a necessary sacrifice, as it was known that planets would die in this war. Even though I knew it just as well, I still couldn't stand for it. So I made my own Great Forbidden Weapon, the Omega Wave."*

In the replay of the conversation, it seemed that even though Tactician Radien had never heard of that weapon until then, he somehow seemed to understand its purpose.

"But I didn't have enough time to make sure it was done right. Even as I worked in secret, I knew that at best, I'd destroy the entire solar system, whether Demon or Death Worlder. To call what I felt rage doesn't do it justice by infinite magnitudes... and because of that rage at how unfair it was, I didn't just destroy the solar system with the Omega Wave."

Arch-Militant Kassari Elayn recoiled in her seat as she realized how literally dark this timeline was, and just what this version of Radien meant when he said he was all that was left.

"I haven't seen starlight in seventeen million ASC, Tactician. And I know in my mind of minds that I've no business seeing it again... all I should be permitted is the prevention of my destruction of everything out of spite, and to simply fade away along with all that sorrow... let

alone see again the planet that I was honored to call home, for as short a time as I did."

Major Radien then scanned the system, and called up a holographic map of Raon-Arashal, still in space and in its orbit around the white giant star, kept stable by Redarian Gravity Satellites. He gazed at the world for a few moments, and sighed with relief that it was there.

"I won't insult those hallowed grounds by daring to set foot on them again before my fading is complete, now that my timeline no longer exists," Major Radien affirmed to himself before turning off the 3D projection. *"Though I still think the Omega Wave is within your future, it won't be the same now... I'd thank the gods that it may work this time, but they deserve no thanks from me."*

"I'm not sure what to say."

"Then say nothing. This is not a bad thing. Remember the Oldest Truth..."

"The Oldest Truth, the fact that has been known since fact could be known, is that we stand alone, but this is not a bad thing."

The playback ended after the two Death World Vulpians recited the Oath of the Oldest Truth, and the *Aura Runner* from the timeline no more vanished from existence.

The Arch-Militants looked to each other with a mixture of surprise, concern, and internal conflict at the implications of what had happened in both timelines, mixed with bafflement at what do to about it. What was done was done, and nobody could argue that it was the wrong thing to do, just as much as nobody could bring themselves to say aloud whether or not it was right. All that could be known is that it *wasn't wrong*. Radien himself had no words, he only looked on with quiet reflection.

"Radien…" Arch-Militant Veks began. "Do you consider Raon-Arashal to be your home?"

Radien was surprised that this was the question being asked of him, but there was an answer to give.

"When I first came to this world, I wondered if one day I'd be able to call it home. When I became *Zhernrel-Vuljar*, I wondered if maybe that was within my future. And when I underwent and conquered the Gauntlet of Doom, I had started to do so, but only to myself. I guess that's why the Major was comfortable saying it around me, because it still was only between us. I didn't want to risk insulting everyone who was already here by trying to act like I was a part of something that—"

"Tactician, *Defender…* that there is any doubt still within you of your right to call Raon-Arashal home tells us that *we* have paid insult to *you*," Arch-Militant Elayn interrupted. "We all know that you hold no pride for your past, having been born Human and spending your formative years surrounded on all sides by them, and I know I speak for not just the High Commandant, but also the whole of Raon-Arashal when I say that after everything you've done already in so little time… how could we *dare* to not allow you the right?"

Now Radien was the one surprised and confused, and Arch-Militant Elayn chuckled as the expression became clear on his face. "That's the question you ask me?" Radien said to her. "I—"

"What else is there to ask?" Kassari responded.

"It cannot be said that what you and your future self did was wrong... it would seem that in a gamble of one in a million with the universe at stake, we have been granted our allowance of once."

The rest of the High Commandant slowly agreed to this statement, that this was indeed the once in a million, though Arch-Militant Pelikarn was the last to nod, and though everyone was hesitant to admit it, what was done got results, and even Pelikarn Desh had to acknowledge this, though he clearly was not fond of it, and seemed quite aware of how it was the *once* in a million. Radien, though relatively oblivious to the emotions of others given his intense training in logic, quietly acknowledged to Desh that he understood his trepidation with a roll of his shoulders, the equivalent of a wink to the the avian Du-Vak-Maran species that the Orbital Corps leader was the leader of. However, this context of a wink equivalent was of a 'Yeah, fair enough that you don't like this one' nature. Granted, this nonverbal message was successfully communicated. It seemed that if there was anyone more vigilant than Arch-Militant Pelikarn on this matter, it was Miles Radien. Desh remained quietly impressed that Radien understood this custom within his species, and allowed himself thusly to be just as impressed by Radien's own vigilance on the matter at the time, considering the Protocols of Vigilance, which had only become known to persons beyond Radien in this very meeting, since the replay of the conversation past involved their invocation.

After the inquiry was finished, Radien loafed in the darkness at the Torvaltyne Mead Hall. Its architecture was deliberately designed to make it very easy to brood mysteriously in dark corners. He soon found himself joined by Arakai, who had two fresh pint glasses with him of the Fortress's house mead.

"You didn't have to get me a replacement," Radien started.

"I didn't," Arakai countered, and Radien chuckled, knowing full well he would've said exactly the same. "Protocols of Vigilance, huh?"

"How the hell do you know—"

"Inquiry's an open-books thing. I was curious since it was a Temporal Interference matter, I find them fascinating."

"Gah, and I enjoy temporal buggery about as much as Janeway and O'Brien combined," Radien commented as he motioned to the barkeep for another pint of mead. After all, mead is good, and this is known. "So, what about the event did you find—"

"*Protocols of Vigilance,* Tactician?" Arakai emphasized once more as the item of his curiosity, with a next-level eyebrow raise to boot.

"What of them?" Radien countered.

Arakai waited for a follow-up sentence that never came, and he sighed. "I'm no Psionic Empath like Veralis, Radien, but I'm not a fool."

"Never said you were."

Arakai couldn't help but chuckle now. Radien was definitely a unique case compared to all the other people he had met across his life. "You're gods-damned unreadable, you know that?"

"I consider that a compliment."

"I knew you would."

The two continued to share each other's company in relative silence, making sure there was a glass in their hands at all times. A few minutes later, Arakai spoke again.

"Sometimes, when I look at you, Radien... I find myself wondering just how much anger, hatred and rage had to course through you before you could finally be so calm and collected?"

This caught Radien's attention far more than the comments about his Protocols of Vigilance did.

"And just how loudly did you have to scream and shout before you could finally afford the chance to be silent? I've learned that there are three things to fear in this universe beyond any other; the sunless day, the starless night, and the anger of a kind person. I've also learned that kindness and altruism are *not* one and the same. When we first met, well... I know you don't hold it against me, I was just doing my job as a Plainsguard, ensuring the preservation of the Plains of the Stars. But you were very prepared to be met with a rifle pointed at you."

Radien recalled that day, and then chuckled himself. "Oh shit, that's right... first act on Cynofrax was a next-level parking violation."

"I feared the worst when I saw the ship of myth itself, the *Aura Runner* landing on those plains, because whoever piloted it would know not to do so, so I wondered if it had fallen into the wrong hands, and the first act was to make a display of power... though that seems pretty damned silly now that I think of it... yeah, landing on the border of the Plains but still within, definitely someone putting their foot down in defiance of Cynofrax's laws."

Both men shared a laugh at this, but Arakai still had more to say, so he did.

"But... you were very, very ready to have hostility be the first thing you encountered... I've never been to Earth, and I certainly never want to, knowing that what it does to people is make them prepared to have hostility always be the first thing encountered..."

"You're not missing out, Arakai," Radien commented, finishing his pint glass of mead. "No one in their right mind wants to step on Earth... I still find myself so constantly baffled by Humans who visit to pay homage to their species's birth world... it's such a senselessly cruel and awful place, the only thing worth remembering about it is that it should be left in the fucking dust!"

Radien took a few breaths to calm himself down before speaking his next. "After all, why do you think I'm always prepared to have hostility be the first and only thing I encounter? I spent too long on Earth."

Arakai placed a hand on Radien's shoulder, to the Death Worlder's inquisitive look at Arakai's toned and dense arm setting itself upon it. The two were of similarly athletic and dense build, though Arakai was about three inches taller than Radien, being half Cynofrax Vulpian, and Cynofrax Vulpians tending to be tall. All the same, Radien didn't stop him, and Arakai knew he could use the pick-me-up.

"You escaped Earth, Radien. And the universe is better off for it. The only thing worth remembering about that time is that it should be left in the fucking dust."

Chapter the Sixth

The Dark Defense

"If I knew all there was to know, existence would be no fun at all."
—*The Aura Prism*

Veralis quickly approached Radien at a swift but not urgent pace.

"How fast can the *Aura Runner* get to Cynofrax?" She asked, to which Radien immediately stopped in place to listen to her and make sure he could answer her question.

"We don't even need the Aura Runner, the Transit Nexus has a Way Gate to Cynofrax," Radien responded. This was true, as Rune Brick-based Way Gates had been constructed within Torvaltyne Bastion for easy transport to several major planets, including Cynofrax, Talvakorrik, Caren'Das, Redaria Prime, Redaria Omega, and Haven Hall. Granted, Haven Hall's Way Gate was both smaller, and elsewhere within the Fortress, considering the 'advanced vacation spot' that was Haven Hall. The honorary capitol world of the Hajikahl was considered an absolutely vital planet for the continued civility of the universe, granted. But one digresses. The Way Gate to Orvitaire was still under construction, but was due to be finished soon, and had only been put off because there was already a Way Gate to Orvitaire in the city of Firatyne on the planet, and since interplanetary transport was free of charge, martial artists already had a pretty easy time making their way to the Martial Planet. Orvitaire indeed was a quintessential pilgrimage spot for those who studied the martial arts, along with Pogo-Pira's Library of Steel.

"Oh, right," Veralis responded to the fact there was a direct line to Cynofrax at the Fortress Borfus, the colloquial name for Torvaltyne Bastion. "You and I need to get to Cynofrax, post-haste!"

Radien immediately began following Veralis to the Transit Nexus, asking her what questions he needed answered along the way since they could move and talk at the same time.

"What's happening on Cynofrax that demands our mutual attention?" Radien asked.

"Are you familiar with the Secret Fire of the Aldzul Rayd?"

"*Aldzul Rayd? Dark Defense?*"

"It's admittedly a misnomer," Veralis gruffed. "It's not bad at all, but someone thought that calling it the Secret Fire of the Dark Defense was very catchy, so it ended up sticking and nobody bothered to change the name."

"Ah, fair enough. But no, I am not familiar with that one."

"The Secret Fire is a bridge between realms, and

once every so often, the bridge becomes stable enough for someone to cross, and it's about to. The Keeper will explain it better, so that's why we're in a hurry, so that Taliah Stratenheim can explain it to you better than me."

"I wasn't aware you had a sister!"

"I don't."

Radien froze in place, locking eyes with Veralis as he realized just what that meant. Veralis immediately realized why.

"She's nothing like yours, I promise," Veralis informed. "Someone as dishonorable as Amandrianna wouldn't be able to set foot within a hundred leagues of the Secret Fire."

Radien began walking towards the Transit Nexus with Veralis again, but at a steadier and more controlled pace than initially. Veralis then stopped in place and put her hands on his shoulders, to which he immediately stopped in place again, surprised as all hell.

"Radien, *I understand.* Look at me. I was *honored* beyond words to relieve this universe of Amandrianna's filth, of her lies, of her wicked soul. I could *see* the weight lifting itself from your shoulders when you saw that I had done Cynar a favor and put an axe through her head, I *know* what you're feeling right now, and I *know* your vigilance. So let me promise you, right now, Vulpian to Vulpian, ally to ally, that Taliah Stratenheim taught me half of everything I know about honor."

Radien slowly nodded, and then soon after resumed following Veralis towards the Transit nexus. "If what you say is true, I am willing to believe it. If nothing else, I'm glad you understand my trepidation."

"I can't hold it against you, Radien. Nor can my

mother, if she's half the person I remember her to be."

Once the two crossed through the Way Gate's portal to Cynofrax, they immediately went to the land-vehicle rental facility nearby, where Radien quickly acquired for them a Xnopyfth Speeder with sidecar. At first, Veralis was perplexed that Radien was about to ask her to get into the sidecar of such a vehicle for the trip to the town in which both Taliah Stratenheim and the Secret Fire of the Aldzul Rayd were housed, to which Radien casually responded "What? You said we needed to get there in a hurry!"

To her surprise, Radien had no comments about how Veralis had to somewhat cram her six-foot-two muscular frame into the sidecar, as Radien was far too concerned with making sure he could balance urgency with safety. After all, the Xnopyfth had an average speed ceiling of up to three hundred kilometers per hour, with Cynofrax's general flatness within this province, this was easily pushed to a solid five hundred on the open road. Naturally, the Xnopyfth was generally only used for when one had somewhat of a rush job on their hands. And as far as Radien was concerned, he had a rush job on his hands, per Veralis's testimony.

Once the two stopped in the town of Arsketh, Radien climbed out of the driver's seat ready to go, while Veralis took a few moments to stretch after she followed suit.

"I thought we were in a rush?" Radien said. To this, Veralis burst out laughing while she stretched her athletically-built self out after the ride.

"Only in the sense that we needed to just be on our way!" She laughed. "This wasn't exactly do or die, Radien!"

Radien was confused as he stood there. He had sensed urgency in Veralis's voice. "I thought, uh... Well, you said—"

Veralis continued to chuckle. "Well, I'm glad to know that if I call, you'll come running. Our urgency was a product of my excitement far more than it was a need for expediency."

As Veralis walked past the form of Radien, very obviously taking a moment to process all that, she casually brushed a hand across his cheek, which only confused him ever more, resulting in his comment "AH shit, do you have any *idea* how many things I need to ponder now?! By the gods, my brain—"

This sentence was cut off by Veralis walking right past him, knowing full well that he would be flustered beyond words by her actions, that being exactly why she teasingly took them. She casually knocked on the door to the house they were in front of, and soon opened the door and went inside. Radien was cautious, but soon followed suit and entered the house.

Waiting was another Cynofrax Vulpian of similar height to Veralis, albeit a few inches shorter, perhaps. Either way, she was the Keeper of the Secret Fire of the Aldzul Rayd, and she was about to explain what Veralis didn't have time to back at Torvaltyne Bastion.

"You know this reality's given name of Cynar, one of many realms that encompass the fabric of Creation," Taliah began, swiftly moving to prepare a drink from within the house's kitchen, grabbing ingredients from pantries and cabinets, and moving in a calculated manner to prepare.... well, something, that was for sure. Radien wasn't about to stop her, she clearly knew what she was doing, whatever it was.

"Aye, and I also did some studying at The Hideout on some of the other realms. At least, the fact that they exist," Radien answered, deliberately and as calmly as the words were calculated.

"You know then, the Realm of Non-Knowledge?"

"I know *of* it, and not much else."

"The Secret Fire of the Aldzul Rayd is the bridge between Cynar, and *Aldkalst, Non-knowledge.* Every now and again, it flares, granting the chance for someone to cross that bridge and return, having learned something that until they learned of it, no soul in all of Cynar was aware of."

"A unique opportunity one would be a fool to pass up."

"Precisely. That is why Veralis brought you here."

Radien looked over to Veralis, who nodded. This was true and correct. Radien then turned to Taliah, who was now funneling raw Psionic power into the mixture that was being brewed on the stovetop.

"This decoction will accelerate your brain's processing speed, allowing you to act on a faster timescale than the rest of Cynar. It will ensure you have as much time as you need to learn whatever it is you are meant to learn from *Aldkalst.* Even then, you must be wary not to attempt to learn more than one truth from *Aldkalst,* lest you risk spending more time therein than the Secret Fire's portal will, and becoming lost forever."

"Sounds like a plan, then. I can do wary," Radien responded.

"Jazukiir pirfuur duul, Zhernreli. Vigilance becomes you, Death Worlder."

Radien couldn't help but shrug his shoulders in a 'fair enough' sort of manner. *"Jazukiir aldir nejtarn. Tais deliis pir Jazukiir-nah hath nejpiril toulth. Vigilance is never wrong. But there is a difference between vigilance, and merely seeking reasons to be enemies."*

"Truer words are rarely spoken," Taliah commented, impressed. She then turned to Veralis, steadily stirring the pot on the stove, as purple steam clouds rose from whatever mixture was within. "This is the bio-descendant of Amandrianna Sarvalimil?"

Veralis nodded. To this, Radien looked to her as though to silently ask 'you told her?!' Then again, Radien also knew that anyone Veralis would tell of that was not the wrong person to tell it to. Veralis nodded again, and Radien had but another 'fair enough' shrug to respond to that.

"My condolences, Radien," Taliah offered. "And I mean that in the best way possible."

"I understand your meaning, thank you."

Taliah continued to prepare the decoction on the stove, quickly zapping it with a bolt of power from her fingertip, before taking another look at the mix before nodding, and grabbing a ladle to pour a few measures of it into a glass. The mixture, and the vapors emanating from it were a deep purple, with glints of light appearing in all colors across the liquid.

"Needs a few seconds to stabilize, and..."

The liquid in the clear glass soon began to change in its hues and colors, and the only way Radien was able to describe the sight of the potion was that it looked like a bottle of galaxies.

"Pan-Galactic Gargleblaster vibes much?" Radien commented, impressed at the look of the decoction.

"No, that one's a straight glowing blue," Taliah fired back, to which Radien couldn't help but snort with laughter at her response. Taliah cracked a smile, and handed the drink to Radien.

"What do I do, sip, shoot or slam?"

"Slam," Veralis responded, and Taliah nodded in concurrence.

Radien tucked his right thumb into his hand, and with the potion in his left, lifted it to his mouth before declaring *skål,* and draining the bottle down his throat as quickly as possible, in only a few gulps. After this, he sputtered slightly at what got left behind on his tongue. "Ack, slam was right. Tastes like death, and not even the kind that you give to your enemies."

Taliah nodded vigorously to this. "That's about what everyone says, aye-yup. Impressively done. The Secret Fire is in the basement, let's get started."

Radien followed Veralis, who herself followed Taliah. Radien did not deny by any means Taliah's expertise on the matter of the Secret Fire, nor did he really doubt anything she had said.

The Secret Fire of the Aldzul Rayd seemed like an ordinary fire, but ordinary fires aren't suspended three feet above the ground, and also golden in hue. However, it did behave like ordinary fire in how it flickered about.

"I'm still hardly sure what makes *me* the person to cross that threshold," Radien commented as he saw it.

"Typically, it is the Defender who enters the

Aldkalst," Taliah casually responded. There was that title again, that Radien was unsure if he had any business associating with it. Defender. Nine men and women who came before him who bore that title, the exemplars of honor for the stars, the one who drove back the evil night. Or moreover, inspired the stars to do so with their own actions.

Radien stopped in place again. Granted, he knew that he effectively *was* the Defender beyond doubt, because he had experienced one of the six Dreads. But what he knew that few others did, was that two of his predecessors were still alive and out fighting the Second War for Reality, one of them Caltoran himself! If Caltoran was still alive, what made *him* the Defender? With Xatrial Isenhart back in the fight, what made *Miles Radien* the Defender?

"I still can hardly fathom the idea of being that," Radien voiced his concern. "I'm no child of destiny! I can't be! It goes against everything I stand for, if I'm some ever-chosen champion of the universe!"

"The Defenders have never been the children of destiny!" Taliah declared, but not in an argumentative way, to Radien's surprise. Against all odds, her tone was more like one of assurance and encouragement. "The nine who came before you and held that title, they were *not* the ever-chosen of the gods, as you say! In fact, they would say the same thing, that being such would go against everything they stand for! The Defenders are *defiers* of fate, who carve their own out of the claws of an uncaring universe, and to do so, they *make themselves Defenders!* It is not destiny or fate that chooses the Defender, but the Defender who demands that destiny and fate take a seat and stay the *sraiv* out of the universe's business! Now don't tell me *that* isn't what *you* stand for!"

It was unfathomable to Radien. Not that someone had just told him this, but that someone's *mother* did. Rather than berate, interrogate, and discourage, Taliah instead seemed intent on inspiring his spite against the concepts of destiny and fate. Instead of telling him why everything he aspired to do was going to fail, and that he shouldn't bother with endeavor, Taliah told him why he *should* bother. Instead of trying to bind chains around his neck to yank upon at all hours, Taliah was making sure Radien knew how to break any chain that would dare try. It was the antithesis of what mothers do, an incomprehensible experience for the fact that a mother was the one telling him these things that were anything but overbearing and draining. Indeed, this was the polar opposite of how mothers act, which is to say, honorably, and capable of respecting the autonomy and sentience of others, that she understood the value of decency. It seemed impossible. With a Human, it would have been.

But Taliah Stratenheim was not a Human. She was a Vulpian, and the mother to Veralis, one of the most honorable people he had ever met. And if Veralis learned half of what she knew about honor from Taliah, then an enviable youth she had led indeed. But now was not the time for Radien to envy the upbringing of his friends.

Suddenly, the golden flame at the center of the room erupted and expanded in size, and through the dancing flames, *something* could be barely seen

"Defender or not, the Secret Fire has flared," Veralis informed. "Someone's got to go through it."

Radien nodded as he gazed at the portal, making one last comment "I would sure be a fool to waste that potion," before walking through.

When Radien beheld the Realm of Non-Knowledge, he could only assume that this was the form it was taking that his mind could comprehend: A seemingly infinite library, bookshelves towering above him like skyscrapers to a ceiling unfathomably distant, and yet somehow visible. The shelves only seemed to go halfway up to this ceiling, though these shelves that 'only' did so were all taller than any building Radien had ever seen. And having been to many planets other than Earth, he had seen some tall ones indeed. But somehow, he understood that even with that potion, he had little time to learn whatever he was to learn. All of the tomes that he beheld were filled with knowledge that no other being in all the universe knew. How to choose? How to resist the temptation to learn as many secrets as possible here?

Books floated among the shelves, randomly sorting and unsorting themselves, fitting in to a row and then floating away from the row, that nothing was in one place for long. Radien quickly grabbed one of the books, and opened it to about the middle, where he read a single line, and only had one thing to say about it.

"The hell's an Arca?"

The portal that the Secret Fire had formed for him began to flicker, and Radien's head whipped back to face it and realize he needed to leave. *Immediately.* He dove through the portal with the book in hand, but in defiance of his cleverness, the book did not pass into Cynar with him on his return to his home dimension, where Veralis and Taliah Stratenheim awaited his knowledge. It had simply vanished before crossing the threshold, leaving Radien empty-handed.

"Do either of you know what an Arca is?" Radien asked. To this, Veralis and Taliah looked at each other in surprise, as if Radien had just stumbled upon the classified documents of the universe itself. To be fair, he had just done that in entering *Aldkalst*.

Back in the main house, Taliah handed a book to Radien, which he began to flip through and absorb the knowledge of with his Eidetic Memory, courtesy of The Aura.

*The Gems of Creation, they are named the Arcas, and there exists one for each of the Realms. They are the physical manifestation of a Realm's power and existence, and though their machinations are incomprehensible to mortal and immortal minds alike, the best way to think of them is as the 'representative gems' that exist as proof of a realm's existence, but even this is a terrible oversimplification. Most of our knowledge of the Arcas comes from the Aura Prism's reluctantly-given information on them, and it is the Prism that even coined the phrase 'representative gems,' even though not all of the Arcas take the form of gem-like structures. It is believed that the Prism was deliberately vague with this analogy and these descriptions, as the implications of the Arcas and the consequences of their existence are intimidating, as per the Prism's own testimony, an Arca must **never** occupy the dimension that it hails from, or this would result in what the Prism referred to as 'The Ideal State,' and as a result,* *the balance of the Realms would immediately be destroyed as they all would be consumed by the Realm that had its Arca return to it. However, it is also theorized that this all-consuming doom would be halted by returning all Arcas to their home dimensions, if one should do so. However, it is also theorized that one should not experiment with this possibility, as given that several of the Arcas are accounted for, the very nature of their existence invites doom-mongers to attempt to destroy everything, for as assuredly as reality exists, those who would fervently seek it end do as well.*

Auros — The Realm of Power

The mortal universe that we know of exists within the Realm of Power. Though not part of Auros itself, Cynar is surrounded by Auros's domain. It is through Auros that the Psionic and cosmic powers exist. Auros's Arca is the Arca of Power. The Arca of Power is the Aura Prism.

Radien's eyebrow raised. He knew that the Prism was a Grand Psionic Entity, but one of these Arcas, that must never be present in their own realms?

Aldkalst — The Realm of Non-Knowledge

The Realm of Non-Knowledge is a place beyond Cynar and Auros that constantly creates new information and new phenomena, in order to ensure that it is completely impossible to know all things. Aldkalst's Arca is the Arca of Time. The Arca of Time is the Eternity Geode.

Radien had heard of the Eternity Geode before… when he met his future self briefly, from that darkened timeline. Apparently, the Eternity Geode was within the Vault of the Defender, which he had also recently discovered. Two of these Arcas were present in Cynar, and it was starting to make his head spin.

The Void — The Realm of the Space Between Them

The Void is the Realm that occupies the space that Realms do not. Within Auros is Cynar, and within The Void is Auros and Aldkalst, as well as the other Realms, Transistus, and Immaterius. Where these realms are not, there is The Void. The Arca of The Void is the Void Cortex.

Transistus — The Realm of Passage

Transistus is the realm that consists of the bridges and portals between realms, those known and those yet unknown. It is arguably the realm that the least is known about, as there are only five known places that are the realm of Transistus, the five bridges that cross into the other realms, save for The Void.

Radien slammed shut the book, before he started to get a headache.

"You got farther than I did on my first try," Veralis commented, and Radien groaned in brain-strain as he flopped onto his back on the couch he had been reading on. Taliah chuckled as she prepared drinks for the three of them. Rather, preparing a very large batch of a particular drink that would also conveniently act as something to serve, with healthy amounts of leftovers.

"Well, it at least gives enough context for what I learned," Radien finally said, but not before a full six minutes of grumbling had taken place, that though he had made a great many different grumbling sounds, had barely even scratched the surface of the sheer lexicon of discontented noises a Death Worlder is capable of making.

"And what did you learn, if you are willing to

divulge?" Taliah asked as she handed Radien and Veralis each a glass of the Mind-Ease Tonic.

After Radien took a sip, followed by a proper swig, he spoke. "The Arca of Cynar does not yet exist."

Taliah and Veralis both looked at each other quizzically. The implications of this knowledge sure existed, but neither of them could really make heads or tails of what exactly those implications were. Such was the nature of studying the Arcas, it was about the Psionic equivalent of the Collatz Conjecture.

"There is definitely solace to take in this," Radien finally said. "At least for me. It tells me that the universe is still a place of mystery, and despite how long as many of the spacefaring civilizations have existed, we've only barely begun to scratch the surface. It would seem, as it turns out, I have *not* arrived late to the party of these stars that I spent my youth dreaming of."

Taliah seemed to have a moment of clarity about Radien, hearing that he spent every one of his days trapped on Earth wanting nothing but out. How deafening was the call to adventure that could not be answered for the senselessly cruel hands of circumstance? How much did it make the soul bleed and burn in agony, to be a person of sound mind and able body, trapped on *Earth?* Much less *America?* To describe it as 'primal existential frustration' would not even come close to holding a candle. And for all of Miles Radien's life until that fateful day when fate finally took another course, that screaming silence was the only thing he could hear, an emptiness that had not even the decency to be of the useful kind, that could be built on. Instead, only the emptiness that meant *nothing* could be had, and not even the decency to be the kind of nothingness that means one has nothing to lose.

The Death World Vulpians themselves had a word for such a place. *Fjarkauln. The Burning Grey.* It was their version of Hell.

"Make no mistake, Earth was *Fjarkauln*," *Radien* said calmly as he seemed able to tell that the two were having this collective moment of epiphany to just how *bad* life on Earth was. "It shouldn't have taken a miraculous visitor from another world just for my life to start meaning something, but I would've been a fool not to take the chance I was given that day. I had known it for years, to cross at a ford means setting sail even though your friends stay in harbor, knowing the route, knowing the soundness of your ship and the favor of the day."

Radien breathed in and out as Veralis listened, and Taliah refilled her drink. "It was said that the crossing at a ford happens often in a person's lifetime, but I sure couldn't tell. The chance never came until then, when I had already long figured my life was spent. Whether there was no route, the ship's planks were unfit, or the day would never have favor... or all at once, more like. The cruelty of that world was as incomprehensible as it was senseless and needless."

Radien finally sat himself up and finished what was in his glass, save for a small amount that he quickly examined with Second Sight as his eyes briefly flashed amber to do so. He seemed to sigh with relief, that not doing so in the first place hadn't bitten him for it. "But Earth is no longer part of my life, and hasn't been for a very long time, and I am eternally grateful for that. I will shed no tears for the Humans without *Kelvaltor* who were consumed by its shadow, and I will never be ashamed that I did not join them in darkness, though I shudder in retrospect at how very nearly I did."

Radien then caught himself just before he would've said another sentence, one that he tried to leave on Earth with the rest of his time there, in the dust. Veralis seemed to know this, and looked to him expectantly. Her tendencies as a Psionic Empath were uncanny.

<I walk the shadowed path. I walk not the shattered path,> Radien finally said to her in the outward silence of telepathy. Veralis now understood why he was hesitant to repeat that mantra.

Radien's comm-link pinged to break up the silence and introspection before it could reach dangerous levels of divulgence, to his relief. He quickly stood up, but then looked around to Taliah and Veralis before Taliah nodded that it would not be considered rude to teleport while in her house, which is what Radien was looking for. Veralis nodded as well, to say that she'd handle returning the Speeder, but not before riding around the plains with it, since those things knew how to *move*.

Regardless, Radien warped back to Torvaltyne Bastion's war room, where several people were discussing whatever it was that was going down.

"Tactician, my compliments for your speedy response," one of the tactical advisors stated. "Demonic riftgates have opened outside Tenbork Station."

"By the gods, that is *bold* of them," Radien noted as he made his way to the holo-map everyone was looking at, which showed the positions of Tenbork Station, Torvaltyne Bastion, as well as the surrounding terrain, plus the two rift gates that had just opened near Tenbork. "What else do we know?"

"They're just assembling right now, likely because they know how dangerous the area they've dropped into is. Their optimal route through the Devouring Jungle has them about two hour's march from the portals."

"They probably don't know the optimal route, but even if they do, they're anticipating losses along the way," Radien surmised. "Probably why their assembly is taking so long. What do we have in the area that might trip them up further?"

"*Ja-Anan Volarthir* Rholk is already working on that, he's the one who reported their presence to us," Kyla Fjarseng, the Death World Vulpian tactical advisor informed. Cassius Rholk, one of the *Elder Survivors* who lived within the Devouring Jungle was indeed attracting dangerous fauna towards the Demons, that though the servants of Hell would overpower, their numbers would be chipped away at in doing so.

"What about the gates?" Radien asked. Kyla had an answer for this as well.

"Word from Tenbork Station is that they're already preparing countermeasures to destroy the gates," she replied.

"How long until those measures are ready?"

"Six hours."

"Can Tenbork hold?"

"Between Cassius Rholk's efforts, and the defensive contingent, there's no reason they shouldn't, but losses will likely be heavy without assistance."

"In that case, let's send—"

"Tactician! Nineteen rift gates just appeared outside Firatyne!" Another voice called out, and another map popped up next to the one showing the situation at Tenbork Station. Indeed, nineteen rifts were creating a circle outside of the city of Firatyne, and Demonic troops were pouring out from them and forming up, preparing to tear the place to rubble, or worse—occupy it to use it as a forward base for a takeover of Raon-Arashal itself.

"*Fucking nineteen?!*" Radien exclaimed. "Oh for fuck's sake—no wonder!"

"What are we missing, Tactician?" Kyla asked.

"After Asriah finished helping us build Torvaltyne Bastion itself, he transferred to Tenbork Station, where he began working on what he called the Wave Motion Charge. Normally you've got to get right under the nose of a Demonic rift gate to close it with a Counter-Catalyst crystal, but the idea behind the Wave Motion Charge was to... well, send out a wave of that energy to halt an incursion in its tracks at range."

"So if the Demons attack Tenbork..." a familiar red-scaled Dragon spoke up. Crimzin, the Brightminded, was starting to figure it out, too. "If the Demons attack Tenbork at the same time they strike Firatyne, the Wave Motion Charge can't power up quick enough while also fending off a suicide assault!"

"Tenbork Station is basically a bunker with about a hundred special forces guys who are really good at holdouts," Radien said. "But charging that thing enough to have the range to take out the rifts near Firatyne, *and* fight back against that assault is a huge ask..."

Radien turned to Kyla. "Will Tenbork hold?"

"No reason it shouldn't. They'll make sure the Wave Motion Charge fires."

Radien then nodded. "Send all reinforcements we have available to Firatyne immediately, then! That city has to hold until Tenbork Station can fire off the Wave Motion Charge!"

"Shouldn't we at least send *some* to Tenbork itself?" Crimzin asked.

"Tenbork will hold," Radien stated. "We don't have to risk more to make sure of it."

"Even a few extra hands in a bunker like Tenbork Station could spell the difference between barely winning and completely crushing the enemy!" Crimzin insisted. "How many casualties are expected, versus how many could be prevented with even minimal additional reinforcements?!"

"Holographic Arena three, with me, now!" Radien ordered. He then nodded quickly to Kyla to carry out his order of sending reinforcements to Firatyne.

"This is hardly the time to—"

"It's the perfect time! Let your sword do your arguing for you if you think it can!"

Radien hastily made his way to the Holographic Arena that he had designated, with the red-scaled Bol'Drakkin Dragon following close behind, trying to figure out how to get a word in edgeways, whilst also balancing controlling the fires that were brewing in his Flight Ventricles, which was like a second set of blood vessels throughout the body of a Dragon, but were actually filled with lighter-than-air gasses that also served as the fuel for elemental breath, when channeled correctly. Their primary purpose, however, was to make the wings that many Bol'Drakkins possessed functional rather than decorative. Whether they were Flight Ventricles or Flame Ventricles was dictated by whatever they were being used for at that moment. Same organ, two functions. Granted, Crimzin did not possess natural wings. Though it was well known that wings are not present in all Bol'Drakkin Dragons, but winglessness was a recessive gene, one that many of those who it manifests in consider a curse, not least of all Crimzin himself.

When they got to the Arena, Crimzin hastily grabbed a weapon from the wall, since this place was for training. The Holographic Arena technology itself was quite the marvel to Radien, the projected weapons that had the same heft and feel to them as the real ones, but like akin to a table saw with a safety brake, would render inert upon contact with flesh for safety's sake. It allowed for full-speed, full-contact weapons training, just without the lethality. Some arena games even involved trying to 'break' as many of the weapons over your sparring partner as possible through a round, as the disintegration of the weapon from its wielder's hands indicated a strike that would have otherwise been a fight-ender.

But Crimzin had hastily grabbed a double-headed battleaxe from the wall, and Radien pulled a cutlass into his hand from twenty feet away with The Aura. The two soon engaged each other as Crimzin took Radien's advice, and let his weapon do the talking.

Crimzin's swings and leaping strikes were met with evasions and parries by Radien as the Dragon finally found the words he wanted to go with them.

"Even a few more fighters in Tenbork could make the difference between losing ten versus a hundred!" Crimzin began his point after trying to introduce Radien to the point of the spike atop the weapon's haft in the closest thing to a thrusting motion this style of battleaxe could achieve, and Radien met it with a sidestep, followed by a shielding parry from the cutlass in his left hand, just in case the sidestep wasn't enough. The battleaxe then quickly weaved around Crimzin's head as Radien just as quickly needed to duck that swing. "I find it hard to believe a squad's worth will make a similar level of difference in all of Firatyne!"

"Firatyne needs every hand that can hold a blade it can spare!" Radien countered, going on the offensive. Crimzin was able to hold off the attacks despite wielding a heavier weapon, with an impressively-timed set of blocks that carried into each other, even slamming the head of the axe into the ground and ducking behind the haft to avoid a strike, since lifting it up again wouldn't have been fast enough. This was able to transition into a new grip on the axe, and a follow-up aerial attack that Radien needed to either get the hell out of the way of, or get chopped in half vertically were it not for the Holographic Arena's safety features. Radien did dodge the attack, though, and also evaded the follow-up horizontal cleave. "A squad's worth could be the difference between a whole district either standing tall or having to be rebuilt from rubble after the battle!"

"Even if the Artisan's Row is what must be rebuilt, what does that matter compared to the lives of Tenbork's defenders? Will they appreciate dying emptily to save the Photon Saws and Rune Lasers that can just be replaced?"

Crimzin's attack continued, feral yet experienced. The strikes were that of someone trained well to use that battleaxe specifically, but these techniques would *not* be working with a different weapon, Radien knew well. When the next horizontal overhead slash came, Radien sidestepped inward, so that not only did the strike miss, but the haft of the weapon was right in the path of the cutlass the Holographic Arena was providing his hand. It didn't carve the haft in two, but it did cause Crimzin to drop the weapon from the sheer amount of force that just struck downward on his arms. He had to either drop the axe or risk wrenching his shoulders, so now he had to improvise. The flames that he was barely holding back already *demanded* to be let loose, and so before Radien could point the cutlass at Crimzin's throat and demand he yield, a raging plume of fire erupted from the Dragon's maw, on direct course with the face of the Death Worlder who was about to get it. Or so Crimzin thought.

Once he regained a bit more of his senses, realizing that he just about emptied his body's Flame Ventricles on a single target, he saw the ball of fire condensing in Radien's left hand, which had dropped the Arena cutlass, and with great Psionic strain, he was containing it, before he spun around and heaved the orb of flame at a nearby wall to detonate it on the other side of the room, where it posed no threat to either combatant. A blast crater about the size of a car was left on the wall as a result. Crimzin wasn't sure whether to be impressed or terrified at the feat.

"If you think that Tenbork's defenders would find their deaths in this battle empty, you don't know the first thing about my people!" Radien explained sternly, but not angrily. "They know what they're getting into, and they know what they have to do! If Tenbork holds, Firatyne holds, and they know it! *Tenbork will hold!* No Zhenrel-Vuljar dies with a clean sword, and no Zhenrel-Vuljar who dies with a sword in his hands dies emptily! It's who we are!"

Crimzin collected his breath, as spewing all that fire had left him panting.

"You may know something I don't about this defense, you might be right that Tenbork needs more hands! You also might take it upon yourself to prove that fact! And if it works, then no one will call foul, quite the opposite in fact! But if it does *not*, you will incur not only my ire, but that of everyone else who has to suffer for your decision!"

Crimzin's mind spun its gears rapidly as he tried to find his next words.

"Everyone at this Fortress, yourself included, has the right to demand an explanation for a decision I have made, and they will get it! But when I have made the decision, it is because I believe it to be the *correct* one! I lead Torvaltyne Bastion because far more often than not, the decisions I made *have* been the correct ones!"

Both men caught their breath for a bit longer.

"There can be no doubt of the fire in your veins, Brightmind of the *Jurovendr*," Radien said. "It's part of who you are, and the lineage that culminated in you. But don't let that title of Brightminded go to your head, or you may find yourself losing the right to it."

"I will go to Tenbork alone, then," Crimzin said. "No need for a whole squad, just my hands being the extra ones for them."

"If what you told me is true, and that even a few more capable hands could make that kind of difference, I can't think of anyone more equipped to. Just make sure you get a good snack in before you go, you drained almost all of your Flame Ventricles on that one, and you had *better not* go to a holdout with empty Flame Ventricles! The Demons are two full hours march from Tenbork, and that's assuming they've even started marching yet. The Quickgate at the Transit Nexus means you've got time."

Quickgates were different from Way Gates in the manner that they were for interplanet point-to-point transport, and therefore were easier to construct than full-on Way Gates that often had to connect points that were in separate galaxies.

Crimzin had taken Radien's advice and recharged his Flame Ventricles by way of sustenance, and had programmed the destination of Tenbork Station into the Quickgate panel. The portal flashed open, and Crimzin ducked through, at Tenbork Station mere minutes before they needed to shut off the Quickgate on that end, to ensure that Demons wouldn't be able to sneak into other locations on Raon-Arashal during the battle that was about to take place.

"Just in time, Brightminded," Arch-Militant Darek Jor'Galn greeted, to the Dragon's surprise. It was surprising to see the Arch-Militant randomly here, rather than in Firatyne. But then again, it was also possible that

Jor'Galn had the same mind as Crimzin, figuring that a few extra hands could make all the difference. "Between us, we both know that Firatyne will hold. All that's left is to decide whether it will be barely scraping by, or glorious victory!"

"Then let us choose victory, Arch-Militant," Crimzin eagerly replied as he reached into a pouch on his belt, only for most of his arm to vanish inside it like he was rifling through a deep chest. He then produced from the pocket dimension housed within the artificer's belt and produced a two-handed battleaxe, edges glowing with golden power, and blood-red runes in the Primal Draconian language lining the edges, spelling out the motto of the House of Brightflame: *Strength at arms, all of them.* The haft of the weapon clunked against the plating of the floor, and Darek Jor'Galn nodded with approval, before pressing the intercom button on the console next to him.

"*Warriors of Tenbork Station!*" the announcement came. "*The Descendant of the First Defender stands and fights with us today! Channel the spirit of his lineage, and show our foes the Flaming Heart of Raon-Arashal!*"

"*Hol-nah Viir! Stand and Fight!*" Everyone in the station yelled as the footsteps of the encroaching Demons began to make the walls of the bunker rumble.

Crimzin looked to Jor'Galn, wondering if he had confused him for someone else.

"You did not know?" the Arch-Militant asked. "Descendant of Talgoron, the Brighttaloned, of the Kasven Line?"

"Talgoron, the Brighttaloned, yes... He was of

the Kasven Line?!" Crimzin suddenly realized as he put the pieces together. Radien had told him of Talgoron's sacrifice to break him free of Elder Terra's chains, and that there was a reason the *Aura Runner* seemed to recognize him, even though he had never seen the ship in his life, only heard of it in Archaeotech legends. *"That I did not know."*

"Well, now you do," Darek Jor'Galn affirmed *"Anan Volkarn! Time for Battle!"*

"Hol-nah Viir!"

"Anan Volkarn!"

"Pir Jaltai! By the Sword!"

"Pir Iklae! By the Spear!"

Jor'Galn stepped aside from the console, letting Crimzin be the one to press the button that would spell the end of his enemies: *DOLGELSE TOULTH. DOOM FOES.* Crimzin grinned with vigor at the display screen, showing the name of the *Volkarn Orkest, Battle Anthem* that would be playing once he hit that red button, to start the battle.

"Aurok Son-Deyl! Behold our power!" Crimzin yelled to commence the beatdown that was about to take place by the beat of steel and song alike, the song that would ignite the *Nel Jafjaa, Heart of the Flaming Sword* in everyone, the *Zhernrel-Vuljar* word for the soul.

His red-scaled fist hit slammed the button, and the music started.

The opening percussive instrumentals both rang out over the station's speakers, and then the drums started to pound, so did the hafts of spears and halberds strike the floor in tune, and swords banged against shields, and the Death Worlders even recanted the lyrics of the vocals in tune, and the Devouring Jungle around them was alight with the song of *Raon-Arashal, the Arena of Life.*

The first Demon claws began to tear their way through the plated armor of the bunker, and the Trooper who had just entered the bunker was greeted with the fire and fury of its defenders, who would know no falter. The *Volkarn Orkest* made every strike that much more precise, every movement that much quicker, every fire burn that much hotter. And any fire that can burn Demons is one to be reckoned with, which is something the servants of the Dark Six were very much learning the hard way.

Crimzin was carving Demons to cutlets with his runed battleaxe, and Darek Jor'Galn was similarly slicing the scourges to ribbons with his pair of Argentfire Kamas at the ends of Archonium chains, ensuring that no cheeky telekinesis would hinder their accuracy when being acrobatically flung about at long range, before returning to the hand for close combat.

"Darkstar!" a Death Worlder called out. One of the legendary warriors of Hell was present, second only to the Dark Six themselves in power and rank. Jor'Galn nodded to Crimzin that he could handle things up here, so Crimzin leaped down from the raised platform to meet this Darkstar head-on. When his feet hit the ground, the Dragon's eyes met the Darkstar's. At first, Crimzin tried to come up with something clever to say to get things started, but his voice suddenly spoke something else, words that he didn't even know he knew.

"*Saarinthaal...*" Crimzin addressed. Some

presence within him knew this Demon's name, and spoke it aloud with his voice. *"Terror of the Acid Sea... I'm surprised you were allowed to live after your failure at Vosis."*

"Kasven!" Saarinthaal spat in disgust. "You live, clad in new scales! I have had much time to prepare for our next encounter, or rather, my encounter with your descendant!"

Crimzin re-asserted his own voice back into the mix. "You may have prepared to fight Kasven, but now you face me!"

The techniques that Crimzin had been less than successful with against Radien were proving to be the bane of the ill-prepared Saarinthaal, who was not used to fighting an opponent at this level of training, let alone with this weapon. The Darkstar was soon on the defensive, barely parrying and evading the attacks, with the shaves coming much closer than they got to Radlen, and the panic in Saarinthaal was beginning to set in.

It was also the case that Crimzin had yet to unleash the fire in his veins, and against a Darkstar Demon seemed like the best time to see if his fire was one that burned even Demons.

The glow of Crimzin's burning flame was melting through the floor panels, and turning the heads of the Demons around them at the sight: a veritable geyser of fire that could boil the Magma Ocean itself was consuming their commander, and soon, chunks of the Demon Saarinthaal were falling off of his bones, some pieces of flesh even shattering like the charcoal they had become. Saarinthaal's last breaths were barely wheezes of ash, before the runed battleaxe sliced from cranium to pelvis and through, cleaving this Demon cleanly in two along his vertical axis. The two halves fell apart, and all eyes were on the Dragon who had just done the deed.

"Hunderfold Steel, Saarinthaal," Crimzin remarked. "You won't be returning to your masters."

Darek Jor'Galn's kamas carved arms and legs alike from the Demons they were attached to, and as the *Volkarn Orkests* playing in Tenbork station continued, he noticed that something unbelievable was taking place.

The Demons were pulling back. They were retreating.

"What the—they're *running?!*" he yelled out.

"Wave Motion Charge ready, Arch-Militant!" a Death Worlder called out from near a console after hearing the beeps that confirmed it.

"Fire immediately! Ready and fire Quake Pulse as well!"

The first wave of energy that pulsed out from Tenbork Station was the otherworldly blue-green wave of Counter-Catalystic power that tore the rift gates outside Tenbork to shreds, and would continue across the planet to destroy the gates that besieged Firatyne as well. A few moments later, the whole base shook with a percussive hum as a result of the second weapon fired off, the more localized area of effect that resonated the jungle floor for about a kilometer in every direction, and no Demon was spared being hit by this pulse, that shattered every bone in their feet and legs that ran across the ground, desperately retreating from the battle that they had so utterly lost. The Devouring Jungle would finish them off. After all, it was called the Devouring Jungle for good reason.

Crimzin met up with Jor'Galn as everyone assessed the damages and estimated repair times and priorities, as well as materials needed.

"Have they ever done that?" Crimzin asked. "I've studied the First War For Reality, and I can't remember any time that Demons have *fled* from battle."

Darek shook his head. "We've made history today here, Crimzin."

CHAPTER THE SEVENTH
THE BATTLE OF FIRATYNE

"It is time to show the Cynofrax Rogues, and the rest of the universe, why it is we are called DEATH Worlders!"
—Darvok Kestrogale, leading guerrilla resistance against the Cynofrax Rogues during the ill-fated Purification Campaign

At the very same moment that Tenbork's defenders engaged the Demons, Radien was in Firatyne, having arrived via Quickgate along with Jarrek, who was comparing his claymore with weapons that had been brought by other Redarian battlegroups. Along with this, he was also making sure everyone was ready for what was about to come.

"Everyone's taking up their positions and readying themselves, by the time the Demons come, no one will be unprepared to do their part," Jarrek informed Radien as he got some practice drills in.

"Sounds good, how long until contact?"

"Ninety minutes, tops."

Radien nodded, and informed the other leading

commanders in Firatyne. "Ninety minutes until the claws of our foes start hitting the walls of the city! Everyone, battle stations!"

With preparations in their final phase, everyone scattered off to where they were planning to hold.

"Radien, once your group engaging the front breaks off to *Kelar Toreiyn* positions, I'll start making my way towards you for us to meet and basically circle the city with our engagements," Jarrek said, to which Radien nodded.

Kelar Toreiyn, Defense of Spite, was a defensive tactic that the Death World Vulpians were *very* good at. Which is to say, holding the line against a superior force with such sheer burning attrition that the enemy could only hope for Pyrrhic victory at most, if even victory at all. Death Worlders being the stubborn survivalists they are, were practically *bred* to hold down a fort or line.

It was likely this very fact that was why the Demons hoped to assault Raon-Arashal so quickly and decisively, as not only did they know that the current Defender hailed from this world, but so did also an entire species of some of the hardest to kill people in the galaxy. A Demonic victory on Raon-Arashal would be devastating to innumerable parties.

Naturally, every person in Firatyne was planning to fight to their dying breath to make sure that the Demons knew no victory here.

It couldn't be known for sure whether the minutes passed slowly or quickly. On the one hand, with everyone's preparations and positioning entering their final phases, it seemed like the minutes flew past without second thought. On the other, as everyone waited for the first claws and blades of the enemy to tear through the plating of the geodesic dome that was the walls of the city of Firatyne, the tension as everyone reaffirmed their oaths and recited their battle rites, each second might feel like ten. Even so, when the minutes passed, they passed without a second thought, the minutes forgotten as quickly as they had ticked away, even if they ticked away at the pace of a Trylaxian Acidslug.

Miles Radien stood in front of a group of Death Worlders at the front door, that the Demons would make their entry into.

"What's stopping them from just climbing the walls?" One of the fighters wondered aloud.

"The Defense Grid that keeps them from shelling us with artillery," Radien responded. "They've either got to go through the doors we give them, or get vaporized by the energy shield itself."

"All six doors instead of just one or zero, though?" that same fighter wondered aloud again, referring to the six gates that marked the entry points into the city of Firatyne. Radien's group was guarding the Gate of Stargazers.

"We know where they're coming this way," Radien answered again. "If we try to lock it all down, they'll just make one of their own. Personally, I'd rather know where my enemy's coming from."

Everyone nodded their heads, including this inquisitive warrior. Nobody minded the questions, they were completely legitimate, and someone had to ask them, if only to make sure that there was an answer.

"The Demons think they're coming to seize a city

held by desperate militiamen, ill-prepared for war," Radien addressed. "It falls upon us to remind them why they've had to stay out of Cynar for billions of years!"

Radien hit the button on his uplink to the network of speakers across the city that would play the *Volkarn Orkests*. The invigorating instrumental started, and the blood of every defender of Firatyne began to pump harder, faster, igniting the *Nel Jalfjaa, Heart of the Flaming sword* in everyone, the Death Worlder word for the soul.

"*Hol-nah viir! Stand and fight!*" Radien called.

The rumbling of Demonic footsteps grew louder.

"*Anan Volkarn! Time for battle!*" Firatyne responded.

"*Hol-nah viir!*"

"*Anan Volkarn!*"

"*Pir Jaltai! By the sword!*"

"*Pir Iklae! By the spear!*"

The first trooper's feet hit the street, its weapon in hand. In one hand, Radien held forth the Borfblade, and in the other, the Honorblade of Korvideyl.

"*Aurok son-Deyl! Behold our power!*"

Radien wasted no time charging forward to meet his foes in combat, and his foes seemed unprepared to be met with such a ferocious and coordinated defense. The Battlegroup of Death Worlders that were the first foes these Demons would see, they were but a taste of the sheer fire and fury that was yet to be brought upon those who dared to claim dominion over the free souls of Raon-Arashal. By blade and claw, The Death Worlders knew no falter.

"Invoke the spirits of the defenders of Doiran!

Fight them till the end, never to surrender no matter how many waves we face!" Radien called as the *Volkarn Orkest* pounded through the air, and again, again, again, again, the Demons attacked, and the Death Worlders held them back.

As Radien's Battlegroup engaged the Demons at the Gate of Stargazers, Jarrek's Redarian company went blade-to-blade and bullet-to-bullet with the attackers at the Gate of Artisans. As the Redarian Arch-Militant yelled battlecries in the ancient form of the Redarian language, his claymore scooped up a chunk of the street, and was met with a spinning side kick to be flung at the encroaching Demons, and a satisfying *crunch* marked the end of three foes at once.

At the Gate of Stories, Veralis drew *Käyner* and *Käynvi,* and hurled them at the first Whiplance Demon that made footfall. The axes arced around the Demon's spear-like prehensile appendages, embedding into its sides, and the Cynofrax Vulpian Scion of the Psionic Path charged forward, grabbing the hafts of her axes and viciously yanking them through the entire ribcage of the Whiplacnce Demon, and planting her knee into its face, crushing its skull with her strength as she then began to engage more foes, her axes turning her into a whirling dervish of death, honed and precise as the training that made her such. The Battlegroup she was posted with similarly brought doom upon their foes with blade, bullet and bolt alike.

Micah Jorvask stood with her company from the Eyes of the Daggers at the Gate of Aether. In Death World Vulpian architecture, The Aether represented what was not yet known, and awaiting discovery. It was the main residential area, the section in which one could find a rifle behind each lamppost with its cleverly built streets and sidewalks that allowed both for a walkable city, that also could suddenly become an arena of doom for invaders, should the need arise. Micah's Battle Company was twelve assassins of the Eyes of the Daggers, led by the Disciple of Shadow herself, ready to make twelve Redarians feel like twelve thousand for the Demons that were trying to invade.

Micah's longsword and parrying dagger, coupled with acrobatic evasions and tumbles, sliced cleanly through limb after limb of the Demons who were being met not only with the Eyes of the Daggers, but the residents of Firatyne, who were eager to show the Demons what they had spent their lives training for, all to the tune of the *Volkarn Orkests* that boomed through the speakers to fire up the morale of the defenders.

At the Gate of Swords, two well-versed Hykentiu warriors prepared to meet the Demons who were about to enter the *Raon Nurelzi,* or 'arena district' of the city. The Demons were also due to learn why *Raon Nurelzi* was also the Death World Vulpian word for 'playground.'

The double-pointed spear of Miirkae hit the concrete and the Arcane Cestuses of Dorg crackled with fire, frost, and lightning alike. Both entered stances, and the Demons charged.

As the two fought the horde, pummeling the enemy with elemental fury, a Bol'Drakkin Draconian stood guard of an Ascendant technician, who was keying up the Holographic Projectors of the many training grounds present in the Arena District.

"How long, Render?!" the blue-scaled Dragon

called after tearing out the throat of a Demon attacker with a vicious chomp.

"What kind of ship do you want?!"

"Capital-Class!"

"We are indoors, Arcturus!"

"You're no fun! Fine, give me a Phoenix-Class!"

Render punched it in, and the entire network of holographic arenas in the city came online and connected to each other, allowing reinforcements to be projected anywhere they were needed in the city. Even if some of them were illusional, they would give the impression of a much bigger force. However, some projections would have their automatic safety features disabled, such as the attack vessel that had just spawned outside of the building, that the blue-scaled Dragon leaped into the cockpit of from a nearby window, so he could make surgical strikes against enemy targets, particularly siege implements that were trying to breach into buildings and fortified positions. As soon as Dorg saw the vessel appear above the street, he summoned a shield around him and Miirkae, signaling the pilot that he was safe to light the Demons up.

The cannons of the ship tore apart the road, but the only casualties were the enemy's, and if the Artisan's Row held, the repairs would be relatively trivial.

The final entrance to Firatyne, the Gate of Stone, was guarded by none other than Arakai Selendica, the Argent Flame of Cynofrax. He was called this because his swords burned with the titular silver fire that could melt through titanium in seconds. This was the flame that would be introduced to the flesh of his Demonic enemy. Next to him was Iraine Ironscale, a Nuvenr-Bol'Drakkin

Dragon cross of jet-black scales, whose blazing green eyes hinted also that her breath was acid upon her foes. Literally. Her breath weapon was acid. Nobody expects the acid breath.

The spines on her back began to glow blazing white as she prepared to unleash it, and Arakai calmly stood next to her as the Demons charged forth.

The very concrete they stood on began to dissolve, along with the Demons who were foolish enough to be caught in it.

"The Acid Sea! It is wielded, the Acid Sea!" were the last words of one Demonic invader, translated.

"There's an Acid Sea where they come from?" Arakai commented, raising an eyebrow toward Iraine.

"Why wouldn't there be?" Iraine shrugged. "There's one on Trylaxia, too." She then snapped her fingers, and the acid fizzled away, its fumes deconstructing themselves into the base oxygen and nitrogen around them, to ensure that the entire city wasn't suddenly covered in the caustic gas that was the result of Iraine's breath weapon causing flesh, metal, and concrete to boil. However, this also created a pressure wave that was the result of a lot more individual atoms in the air than there was before, and though it flattened the next incoming invaders, the buildings, and the defenders in this section of the city stood firm against it, and it eventually dissipated harmlessly.

"It fucken' *wimdy*," Arakai said with a completely straight face. He then reached for the hilts of his swords, and drew them with lightning speed, igniting the Argentfire along their blades. Those who were slashed by these swords would be immolated in seconds, and Arakai was not so much a tornado of steel as he was instead, *a hurricane of bright silver-flaming Archonium.* Iraine tore chunks out of her foes with the strikes of her talons, which were laced with the acid of her breath, which explained what made them carve through armor and flesh alike so effectively.

As the enemies continued to pour forth, threatening to overwhelm the Battlegroups at the gates, Radien made the call. *"Kelar Toreiyn! Defense of Spite!"* And so the warriors of Firatyne scattered from the gates, taking to their positions within the city itself to wage guerrilla urban warfare against their enemies, which was heavily weighted towards the defenders.

Death World Vulpians were renowned across the stars for their sheer capacity for holdouts.

With everyone in the rhythm of doing their own thing, Radien then began to make his way towards the Gate of Stories, slicing every Demon he encountered to shreds with the Borfblade and the Honorblade of Korvideyl. A throwing spear suddenly splintered against the shield that was covering his back. Someone had just tried to take him out from behind, but the Honorblade ensured that was not possible. He turned to face the Demon that had just made his attempt from afar, and noticed that this was a Darkstar, one of the legendary warriors of Hell, second only in power and authority to the Dark Six themselves.

"And you are?" Radien asked of this Darkstar.

"Izhkath, the Javelin of Despair!" the Demon answered.

"Must be," Radien scoffed. "Let's see

how you do when you haven't got the advantage of concealment!"

Radien engaged with his two swords, the Borfblade and the Honorblade. The Demon hurled two more throwing spears at him, but both were sliced out of the air by the swords. The next spear was raised to block the incoming strike, but Radien changed the position of his right hand mid-air so that while the Borfblade was indeed striking overhead, the Honorblade was piercing Izhkath through the abdomen. Izhkath was only prepared to block one strike.

Radien pulled the Honorblade out of Izhkath's gut, and then slashed the Borfblade across his ribs, severing this Demon in half horizontally. Radien then spun around and side kicked Izhkath's chest, detaching the two halves, forcing the Demon's last sight to see its lower half stumble and fall to the ground a full second after his top half did. Its last breath soon was drawn. One less Darkstar that would return to its masters. Radien moved onward, towards the Gate of Stories.

Veralis was still hacking Demons to pieces with her axes, every now and again channeling The Aura to lash out in all directions to keep the horde at bay. She then threw the two axes, one after the other, and they began circling around her as they whirled in their own circles, creating this Delvonen Hypersteel ward as she went hand-to-hand with what Demons managed to duck and dodge around them. A Demon was kicked out of a window and landed on two of its comrades with a crunch, and Veralis looked up into the window to see that Miles Radien was making the rounds.

"Radien!" Veralis called out. "I was about to tell

you telepathically, but since you're here—I've just sensed a spike of power near the Grand Colosseum! I think they're planting a bomb of some kind!"

"I'm on it!" he shouted. "Jarrek is inbound!"

As if right on cue, a chunk of concrete slammed right into a Demon that was about to try to stab Veralis from behind. Veralis looked at the crushed foe.

"I had him!"

"Still a good shot, though!"

"True."

Radien was already making his way towards the center of the city, where the Grand Colosseum stood. He searched the area with the glowing amber eyes of his Second Sight, and saw that a massive and imposing Demon was underneath the arena, in its mechanical underbelly, and it was indeed assembling *something* there. When he looked back at Jarrek and Veralis, Jarrek nodded, signaling that the two would hold the area.

A few slain obstructing Demons later, Radien was in the Grand Colosseum's underbelly, and noticed that the ceiling had been raised by several feet, which normally was only done for arena matches that involved 'king of the hill' style play. However, it soon became clear that the hydraulics had been set this way because of the sheer height of the creature that was down here. This Darkstar was a Monument Breaker, a fearsome combination indeed. Its blue-toned muscles rippled with azure veins as it worked, and next to it was a sledgehammer to match its build. Whoever this was, he was a force to be reckoned with.

The Demon then turned up from what it was doing to face Radien, and set down the small datapad that was being used to configure this device, replacing it with the sledge. "I heard rumor that the Defender was known, who denied us the price of the Vault of his predecessors. I am told it was... decisive."

"It decided that the Demons would not have the Vault, indeed," Radien retorted. "Those Artifacts will never be in the hands of the Dark Six now."

"And it is you who are responsible for this fact," the Demon continued. "The Ideal Masters will honor me, Charvikaroth, The Mallet Lord, destroyer of Defenders!"

The two squared off at each other. This would be a duel to remember. Both fighters circled around the other in the underground space, positioning and repositioning their weapons for the inevitable clash. Charvikaroth had reach, and strength. Radien had speed, and precision. Both had skill.

Charvikaroth swung his enormous sledge around his head and towards Radien, its head only a few inches off the ground, so there'd be no ducking it. However, Radien could jump over it, and he did, evading the strike that would have annihilated his legs otherwise, and began closing the distance, slashing at Charvikaroth with his swords. His opponent was backing up quickly, evading the slashes as best he could, but Radien was able to move forward faster than Charvikaroth could move backwards.

Radien swiped the Borfblade at Charvikaroth's right arm, cutting a fair amount into the muscle, eliciting a yell from the Demon, who slammed Radien's chest with the palm of his other hand, to push him back while he quickly healed himself. Radien had no choice but to similarly rapid-heal his abdomen after that strike. His solar plexus had been ruptured, and without the assist from The Aura, the fight could've been over. However, the cut Charvikaroth suffered was also severe, that almost had gone through the bone, and needed a similar amount of time to regenerate, without risking losing that arm entirely.

Both fighters reset themselves, and prepared to engage again. Charvikaroth slammed his sledge on the ground and moved his hands in a pattern that summoned a green glow around his arms, and he advanced on Radien with rapid punches, that though they were being cut to shreds by the two swords, that green glow was healing the wounds the Borfblade and Honorblade were inflicting as fast as they could be inflicted. Radien soon found himself backed against a wall, and the Demon slammed his fist into the stone where Radien's head was only seconds before. Radien drove both swords into Charvikaroth's gut, but the Demon was still swinging, a fist slamming into the Death Worlder's jaw and another into his abdomen. Radien let go of both weapons, and drove the claw on his left thumb into his enemy's arm, dragging it across and splitting muscle, artery and vein alike longways as Charvikaroth screamed in enraged pain, and was forced to back off, just to get the swords out of him before he could start healing himself.

Charvikaroth was squarely on the defensive as Radien began responding with a pursuing combination of kicks, front, roundhouse, side, front, roundhouse, side, turning and changing his kicking foot and stepping method depending on his distance. The Demon's ribs were snapping as he frantically healed his left arm, before finally advancing forward with a body check, that Radien evaded, and followed up with a jumping push kick to Charvikaroth's spine.

The Darkstar Demon was thrown to the ground, and would need several moments to pull the swords out of its gut and mend its wounds. Radien quickly rushed over to the device that Charvikaroth had planted, eyeing it with Second Sight and letting The Aura act as his search engine through the universe's databases on just what the hell this thing was.

"It's like a Way Gate generator, but compact..."

"Your counter-catalysts render our portals vulnerable and finite," Charvikaroth commented as he lifted himself back up onto his feet, his body still pulsing with energy being supplied to his wounds to heal them. "But with this, even if your Wave Motion Pulse is successful, it will only be a temporary outage. This is a portal that cannot be forever shut, only temporarily switched off."

"Interesting that you're telling me this," Radien scoffed.

"Consider it a professional courtesy as we both ready ourselves for the next round," Charvikaroth replied. "The reward you will reap, if you can defeat me: this valuable information on our workings and tactics."

"You already knew about the Wave Motion Pulse anyway, or you wouldn't be attacking Tenbork simultaneously," Radien replied, wondering if he was buying enough time for the defenders at Tenbork Station to finish charging the Wave Motion Pulse.

"If Tenbork is delayed long enough for the Realm Ripper to activate, it won't matter if the two locations fully defend themselves, for this will be able to re-establish itself with the Burning Hells. Even if we are defeated here, we can amass in secret under your world's hallowed training grounds!"

Meanwhile on the streets of the Gate of Stories, Jarrek was hearing this entire conversation thanks to the earpiece that Radien was using to communicate with him during the battle. This was valuable information indeed, just in case Radien failed.

Back underground, Radien quickly sliced at the Realm Ripper's assembly with the Borfblade, which he had telekinetically retrieved while Charvikaroth thought he was stalling Radien. The metal frame crashed onto the ground, destroying the Realm Ripper.

Charvikaroth's eyes lit up with fury. "I'm going to have to spend *days* repairing that, you son of a bitch!"

"She certainly was! But you'll have to beat me first, Mallet Lord!" Radien challenged. "The reward you will reap, if you can defeat me: the chance to continue battling the entire city of Firatyne!"

The two faced off against each other again, and let loose their skill upon their clash. Both were using their psionic powers to speed up their movements, allowing the much larger sledgehammer to move at the speed of the Borfblade and the Honorblade, and Radien was similarly accelerating psionically to be able to move fast enough to dodge the entire massive head of the sledge.

A concrete wall was cracked by the impact of a wave of wind that was the result of these two moving at such speeds. The Grand Colosseum was shaking with the force Radien and Charvikaroth were throwing at each other, with all the strength, speed, and skill they had.

Neither of them could land a hit on each other, for a full seventy seconds, until a massive wave of force more energetic than either of them rippled through the city of Firatyne, knocking combatants flat on the floor, but only causing minor quakes outside. The city's architecture was clever, and quite resistant to geological phenomena. Granted, since this wave of energy was a Psionic phenomena, it made things behave a bit more weirdly. Fortunately, since the Wave Motion Pulse had been configured as precisely as possible, and it at the very least was sure to not damage the city itself as it ripped through the Demonic Rift Gates that surrounded the geodesic dome that covered Firatyne. The Demons who were pouring through to assist in the invasion were torn asunder by the explosions that ensued from the tears in reality forcibly shutting and sealing themselves.

The two quickly kicked themselves back up, realizing what had just happened.

"The battle is not yours yet, *Greígoth!*" Charvikaroth cursed. "I still can destroy you, and repair the Realm Ripper!"

Several footsteps could be heard. Radien looked into the darkness with Second Sight, and saw that a squadron of Shadow Striders was making its way towards the two. Radien wasn't sure if he could take them on, *and* this Darkstar. But there were thirteen signatures, and Shadow Striders only move in packs of twelve...

One dropped off out of the Second Sight, like a light that had been where the Demon once was, suddenly turned off. Jarrek had made his way to the location, and was becoming the hunter of the Demons who thought that they were hunting Radien.

When Radien snapped out of Second Sight because one of his Autopsionic Cantrips, which he had named Proximity Alert, would automatically snap him to attention if something new got within ten feet of him, while using Second Sight. The two were tailor-made to work together, keeping Radien passively alert, even if he was actively looking elsewhere. Charvikaroth had been using his own version of the Second Sight as well to scan the situation, but was also slowly moving towards Radien at the same time. Charvikaroth nodded in a 'not bad' mannerism.

"You're as vigilant as one of those *Rogues*," Charvikaroth growled, the word *rogues* itself with extra emphasis on how bothersome they were to the goals of the Dark Six.

"The Rogues are real, then?" Radien asked.

Charvikaroth froze. He had just let slip the fact that the Burning Hells truly did have rebels, indeed were they no myth.

"So Rogue Demons really are a thing, then!" Radien audibly pieced together.

Charvikaroth growled. "Tactician warned that you were clever, *Greígoth!*" The Mallet Lord's sledge was raised again by its wielder, prepared to make his last stand, and maybe take Radien with him in the process.

Radien fired off a bolt of The Aura at Charvikaroth, who swung the sledge at its path, deflecting the strike. He then returned the Borfblade and Honorblade of Korvideyl to his hands, and readied himself in a stance, charging his weapons with the

Psionic power of The Aura coursing through him, making both weapons crackle with energy.

Charvikaroth arced the hammer over his head with a yell, throwing one last all-or-nothing blow at the Death Worlder who stood against him.

The ground shook as the weapons collided. Jarrek dispatched a Shadow Strider who had just been knocked onto the ground by the sonic wave, wondering just what the hell was going on in that central room.

The Mallet Lord's weapon was on the ground, and both of the Demon's arms were still shaking. Radien had coursed enough energy through his weapons to anchor himself so resolutely, that the sheer force that was stopped, that had to go somewhere, was rocketed back into the arms of the weapon that had just been blocked. Every single bone in both of Charvikaroth's arms had been shattered into shards from the feedback's force, and the sledge of the Mallet Lord dropped on the ground, the Darkstar so startled by what had taken place, the pain of his arms exploding from the inside hadn't even time to set in yet, and the only thing he could hope for was that the Death Worlder before him was going to end this before it had the chance to.

Radien sliced into Charvikaroth once with each sword, to ensure that a wound had been inflicted with the Hunderfold blades. So long as the Demon died with wounds inflicted by a Hunderfold blade, he could land the killing blow with whatever weapon he pleased, and it would still have the same effect. But the sheer force that had been absorbed by the swords was converting to an unstable arcane energy, that was being diffused by way of purple lightning strikes crackling off from the blades of the swords themselves, desperately venting away the impact that had just been taken on as quickly as it could be done safely, without blowing the entire arena to pieces.

Radien tossed the swords away from him, and then one of the magenta lightning strikes zapped a Shadow Strider to dust. Jarrek quickly took cover behind a pillar, figuring that he'd let the his enemies have a go at dealing with the errant energy first.

Radien then entered one last stance facing Charvikaroth, baring the claws that he had sharpened on the sandstone walls of the canyons of Jaltai-Vuul, that would easily shred through the Demon's flesh. And that's exactly what they did. Left and right swiped horizontally through The Mallet Lord's neck, followed by a wheel kick that split the wounds open, almost tearing his head off completely, which was itself followed up by a roundhouse kick that finished the job, and the Darkstar Demon's head was no longer attached to its shoulders. It rolled across the ground with a *thud*, into the shadows, eliciting screeches from the Shadow Striders as they realized what had just taken place. These noises were short-lived, however, since they revealed their positions to Jarrek in doing so, who skillfully dispatched each of them with his claymore, before approaching the clearing that Radien and his fallen foe were within.

"Did we win?" were the first words out of the Death Worlder's mouth after Charvikaroth's corpse disintegrated into red sparks.

Jarrek burst out laughing, because he already knew that the Wave Motion Pulse meant the battle was won.

"I'll take that as a yes, then," Radien responded.

"That has got to be the most *you* thing I've ever heard from you, Radien!" Jarrek chortled. "Oh yeah, we just completely *eradicated* them, and you're just like 'that means we win, right?'"

The Redarian giggled all the way back to the service hatch that would let them reach the surface. When they did, the whole city was alight with the song of victory, as the warriors of Firatyne celebrated the successful defense.

Pir Dolgelse sol thej! Pir Dolgelse sol thej!

Pir Jaltai-nah pir Iklae, djozernaaverash toulth sol kallej!

Viir duunraeynar Torval'e krae, dwerai thej kel Yagitay!

Jasaln givol sol hol-nah orgaen, pir Dolgelse sol thej!

With Doom we come! With Doom we come!

By the Sword and by the Spear, to destroy our enemies alongside our allies!

Fight the fear for Honor's sake, finally bring forth Victory!

On Mountains of virtue we stand and shout, with Doom we come!

Chapter the Eighth
Judgment of the Defender

"Make the ':3' face at your foe, asking them if this looks like the face of mercy. When they answer 'yes,' explode their head with telekinesis, claiming that you killed them by making such a cute face that their physical form simply could not handle it. Alternatively, if they should answer 'no,' inform them that they are correct before disassembling them with your sword"
—Entry 13 in 'The Big Book of Tor-Jazherns,' a popular non-fiction volume on Raon-Arashal

The festivities in the days following the battle of Firatyne were abound, and everyone was telling and retelling about their best moments during the fighting. Suddenly, the every monitor in the city switched on, as the Aftermath Broadcast began.

FIRATYNE IS DEFENDED.

"Toriyah!" Everyone called out. It was the Death World Vulpian equivalent of a 'huzzah!' that also worked as a rallying cry along with being a celebratory one.

TOR-JAZHERN COMMENDATION – HONORABLE MENTIONS

The first segment, that would show the runners-up for the award that would be given to the most impressive *Tor-Jazhern* that took place during the fighting, *Tor-Jazhern* being a Death Worlder word for 'glorious kill,' that denoted a dispatch of an enemy that had particular flair to it, a certain *je ne sais quoi* of bringing doom upon one's foes.

The first honorable mention was when a Hykentiu warrior from the Library of Steel nailed a Demon to the wall with a double-pointed spear—quite literally, and following it up with two knives thrown that pierced enemies approaching from both sides, and then a crescent kick on the spear that had jammed into the pillar, dislodging it and causing the haft to slam into the face of another approaching Demonic attacker, and Miirkae then ducked under his weapon that still resting in the indent it had just made in the wall, side kicking the opposing Demon away, before he finally retrieved his weapon and slammed it into the skull of his next foe.

The second honorable mention was when a fighter from the avian Woran Cos species jumped twenty feet from one rooftop to another to impale a Whiplance Demon that was on the other roof, firing off its attacks at the flier, but Varkassaniar parried each blow before landing on the Whiplance Demon with an impaling strike from his foot talons, then using his wings to lift himself *and* the Demon into the air, before kicking his legs out and apart into a full split, that split also the Demon in his talons in two.

The third and last honorable mention before the

Tor-Jazhern commendation's winner would be announced was one where a Demonic Siege Laser pointed directly at a group of Death World Vulpians, and one of them grabbed one of the Bulwark Demons, heaving him into the barrel of the Siege Laser, causing it to not only tear this Demon apart, but the battery's assembly couldn't hand the stress of suddenly having that much interference, and it soon exploded, immolating its crew.

A few seconds passed as everyone awaited the announcement of who would receive the commendation.

TOR-JAZHERN COMMENDATION AWARDED TO MASTER OF ARMS ARNGEIR RHUIVAL

The veteran Death World Vulpian warrior was cheered on as the replay of the moment came, which was damned impressive. As the Demons entered his home, one was immediately met with a blast of Psionic power that punched a hole through its chest. But that was only the start of this old guard's display, as a Darkstar pushed aside the mortally wounded Demon and began a flurry of attacks with blade and bolt, that Arngeir skillfully blocked and evaded. Eventually, Arngeir threw down his weapon and put his hands behind his back, at which point the enraged Darkstar desperately tried to slice this old warrior to shreds—which wasn't happening, as Argneir simply ducked around all the slashes and thrusts like it was nothing, and he didn't even need his hands to defeat this foe. He soon crescent kicked a thrust from the Demon that knocked the weapon out of his enemy's hands, following it up with a wheel kick that slammed into the Darkstar's jaw, fully detaching it and sending it flying right into a nearby trash bin. Arngeir then charged up a surge of power through his hand, and slammed it completely through the Darkstar's chest, pulling its heart out in the process. Arngeir then tossed the heart at an approaching Demon, who was so confused by what had just happened that it ended up tumbling out a nearby open window.

The screen then displayed new text once the replay was over.

BEST ONE-LINER COMMENDATION: POET OF ARMS SECOND DEGREE ARAKAI SELENDICA

The monitors replayed the moments that led up to Arakai's line about how the wind had just picked up after Iraine created the pressure wave, and everyone let out either a solid laugh or a 'toriyah!' for it.

MOST PRESTIGOUS KILL – HONORABLE MENTIONS

The Demons had suffered a vicious defeat in completely failing to take Firatyne, and now it was about to be learned which of the Dark Six's most valuable warriors had been lost as a result. Though it was clear that dozens of Darkstars had been destroyed, some of them were more renowned than others.

MASTER OF ARMS ARNGEIR RHUIVAL – DARKSTAR VIZZERDRIX, HERALD OF THE FLAMING FIELDS

SPECIALIST KESTRA TARGALE – DARKSTAR PALTHAGOSTROTH, MESSENGER OF THE POISON FLOOD

BRIGADIER STELLA FOLTHST – DARKSTAR ENKASMIINE, THE TIMELESS SCOURGE

Not everyone knew exactly how massive this blow was to the Dark Six's elite, but there was no doubt that it was significant.

MOST PRESTIGOUS KILL – MAJOR MILES RADIEN –

DARKSTAR CHARVIKAROTH, THE MALLET LORD

"Wait, *Major?*" Radien wondered aloud. He thought his rank was Tactician. Jarrek burst out laughing again as Radien counted the number of battles that he had been victorious in. Sure enough, the battle of Firatyne made his tenth, that qualified him for the promotion. The feed from underneath the Grand Colosseum showed the conversation that Radien had with Charvikaroth.

"You're as vigilant as one of those Rogues."

"The Rogues are real, then? So Rogue Demons really are a thing, then!"

"Tactician warned that you were clever, Greígoth!"

After the replay concluded when Radien decapitated The Mallet Lord by way of claw and kick, the crowd went quiet, with hushed whispers and realizations that the Rogue Demons had just been confirmed to exist.

"The Rogues are real! We have allies in the Burning Hells!" one of the Death Worlders shouted. *"Toriyah!"*

A chorus across the city soon started, chanting the huzzah of the *Zhernrel-Vuljar*, that the Rogue Demons were real, and that they indeed had battle brothers and sisters alike in the Burning Hells. It lasted for two solid minutes before the festivities resumed as normal, with everyone making sure to have a good time in the wake of such a glorious victory.

Eventually, Radien did take his leave, returning to Torvaltyne Bastion and preparing some mode modifications to the Aura Runner. Specifically, he was making something he called a Waypoint Platform. After placing a Waypoint Stone within the Vault that he had taken up the Honorblade of Korvideyl from, he needed a way to reconnect with that stone, so that he could travel back to the Vault to learn more of it, as now was as good a time as any, having just struck a massive blow against his enemies, and earning a breather for it.

A stone platform was soon among the accouterments of the *Aura Runner's* helm, with an azure pentacle drawn across the granite surface, two bright blue flames on the sides that lent it a familiar look, one that he remembered from a lifetime ago, back when he only could dream of being able to slay the enemies of creation.

Once he stepped into the center of the platform, he could feel the energies searching through the universe for its kin, the stone that had been left in the Vault. Radien used his memories of visiting the place initially to guide the finding of the Waypoint Stone, and once it was found, the Death Worlder found himself within the Vault's halls, the stone he left behind having transformed into a similar waypoint platform.

"Designate Waypoint Network destination: Vault," Radien commanded to Techbooth aboard the *Aura Runner*, who made the necessary finer energetic connections to keep this passage stable, and name it such within the internal memory of the *Aura Runner* itself.

Radien perused the section of the Vault that he had found himself within, glass display cases containing seemingly mundane objects that quite obviously were anything but. Display pads upon them read the artifact's name, the level of danger it presented to the wielder or the universe at large, and a description of just what it was.

In one case, Radien saw a single-bladed sword of darkest metal. It was jet-black in appearance, save for the eerie silver sheen that surrounded it like enchanted ice.

ARTIFACT SD-4-2

TRYLAXIAN VAMPIRE BLADE

LOGGED UDM 5-3,621-03-03 BY PELDANE THARI

Radien then pressed a button on the display console to play the audio file that was stored within.

The Trylaxians are a clever lot. This is their single most notorious weapon, even though it is far from the deadliest. It is also their most unique, one whose enchantment has yet to be reliably replicated. They guard this secret ferociously, and I had hoped that in placing one within the Vault, I might study it and make my own attempts at recreation of this most interesting weapon.

The voice that was playing was of the Kendrosian who in life was known as Peldane Thari, the sixth Defender. Though not the longest-lived, he had arguably seen more history than any other, for better and for worse.

This sword's ability is to use the blood that is spilled upon it to heal its wielder. Further testing showed that rather than merely spilling blood, the sword needs to make contact with it. You could simply pour a vial of blood you borrowed from a medical facility onto the blade, and it would work just as well as if you had taken someone's head off. I have also discovered that this process only works with the actual biological compound that is blood, so the Vital Fluid that a mechanical or partially mechanical species uses does not work to this end.

Radien looked back at the jet-black sword, hovering in the display case, rotating slowly. He then pressed the button to play a few more supplemental files that were added by Peldane's successors. There were two of these recordings, the first one from Thayvek Rentarili, a Kendrosian himself, and the seventh Defender.

I was able to further verify the capabilities of the Vampire Blade by testing on multiple different forms of blood. It is very clear the blade, rather than adhering to a chemical definition of blood, is able to operate off of a functional definition of biological blood. I do have to say biological, since what would be considered blood for a mechanical being doesn't work, that being maintenance oil, or gear grease, or whatever.

Thayvek appeared to be unsuccessful in replicating the vampiric enchantment, however.

After reading some Trylaxian war chants, I've deduced that the non-functionality of mechanical blood such as Ascendant Vital Fluid that Thayvek and Peldane seemed perplexed about is the result of Trylaxian ideals and morals, specifically pertaining to what is considered to possess blood worth spilling. The Trylaxian species seemed to believe that mechanical beings were beyond conventional sin, even when sentient. Furthermore, some of the wording seems to suggest a god-like adoration of the mechanical sentient species of Cynar, especially the verse I found that reads, and I am paraphrasing due to the complexities of translating the language, 'that which was constructed in the factory and yet still feels, can only feel what is right to feel.'

This may explain why Trylaxia Moon was in a strange state of governance not long after the Sentience War ended, as Ascendant warriors and refugees who had found themselves on Trylaxia Moon were elected as the absolute leaders of the world basically against their will. Accounts say that it was a comical exchange of being forcibly given absolute power over Trylaxia and its peoples, followed by Ascendants fleeing the planet out of a sheer want to not rule over others like the Shard had such a drive for.

The Laksorian voice took Radien by surprise, as he remembered his encounter with Caltoran while he underwent the Gauntlet of Doom on Raon-Arashal. His cadence of voice in this recording was much more... well, youthful seemed like the wrong word, but it sure was obvious that this took place thousands of years before Demonic possession was even a possibility he might one day become the subject of. After all, no Defender had ever been *taken* by the Dark Six. Sure, the first two were killed by the Frontliner, but never had a Defender's hands been turned to their service before. Not the kind of first one wants to be.

Radien's ear twitched. Something was behind him, or someone. Either way, they had been attempting to approach silently, and even Radien's Proximity Alert Autopsionic Cantrip hadn't detected it. Multiple layers of instinct are always helpful, which is why Radien was thankful that his hearing was still as good as it had always been. He had excellent hearing even back when he was an un-powered Human of Elder Terra, and as a Death World Vulpian, this was only accentuated.

The Borfblade was unsheathed and pointed back at his stealthy adversary faster than one could blink. The spectral form he beheld shifted itself into a female Taigron's form.

"A challenge?! This should be fun!" the Taigron yelled, drawing a pair of her own swords, and engaging Radien, who now held the Honorblade of Korvideyl in his right hand as well. The two dueled for some time, their blades biting into each other with their parries, but neither were letting the metals they were made from barely even chip, causing a screeching ring to resonate across the vault as the Borfblade went edge-to-edge against this Taigron projection's own sword. Both fighters did *not* like that noise, and both stepped back slowly from each other. Radien's eye twitched. The Taigron's left heel tapped against the floor. Both threw their weapons down, grabbing their ears and cursing at the sheer *sting* of that unbearable noise.

"My fucking *hearing triangles*, that noise *sucks!*" the Taigron yelled.

"*Ja-jahada djalsej*, you're telling *me!*" Radien responded. The two soon pulled their acts together, at which point Radien realized that there was a Taigron in the Vault. "Wait, who in... wait, no, *I know you!* A while before The Unmaker started his bullshit, the Aura Prism needed me to verify one of his memories by having me live through it... *your* memories! Kirinaultr, the third Defender!"

The Taigron nodded, then shook her head. "Well, yes, but actually no. Surely you had heard the Vault of the Defender had developed a consciousness?"

Radien thought for a moment, and then

remembered that he had indeed heard those legends. Or at least, one of them that ensured he was at least aware that it was rumored.

"I take upon the personalities of the Defenders who have come before you, to better offer council depending on what each of them were experts on in life."

"And to meet a challenge head-on, you took Kirinaultr's form."

The Taigron form morphed into a different one, that was of a much taller warrior, a Hydenti, the genetic precursor to the selachimorphic Hykentiu.

"And if I need to judge character, I may assume the memories and experiences of her predecessor," Shparghen-Shperg addressed, eyeing Radien up and down. "T'Sen spoke of the *Zhernrel-Vuljar*, that they are as stubbornly difficult to kill as they are honorable."

"That would be high praise indeed," Radien replied, and Shparghen-Shperg's eyes narrowed as they glowed amber.

"But there seems to be something *else* there... it is as though your consciousness evolved *into* a Death Worlder... having been born something else."

Radien's eyes crackled with azure power as every defense that kept his mind inaccessible to others went on full alert.

"Interesting..." Shparghen-Shperg's form shifted now to that of one of her successors that still lived, Xatrial Isenhart. Radien was unsure whether or not it would be of any use to inform the Vault's consciousness of this fact, let alone that Caltoran, the Betrayer Defender did live as well.

"Not very many people have that level of training in psychic defense," Xatrial commented. "It's a very specific art, to have your mind that unascertainable, one that already relatively few bother to invest much training in... but you are *very* prepared in that aspect."

"My mind is my own," Radien said. "Do you have a name of your own, consciousness of the Defender's Vault?"

"Each of them have called me by different honorifics, I'm sure you'll think of an appropriate one soon enough."

"Fair enough."

"All minds are their own," the form of the Kendrosian Peldane Thari began. "And though few practice constant telepathy out of its sheer rudeness, many still permit themselves to leave their thoughts relatively... well, 'open' isn't the right word. More like..."

"Unguarded?" Radien finished. "Unprotected? *Vulnerable*, perhaps?"

"Unrestricted," Peldane finished. "The door kept closed, but not locked, let alone on scale you implement... it is impressive. *Jazukiir pirfuur duul. Vigilance becomes you.*"

"Why, thank you," Radien responded. The phrase was a Death World Vulpian compliment, after all. "But I didn't come here to be analyzed. I came here to learn more about the Vault. Specifically, to answer the question of 'why I was able to take this sword from it?'"

"The Vault's purpose... my purpose, is twofold," the vulpine form answered. That of Farrox Tesamaug, the fourth Defender. An Old Cynofraxian, the ancestor to the modern Vulpian races. "It is a museum of the greater universe, alongside being the containment chamber for its most dangerous creations that must never see starlight again. The Honorblade of Korvideyl is not among the potential bringers of apocalypse that rest within these halls, and it is a blade that demands to be wielded, by a soul of honor."

Farrox then shrugged his shoulders sagely. "And who am I to deny the blade of T'Sen Torgaen its purpose when it finds new hands to wield it?"

"Who is anyone to deny purpose when it is found?" Radien wondered aloud. "No friend of mine, that much I know." He then sheathed the Honorblade. The Borfblade had already returned to his side by this point. "The shield that the Honorblade of Korvideyl provides is not only a concept I thoroughly enjoy, but it has proven most useful through several battles already."

The Vault's consciousness shifted to the Hajivakk form of the Honorblade's original owner, T'Sen Torgaen. Radien then handed the sword over, so that it could be returned to its resting place alongside the weapons of the Defenders before him. T'Sen took the blade, and then eyed the Borfblade on Radien's right hip.

"Leftie, eh?"

"Aye."

Radien then remembered something.

"If you possess the memories and personalities of each of the Defenders, then you also have T'Sen's skill, right?"

T'Sen nodded.

"T'Sen Torgaen was a legendary martial artist, arguably the deadliest fighter of all of the Defenders. I would be honored to learn..."

T'Sen cracked a smile as he held the Honorblade of Korvideyl.

"Caltoran was also known to be one of the most potent wielders of Psionic power, and I could learn much from your memories of him, too," Radien continued. "You said it yourself, this Vault is a museum as much as it is a barrier between the universe and its most dangerous creations. I would never ask to wield the artifacts that could bring an apocalypse except come the apocalypse itself, but there's much to learn here, if you are willing to teach me."

"There is much to learn here, indeed," T'Sen said as he returned the Honorblade to its resting place, next to Caltoran's Arcane Cestuses and Thayvek's Whip Chain. "Your eagerness is on par with your predecessors, Radien."

"I don't recall telling you my name..."

"When you were last here, your friend had to snap you out of the Dread of the Mortal Wound by calling it."

"Oh, right."

The Honorblade of Korvideyl hovered within its display case, and Radien could somehow sense an air of satisfaction about it, that the sword was proud to have been wielded against Cynar's foes once again, and that T'Sen was considered now avenged.

"What happened to T'Sen Torgaen?" Radien asked. "I know the satisfaction of vengeance well, and I can tell his sword is satisfied thusly."

The Vault's consciousness, in T'Sen's form, immediately reached an arm out to press against Radien's forehead to show him the day that the

Demons returned.

After the forging of the Aura Prism that first purged the Demons from Cynar, there was a window of time between that moment, and the Sehlsaln Anchor's destruction that allowed four hundred and seventy-two Demonic Battle Barges to enter this reality and exile themselves to the great spans between galaxies where even neutrinos seldom reach. These ancient vessels carried the Demon's remaining presence within Cynar for eons on end, watching the universe's history unfold. Some were discovered and destroyed. Others attempted to resume their masters' work, but failed, and were then destroyed.

The memories that Radien witnessed included the destruction of the Battle Barge that attacked Fortem Terra Nova, back when he was still a Human.

T'Sen Torgaen was the first casualty Cynar suffered of this new war, upon the battle that took place on the planet of Outphase VII, where the first of the new gates formed, that showed Cynar that the Demons were once again ready to resume their campaign of domination.

Back at the Fortress, Veralis noticed a twinge in her right arm. Like something sharp and pointed had just poked down at her shoulder, though nothing was there. She raised an eyebrow at it, before feeling the poke again in her forearm.

Channeling some of her own power of The Aura through her right arm, she held the energy trying to course through her muscular and well-built limb at bay, so that whatever was about to happen, it wouldn't happen within Torvaltyne's walls. Too civilized, she thought. Somehow, Veralis couldn't help but understand that this was a matter that would need to be addressed without civility. Something dark was at the heart of the flood on this one.

Running at a brisk but not urgent pace, Veralis jogged out the front gate and into the Devouring Jungle itself that the Fortress was built next to, in the foothills of the Blizzardblade Mountains, better known as the Blizzardblade Foothills, as cartographers who mapped the region did manage to let reason win out on the naming of these foothills, to be the Blizzardblade Foothills instead of the Foothills of the Blizzardblade Mountains, which would have been an excess of syllables. Thankfully, Death World Vulpians are a practicality-oriented species, and thus Raon-Arashal was spared of such silliness.

Once she found a clearing of grass, she then held out her arm and let go of the barriers she was setting for this energy, allowing a bright orange stream of particles to seethe from her hand and onto the ground a few feet away. The process itself was actually quite painful to the muscles, like they were being pulled at as the intruding power forcibly expelled itself from her body. However, Veralis was no pushover, and she had been hit harder in training. It was trivial to her, and for it, she was very cool indeed. Inevitably, the flow stopped, and the pile of energy coalesced into the shape of a reviled Human.

Radien's reliving of the past was like moving through a dream, where one's legs were as though they were running underwater, seeing the Haji-Son Defender make his stand against the Demons that poured from the first of the new rift gates that marked the beginning of the

Second War for Reality.

He knew this was where he would make his stand. And so his last act was to order that all others leave the planet, and him with it, to warn the stars of the return of the Demons, that the stars knew one day would come.

Radien watched as T'Sen placed the Honorblade of Korvideyl aboard his ship, and ordering the autopilot to take it to the Vault.

"Every memory of mine, I impart unto this blade," T'Sen recited. *"My lifetime as the Defender, the eighth of that line, I commit to this sword, and banish from my sight, that it does not fall into the hands of my enemies, when my hands fall to the dirt with breath and life no more."*

The ship sped off, and Radien realized from who's perspective this memory was derived. The Honorblade of Korvideyl itself. The last the universe saw of T'Sen Torgaen, was his claws bared at his foes, as he rolled his shoulders and coursed power through them to make sure his strikes were as deadly to Demons as Hunderfold weapons. The last words that were heard were a humorously dismissive 'What, you guys again?' from the eighth Defender.

"Amandrianna *sraivenn* Sarvalimil..." Veralis groaned as she saw her. "You know, it's generally considered the polite thing for a villain to die when they are killed."

"A whole universe of technology and magics, and you didn't think I'd have some kind of plan? I may not have grown up among all this endless wonder, but how stupid do you think I am?" Amandrianna scoffed, impressed with herself. "Honestly, I thought it was going to be Miles, finding some remote world to do away with me on, but you surprised me."

"I surprised Radien, too," Veralis responded resolutely. "It was my honor to rid his life of someone so charred and blackened of soul and so utterly without decency or morality, his oldest foe."

"You sound a lot like him…"

"No wonder we're friends."

The two glared at each other. Veralis was countering every ounce of Amandrianna's verbal poison, she would not be fooled by this vile manipulator. And there was nowhere for the wretch to run in the Devouring Jungle.

Veralis did speak first soon enough, however. "I once looked through you and saw who you were… but it still confounds me, just what kind of monster *are* you?"

"What kind of a question is that?"

"What kind of a question?!" Veralis growled. "As in, who are you, so vile and cruel, that my best friend would sooner die in agony than ask for my help, even though I would be clamoring to give myself completely to aid him?! Who sooner flees to the furthest corners of space, rather than risk letting someone see him bleed?! What kind of *wretched mother* were you, that someone who I have fought *Demons* and *Voidspawns* alongside is still always looking over his shoulder, even after I've said I've got his back, and I know he's heard me?!"

Veralis stood there, her palms atop her axes Käyner and Käynvi, tempted to draw them and fling them at this scourge again. But something told Veralis that she had to play her cards right if she wanted to make sure it killed this accursed foe properly this time.

"What kind of monster are you, that when he saw your corpse with these two axes embedded in it, I could *see* the weight lifting itself off of his shoulders? He thanked me, you know. He told me that he owed me a debt he could never repay in ridding the universe of you. I could *see and feel* what it meant to him when I could see through you, and I showed him he wasn't crazy to despise you."

Radien looked back at the Honorblade of Korvideyl, now with more understanding than ever of why it longed to taste Demon flesh. "That sword saved my life during the battle of Firatyne," he remembered aloud, recalling when a javelin from a Darkstar Demon shattered itself upon the shield that covered his backside. "I have no doubt that it assured our victory over the Dark Six there."

"The Dark Six were humiliated at Firatyne." T'Sen chuckled, even though he was actually the projection of the Vault's consciousness. "They've been taking quite the thrashing ever since..."

T'Sen's smug grin faded as he remembered what happened to his successor. Radien wasn't sure what to say. He knew that Caltoran lived, and did so in exile, and that this information might be best left unsaid to the Vault.

"Do they call him the Traitor Defender?" Radien asked.

T'Sen's form rearranged itself to that of Xatrial's. "No, they don't. In the wake of his destruction, it became well known, the circumstances of his corruption. Even as planet after planet was scorched to ashen husks, many suspected as much. It is... never easy to learn that someone you trained had their training used to evil ends. I still do not know if it makes things better or worse, that he had no control over the Demon's actions after his consciousness died."

Radien could only wonder how much Caltoran wished he *had* simply died.

Amandrianna rolled her shoulders and sighed. "All right, kill me again, then," she said dismissively.

Veralis scoffed, unimpressed. Her eyes subtly transitioned into the amber glow of Second Sight, as she looked over this Human to see what the catch was.

"What are you waiting for?"

"You used a Rakta Crystal to survive our last encounter," Veralis concluded. "They're typically in the hands of people with a lot of enemies who still want to live their full lives. The crystal will bind itself very slightly, in a completely unnoticeable way, to whoever kills the holder, the moment before they would've otherwise died. Over a very long and subtle process, that Rakta Crystal's carrier will be slowly rebuilt until they can take physical form again. Even allows for some cheeky karma of being killed by your own victim, mostly in cases of assassin versus assassin."

"I'm no assassin, though!" Amandrianna scoffed.

"No, you're a disreputable Human, too honorless and pathetic to be anything other than the scum that people like myself and Radien kill scores of before breakfast," Veralis spat. "And I just found where yours is surgically implanted. That's what I was waiting for."

Veralis then threw out her left hand and yanked

at where the crystal was sitting, implanted into the tissue of one of Amandrianna's kidneys, ripping both the crystal and the organ out and into her hand, where she crushed both, to Amandrianna's shock. It took a full five seconds before the Human fell to her knees, pawing at the ground where chunks of kidney and shards of inert mineral lattices were, like they could still save her somehow.

"A whole universe of technology and magics indeed, and you thought *I* didn't know about this kind of stuff?" Veralis roasted the despairing Human, who was frozen, staring at her own ruined organ and lifeline like a deer in headlights. "I *did* grow up among this endless wonder, how stupid do you think *I* am? Now, I don't remember off the top of my head when it comes to your species, but I'd anticipate you've got at least two minutes before you bleed out, or I'm going to be *very* disappointed," Veralis said as she approached the nemesis of her ally, grabbing her head and pointing it upward, forcing Amandrianna to look at the one who was killing her, again.

"He's going to be incredible, you know," Veralis stated. "He's the Defender, one in a long line of warriors, honor-bound and proud of it. You died nameless and forgotten in a transit tunnel on Mjarfus centuries ago, the waters and the algae made your bones vanish within a month. There will be no monument to your sins, Amandrianna Sarvalimil, no shrine to commemorate your evil, and no poem or ballad written to celebrate your end. You will never have the honor of infamy."

"He's going to be all that because of me!" Amandrianna sputtered.

"No, Amandrianna. He's going to be all that *despite* you."

Amandrianna tried desperately to cough out some kind of retort, some way of getting the last word in, but the loss of blood was too great from the hole in her body, and the kidney-shaped cavity where it once rested. Veralis finally let go of Amandrianna's head, throwing her face-down onto the grass to gurgle and sputter until she died at long last, for the second time. Once that had finally happened, Veralis used The Aura to lift the Human's corpse into the air and hurl it into a patch of the carnivorous Bladehook Moss native to the Devouring Jungle, and no small part in why it held that name. There would be nothing left of the vile Human that was Amandrianna Sarvalimil. She would never know the honor of infamy indeed.

"It's one thing for someone you trained to simply have been killed," The Vault's consciousness in Shparghen-Shperg's form said. "That's something I've never had trouble reconciling with. I trained Kirinaultr when my only form was her predecessor's, and Farrox after her. Xatrial was quite the silent workhorse, Peldane and Thayvek were worthy students in their own rights, and T'Sen was the one who taught *me* a few things. Caltoran, just like the rest, was someone I was always prepared to hear had fallen, and I could ready myself to meet his successor. I have always been eager to meet the next Defender, and I've never lingered too long on the passing of one."

Radien listened as he perused the shelves full of artifacts, guided on a tour of sorts by the Vault's chosen form.

"What made Caltoran unique was the fact that he didn't just die, but instead suffered a fate far worse."

Radien nodded, but had nothing to add.

"That being said, shall we begin?"

Veralis made her way back to Torvaltyne Bastion, to the Honor's Stand Mead Hall. It was Mysterious Loafing in the Darkness Night tonight. The lights would dim to a more moody hue, and everyone would be loafing mysteriously in the darkness, brooding and pondering over drinks, sometimes making a random noise such as a 'marf,' 'rer,' or 'mjergh.' Radien never missed it. Sure enough, he was loafing in the darkness like a pro, pondering a pint of mead after having trained with the Vault's consciousness. He still hadn't thought of a good name to call them by. Veralis loafed next to him with a stein of ale.

"Merf," Veralis merfed.

"Marf," Radien marfed in response, and Veralis nodded in agreement. Radien then thought for a moment, considering his next action heavily.

<I'd ask if there's something on your mind, but there's always something making those gears spin,> Veralis said to Radien telepathically, so that neither of them had to speak aloud. <But you know what I mean on this one.>

<I do, yes,> Radien responded in kind. This ensured their conversation was private. <During the campaign against The Unmaker, when I first toured the Dart after you visited the Aura Runner when I was patrolling the Dyson Shield...>

<Not exactly an easily forgettable time, that one.> Veralis's chuckle was also telepathically transmitted. Nobody in the Mead Hall could tell that there was even a conversation happening between the two.

<I sensed a great danger not long after, something that threatened to tear every planet and star asunder,> Radien continued. *<A threat I cannot ignore.>*

<I know what you mean.> Veralis then took a drink from her stein, and Radien followed up by draining his and motioning for another. *<Six hundred years we had known each other up to then, and that's how long it took for us to reach the level of friends with benefits? Even then and especially now, I'm glad to be able to say we got there, if nothing else.>*

Radien sighed aloud, making a 'peff' noise at the table. *<No words that I know can adequately do justice to what's going on in my head, Veralis. The Dreads from the Dark Six are one thing, but description fails me on this particular matter.>*

<I know what you mean,> Veralis said again. *<Remember that I'm a Psionic Empath? You compared me once to a fictional councilor from Old Earth folklore similar to what I can do to that end.>*

<Well, you're able to do it at-will, and it never actually tells you when someone's lying. It'll tell you that someone's experiencing the emotions of nervousness and apprehension that can lead to the conclusion that they're lying...>

<And that's why it isn't mind-reading.>

<Right, yes.>

Another few moments of sipping drinks and silence passed.

<I can't help but feel like my sanity is greatly endangered—no, endangered is the wrong word. Metastable is far more appropriate, because I know that it would only take one calculated push to send it careening over the edge of madness, and I know what that push would be.>

<I hear that.>

<Gods damn it, I am Steel and Doom, Skill and Stone! I shouldn't be having debates like this in my head, I shouldn't even be needing to have them! I shouldn't even have to consider this!>

Despite the turmoil Radien was very clearly sifting through, he was completely stoic and collected externally, calmly sipping his mead every now and again. <I can't make heads or tails of this forbidden-feeling dilemma, and that's what's frustrating me more than anything else... I can't find the damn solution, or even figure out if there is one!>

Radien audibly sighed again. <Hellfire, I know I shouldn't be putting this on anyone, much less someone who in one day, that first day on Cynofrax, showed me more kindness than I had known in all my years on Earth combined...>

Veralis raised an eyebrow to this comment. She knew that Radien didn't live his best life on Earth, but wasn't aware that he lived that shut-in.

<And despite all you've taught me in this time I've been finally away from Earth, teaching me how to wield my powers, finding me the books and the manuals that explain this and that of which I had so many questions... what can I say that I've done for you? I owe countless debts to you, Veralis, and I can't convince myself that I've paid

off any of them, or even come close. I swore never to be just another taker, another talker... and here I am, spilling my guts to you and being one who just takes.>

Veralis drained her stein, before motioning for another. *<Did I ever tell you what I was doing that day before I went to that pub in Kaldres-Viane?>*

<No, I never asked.>

<I was sitting at my house that you later stayed your first night off Earth within, twiddling my thumbs with frustration born of boredom that I couldn't find any adventures, any calling or real purpose. I had the Celestial Dart, freshly commandeered from the warlord whose capital ship I trashed in glorious fashion, and I was whizzing across space, pining to scratch that itch again, but it just wasn't happening. So I decided to hell with it, and just went over to that old place for some introspection and pondering. And figures, in comes a person from a species I'd never seen before, playing songs I'd never heard before... how could I resist? And to think it happened the one time I wasn't looking.>

Veralis's Psionic Empathy picked up massive shock from Radien. He was truly flabbergasted by this, though he didn't look it on the outside.

<Who else could teach me to be like water, able to flow to any river's current, but can carve canyons from mountains? Besides, Radien... you said it yourself. You never asked. How can you call it taking when you never asked for what was was given to you freely?>

Radien stared into his mead, before grabbing the glass and downing it with swift surety. His breathing was more deliberate and controlled than ever, and he wasn't sure what to say or do next.

<Though I have said that I learned half of what I know of honor from Taliah, but it's more like an eighth, to be honest. Before he vanished, Galtyn had left a few pearls of wisdom to grow in my mind, but it was only basic stuff,> Veralis continued. *<Kurai taught me what I know of fighting, and doing so for honor... but you remember what happened after you destroyed the Cult of the Chaosmaker. You know damn well that you taught me the sheer scale of the evil of ignorance, and to never accept bullshit. Much as I already knew that bullshit wasn't to be accepted, and that ignorance was evil... I could never have learned such conviction from anyone else.>*

To all this, Radien wasn't sure how to respond. As much as he did remember vividly when Veralis understood his rage at the awful and defeatist phrase 'it is what it is,' he still found himself wordless in the wake of the idea that he had done something helpful, let alone something right. *<Miles Sorvenjar Radien, the Steel and Doom, Skill and Stone,>* Veralis softly commented. *<That's what you've given me.>*

Chapter the Ninth

If Decency Be Treason...

"Though they may seem without number, beyond count, every one of their ranks slain is one step closer to victory, for there is no such thing as an infinite army. If one warrior of this universe can bring the universe ten steps closer to victory before he is himself felled, then the war shall be won by virtue of mathematics."
—Ahron Kasven, the first Defender

Personal log of Major Miles Radien, UDM 8-317,392,506-9-22. The Battle of Firatyne was without a doubt, a legendary victory for our side in this Second War for Reality. So too was the routing of the Demons at Tenbork Station, which though I do not discount the value of, makes me uneasy that the Dark Six are due for their own. Though I shall continue to fight them at every turn that they try to make our universe their dominion, my instincts tell me that The Tactician has something big planned. I do not deny the value of our victories, but I must observe the fervor of our enemies.

"Major, I thank you for your prompt response,"

Arch-Militant Darek Jor'Galn began.

"You did say that the matter was urgent," Radien responded.

"What do you know about Rogue Demons?"

Radien thought for a moment. If Rogue Demons were a potential factor in whatever it was Darek needed to brief him in on, it must have been important. "No cause can exist without rebels. If the Dark Six exist as the lords of Hell, Demons who are against their desires of conquest will exist as a result. Mathematically, they *must* exist. We just haven't made contact with any."

Darek nodded. "Continue."

"It's currently theorized that the intel breakthrough regarding the *Gadrigaridox* was the work of Rogues. The Eyes of the Daggers suspect that it was a coordinated effort of high enough value to demonstrate their existence, yet covertly delivered enough that it didn't name names or give locations on either end. Furthermore, the intrigue I learned from The Mallet Lord during the battle of Firatyne confirmed that the Rogues are neither myth nor rumor."

"Your level head is exactly why I need you for this assignment," the Arch-Militant commented. "A message came to Raon-Arashal directly, requesting you by name, for the reason I just told you."

"Message?" Radien asked.

Darek Jor'Galn placed a voice recording device on the desk and hit the play button.

"This message is intended for the individual known as Radien," the recording played back. *"Radien destroyed the Deceiver known as Avanchenvaldr, as well as the Darkstar known as the Mallet Lord. This is what we know*

of him, yet we suspect he has further exploits. We delivered information on the Gadrigaridox as a message of our existence, for we are rebels against what you call the Dark Six, and what we would call the same, for they are vile enough to earn this title. Enemy of our enemy, ally in all but declaration, may you know the voice of rebel kin, and know when minds and morals align. Find us, that we may show them why they are right to fear our power."

"Hell of a finisher," Radien said. "They're trying to get my attention."

"I assume you relate to that message more than most," Darek noted. "There's nothing else, by the way. No hidden message showing which system they're in, no radio isotopes that can link it to a specific planet, and no tech signature."

"That recorder is of Human design," Radien said, grabbing the device and sliding the battery case open. "The Humans were meant to be the secret weapon of the Dark Six, it was Avanchenvaldr's personal project."

"You're going to have to tell me the story of how you figured that out, Major." Darek chuckled.

"Remind me when you visit Torvaltyne Mead Hall next time," Radien replied. "We just perfected our strawberry melomel recipe, and the first batch is due to be finished aging in about sixty days."

"Don't threaten me with a good time now, Major."

"Save those advances for Arch-Militant Wöllschlager."

"What makes you think I haven't already used them on him?"

Radien thought for a moment. "Oh, son of a bitch..."

Darek Jor'Galn had a good laugh after Radien had just figured things out.

"Regardless, the manufacturer's brand on this recorder is one from the Human planet of Hy-Brasil, so I at least can narrow my search down to that planet for clues."

"Still a whole planet, Major."

"Beats a whole galaxy to search, Arch-Militant."

"Fair enough. Wöllschlager personally recommended you for this mission."

"Wonder why he'd do that..."

"Because he thinks you're qualified for it, would be my guess."

"High praise from him, then."

Darek raised an eyebrow.

"Yeah, yeah, I know, I spent too long around Humans," Radien said. "You don't have to remind me, Veralis does that plenty enough."

"Might she have a point?"

"Oh, *believe me,* I agree."

When Radien boarded the *Aura Runner* and set course for Hy-Brasil, he then adjusted it to exit the Warp Channel just outside the solar system itself. He didn't want to get too close unless he knew he had to.

"Techbooth, while we're on our way, what can you tell me about Teryn Industries?"

TERYN INDUSTRIES IS A SCIENTIFIC EQUIPMENT MANUFACTURER BASED ON THE HUMAN PLANET OF HY-BRASIL. THEY SPECIALIZE IN RECORDING AND DATA COLLECTING INSTRUMENTS OF SEEMINGLY ALL TYPES,

FROM SIMPLE AUDIO MICROPHONES TO MUON DETECTORS.

"All right, why would the Rogue Demons use a Human device to deliver a message to us?"

HUMANS, AS A SECRET WEAPON FOR THE DARK SIX BEFORE AVANCHENVALDR'S DEATH, SHARE A PASSIVE CONNECTION WITH THE DEMONS THEMSELVES THAT MAKES THE SPECIES THE ONLY KNOWN PROXY LINK TO CYNAR FOR THE BURNING HELLS.

"So, a middleman species, then?"

IN GROSSLY OVERSIMPLIFIED TERMS, YES.

"So the Rogues can make contact with us, through the Humans. Specifically, on Hy-Brasil... where's this company's headquarters on the planet?"

TERYN INDUSTRIES IS HEADQUARTERED IN THE CITY OF ARISTOPHEUS.

Radien sighed when he heard that name. Something about it just felt... off.

"Scan the planet, wide-field. Do it on an unused frequency that nobody's transmitting on right now within a two light-hour radius of the planet.

A few moments later, Techbooth beeped that the task was done.

"How likely is it I will need to be disguised while down there?"

EXTREMELY UNLIKELY.

"Show me the population demographics."

61.6% HUMAN

26.9% HAJIKAHL

7.2% VAROK-TORIVIDAN

4.3% MIXED OTHER

Radien rolled his shoulders.

"All right, set course for Hy-Brasil, bearing towards Aristopheus."

The *Aura Runner* Began making its way towards the planet at a relatively leisurely pace, at least as far as cosmic distances were concerned. Eventually he was hailed by the starport at Aristopheus.

"Zhernrel-Vuljar pilot, this is Aristopheus Starport requesting your identification and course."

"This is the *Aura Runner*, requesting permission to land at Aristopheus Starport."

A few moments passed.

"Aura Runner, permission to land on platform Oscar Echo seventeen-one. Maintain your course."

The OE designation meant that it was a circular landing platform, like a helipad but for ships whose engines could perform vertical landings in planetary atmospheric conditions. Landing pad 17, spot 1.

Once the *Aura Runner* landed, Radien was met by a uniformed Human, to which he raised an eyebrow. He did not expect, let alone request a reception.

"Major Radien," the man greeted, extending a hand. Radien took it and permitted the handshake, his index finger extended along this military officer's wrist, an old self-defense trick to determine whether or not this Human was planning to try to kill him, which would be evinced by a rapid or more intense heartbeat thanks to the adrenaline of anticipation of combat. However, this man was not planning to kill Radien. "I'm Colonel Sven Polaris, retired Hy-Brasil Defense Corps. These days, I run Teryn Industries."

"Did Arch-Militant Jor'Galn tell you I was inbound?" Radien asked, to which Sven nodded. "I wasn't expecting a reception."

"You don't strike me as the kind of guy who would, let alone ask for one," Sven complimented. "Honestly, I've got nothing but disdain for uppity officers who expect formal dinners and parties to be thrown just for their arrival. One of my ancestors was a Colonel in one of Elder Terra's armies, I forget which. From what stories I've uncovered, the man was an insufferable member of the brass, whose uniform smelled of mothballs and champagne. Allow me to assure you that I was the *antithesis* of that during my career."

"I know the struggle, Colonel," Radien commented. "I was once helping set up such a reception back in my hometown, and I ended up throwing a guy over my shoulder onto and through one of the tables because of how abusive he was being to the other staff. Only thing that stopped me from getting in trouble was the fact there was a Master Chief in the room who applauded me for doing it."

"I would've paid to see *that*."

"I don't remember if anyone caught it on tape."

"Anyways, Arch-Militant Jor'Galn did tell me that a recording device from one of my manufactories was in the hands of Demons... let me assure you Major Radien, we do *not* collaborate with the Dark Six, or Dark Six servants."

"Take heart, Colonel Polaris. The Demons we're talking about are as much enemies of the Dark Six as we are."

"I'd heard rumors about the Rogues... and that the battle in Firatyne ended up confirming their existence once you finessed the confession right out of the Mallet Lord's mouth."

"Interesting verb choice…"

As they had been chatting, Sven had been leading Radien to the main office of Teryn Industries, which was in walking distance of the starport. One thing that had changed about the Human race for the better after they broke free of Earth was the return of walkable cities en masse. It was indeed an excellent point of progress on their part.

Once they got to the laboratory within the facility, Radien handed the device over to Sven, who placed it in a machine that would scan the device for a unique identifying marker, which for some reason wasn't just a plain old maker's mark or hallmark.

"Normally, our remote satellite factories are supposed to have unique hallmarks and maker's marks for each of them, so that they can be traced to some extent. However, seven of these satellites cannot for the life of them agree on a design for theirs, so the alloy that makes up the casing itself is laced with a unique element or compound until the management there gets their shit together," Sven explained.

Radien raised an eyebrow.

"Allow me to assure you that I do *not* approve of the lack of a physical label, especially the reason *why* that's currently the case for those ones… I should probably get to lighting a fire under their asses, honestly," Sven commented further. Once he was done looking through the viewport on the machine, he then wrote down a string of numbers before entering them into a terminal.

"This one came from the *Manta* satellite manufactory, and it's right now... let me check its most recent location ping... Oh."

"*Oh?*"

"I'm probably going to have to order them to retask to a different location. They're getting dangerously close to a solar system that's confirmed to have a pre-industrial species on it. Selio-Vaqueri, the planet's called. Home of the Tanandar Gael."

"That's at least two leads," Radien commented. "Manta satellite, Selio-Vaqueri... I think I've got what I came here for."

"Glad to be of assistance," Sven said, handing the recording device back to Radien. "On another note, if you've got a minute..."

Radien nodded.

"I have heard that you've been investigating Elder Terra, specifically the oddness that surrounds the entire solar system. You're not the first person to wonder whether or not there's a bigger reason that the Human race was so fucked up, and still is in a fair few ways. Hy-Brasil's scientific body also has an expeditionary force on that. Whenever you're next in the area, I would like to extend the offer of collaboration with our boys there to you."

"Sounds good," Radien said. "I'll compare notes with them whenever I head over there next. Keep in mind, it's more a personal project that I'm only doing when I've got spare time to."

"No rush, Major. I am also curious if you know why there's a giant crater right in the middle of one of the old cities... can't remember the name... Eternal City, was it?"

"You mean Rome?"

"Yeah, that's the one!"

At that moment, Radien remembered how long it had actually been since his days on Old Earth, and that the name of one of its oldest cities wasn't common knowledge anymore.

"Anyways, scans show that sometime around twenty-seven hundred and twenty-eight hundred AD by their calendars, so back when it was still inhabited, a Photon Bomb was detonated in a section of Rome that vaporized about four hundred fifty-thousand square meters, and left a crater to match. Similar craters were found on the eastern coast of the Mediterranean, and a few dozen miles inland near the Red Sea. You wouldn't happen to know anything about that, would you?"

Radien paused for a moment, carefully choosing the words of his answer. "I will say this: There is a very good reason why those places were torn to atoms."

Sven nodded, and Radien soon took his leave. It was only after he got back aboard the *Aura Runner* that he realized that his eyes had started sparking with volatile energy when he had said that to the Colonel. Sven Polaris was far from a fool, he knew what it looked like when wielders of Psionic power were starting to get heated over something. Whatever used to be in those places, they were clearly a source of great and terrible evil, of a kind that would need to be vaporized just to rectify.

As the *Aura Runner* cruised through the Warp Channel en route towards the solar system that contained the planet of Selio-Vaqueri, Radien mulled over whether to investigate the satellite manufactory first, or the planet that he began to wonder if the Rogues were hiding out on. It made sense. Non-interference pacts and clauses were present in almost every spacefaring species's laws, which would make such a planet the perfect place to hide for Hell's dissidents. But it was also incredibly risky, for that reason. If it was discovered that Demons had stooped to the level of interfering with developing races, furious retribution was sure to swiftly follow. Granted, that sure didn't stop the Dark Six from draining the lifeblood of the universe from an entire solar system just so that they could mold the Humans into their secret weapon.

The Humans... yes, that was still an issue that plagued Radien's mind. For all the trouble they were having adjusting to a moral universe, filled with peoples that valued decency and honor, they were making progress at a non-zero level. Though their nature remained all too Human, Radien also knew he could not ignore what progress had been made, paltry and minuscule as it was.

Fortunately, the trip through the Warp Channel was short enough that he didn't need to reflect on this for *too* long, now.

"Only question is *which* lead to pursue..." Radien wondered aloud. "Hardly makes a difference in distance anyway, from the looks of it. All right, let's go with the wildcard!"

Radien then activated the *Aura Runner's* cloaking module, before flying into the inner half of the solar system that contained the planet of rumor, Selio-Vaqueri.

"Techbooth, scan Selio-Vaqueri once we're in range," Radien instructed. "If the Rogue Demons are on the planet, we'll be able to find them rather—"

DEMONIC LIFESINGS DETECTED ON PLANET.

"...quickly."

Further scans did indeed confirm a resident species that had yet to enter naught point seven on the Kardashev scale. The Tanandar Gael were technologically comparable to Old Earth's Renaissance era.

"The Demons are on a continent yet unexplored by the Tanandar Gael," Radien processed aloud. "No doubt they're aware of the local species presence... I can only wonder which reason out of many they could have for making contact now, that they justify with in the here and now."

Between needing to get off of the inhabited and still developing planet, potentially urgent intelligence that needed to be shared, and the general desire to graduate out of the realm of myth, the Rogue Demons that had taken shelter on Selio-Vaqueri had many motivations to pick from.

The Tanandar Gael themselves, according to the *Aura Runner's* Wide-Field Scan-Pulse, were fully sentient and mentally developed marsupials, and by what Radien could tell from the images and information that Techbooth was able to acquire, they had potential as a species. They would most likely find their way to the stars.

The continent that was not known to their maps, that housed the Rogue Demons was what Radien needed to focus his interest on. With the Tanandar Gael possessing no signal-receiving technology, there was nothing stopping him from hailing the Demons where they were situated directly: in the middle of a desert on said uncharted continent.

The hail was a basic ping, no audio message attached. The response was swift, from a Darkstar Demon whose skin's color was oddly similar to the pattern that was found on the spaulders of Veralis's Demonhide Leather armor, that had been made from Demons she herself killed.

"Major Radien," the Darkstar introduced. "Your arrival is as fortunate as it is swift."

"I got your message, to whom do I speak?" Radien asked. He recognized the voice of this Darkstar, it was the same one that was on the recording device.

"As a Demon, my name is Aldarezzix. As a Darkstar, my title is Ruler of the Midnight Air. There is much we have to discuss, and we don't have much time until the Tanandar Gael might detect us."

"Aldarezzix?" Radien questioned. "The Tanandar Gael haven't even *been* to the continent you're on yet, and they probably won't even be able to for at least a century, considering where their cities are, and their technological progress."

Aldarezzix paused for a second. "You must forgive me. It is not easy to predict the speed at which a species progresses. But this news does relieve me of a *lot* of pressure."

"Glad to be of help," Radien commented. "I'll be warping down promptly."

Aldarezzix nodded, and the communication terminated.

Radien did warp directly down to the planet's surface, in the city that the Demons had built as their refuge, Molthlagulia. This allowed the *Aura Runner* to remain on alert in orbit, just in case some threat from the outside decided to try to make its move on Radien and Aldarezzix. If these Demons truly were Rogues, they would be targets of high priority for the Dark Six, especially if a Darkstar were among them.

"Blegh, heat," Radien quietly commented to himself, that no one else was able to hear. The refuge was indeed very much so, that had been converted from what must have been formerly a ship, that did not have a friendly entry with the planet's atmosphere and surface. Aldarezzix soon exited one of the buildings and approached.

"No need to be on highest alert, Defender," Aldarezzix explained. "You're in the company of the Dark Six's most hated enemies, who celebrated Firatyne's defense when it was known."

Aldarezzix led Radien into the Molthlagulia's Vorai of Drell, or 'House of Dross,' translated. It was the term for the building that the leader of whatever collective was in the area lived within, putting it on par with a governor's mansion.

"As you're no doubt aware, our situation is a sensitive one, that requires absolute precision in all movements, lest disaster be our reward," Aldarezzix explained. "It must be known, we were not aware that this world was occupied, let alone by a pre-spacefaring civilization. We also know how fiercely Cynar protects the right of a species to develop as naturally as possible. On top of that, ours is not a well-reputed people. Even though we fight the same foe with ferocity to match, and we celebrate the defeats of the Dark Six alongside you and your universe, we do so in the shadows, knowing well what would happen if we were to do otherwise."

Radien nodded. "When Firatyne was defended, The Mallet Lord let slip that your existence was well-known to the Dark Six and their servants before I dueled him and won. Cynar no longer can doubt, let alone deny that the Rogues are real, and that they seek the chance to prove themselves as allies."

"We are prepared to relocate Molthlagulia in its entirety at a moment's notice," Aldarezzix continued. "It is only a matter of figuring out where to go."

Radien thought for a moment, his arms crossed on his chest as he realized where the Demons could live.

"Jaltai-Vuul, Raon-Arashal," Radien said. "It's hotter than this desert you're in right now, and hardly anyone passes through because of how annoyingly it is very much a desert."

"Sounds like the perfect place for us," Aldarezzix said. "I have found this particular area to be a bit chilly for my tastes."

"Yeesh," Radien sighed. "I hated heat even *before* I was *Zhernrel-Vuljar*, even more so now."

Aldarezzix chuckled. "We should prepare immediately. Consult Raon-Arashal's leadership and secure their approval for us to take this settlement to Jaltai-Vuul instead, and we shall be ready by the time you have it."

Radien nodded again, before turning around to head out to contact the *Aura Runner*.

<Techbooth, hear me. I need you to contact Arch-Militant Jor'Galn, and bring him up to speed on my progress here. I've made contact with the Rogue Demons of Molthlagulia, led by Aldarezzix, Ruler of the Midnight Air. Cross-reference that name with whatever historical records we have on Darkstars and what have you, just in case I'm in danger of bringing a war criminal to Raon-Arashal. The plan is for them to relocate their entire settlement to Jaltai-Vuul, since nobody likes going to that area anyway. It will serve both as a favorable climate for them, as well as being hidden away well enough for it to act as a sanctuary for them and other Rogues while the universe still learns how to recognize Rogues from loyalists. If the Arch-Militant authorizes it, the Demons can be off Selio-Vaqueri before the next moonrise, and nobody will even be able to tell they were there in the first place.>

Techbooth beeped aboard the *Aura Runner*, confirming the instructions and sending the coded transmission to Raon-Arashal via the Interstellar Sound Channel. Given that the ship possessed spatial distortion engineering, allowing its compartments to be larger on the inside, there was enough space to have installed an ISC transmitter. The *Aura Runner* was indeed a well kitted-out ship.

Radien returned to Molthlagulia as he awaited the reply from Techbooth that Arch-Militant Jor'Galn had replied, and met up with Aldarezzix again.

"I don't foresee any major complications," Radien stated. "Much as I don't like to presume, I know Arch-Militants Jor'Galn and Wöllschlager both trust my judgment on this. If I figure Jaltai-Vuul is the answer, then they'll agree; Jaltai-Vuul is the answer."

"I thank you for all that you have done already," Aldarezzix said. "It is more than we had hoped for."

"I know the feeling."

"And that is exactly why we made sure to contact you specifically. Ours is a plight you understand well, for you have lived it."

In the Vorai of Drell, Aldarezzix stood up from his seat and opened a cupboard that contained a bottle of red liquid, pouring himself a glass, and offering it to Radien. He took it, then quickly and subtly looked over it with his Second Sight, to make sure it wouldn't boil his stomach.

Aldarezzix grabbed another glass of the same type and poured himself a much larger amount, before taking a sip of it. Radien soon followed suit, before recognizing the taste of the drink.

"Wait, but—How?!"

"Loyalists and Rogues alike both keep close tabs on the Humans for the same reasons," Aldarezzix chuckled as he knocked back his glass. "Some of their ideas have proven most... fruitful, including the concept of a drink called Bloodwine."

Radien knocked back his glass similarly, enjoying the taste. A sizable replacement pour soon followed.

"We both know what it is to feel like the last man of honor, surrounded on all sides by those who have proudly forsaken it," Aldarezzix continued. "It is for that reason I chose you as our contact point, despite the woes of my kinsmen here in Molthlagulia. Your penchant for slaughtering the Dark Six's servants is as impressive as it had worried some, who wondered how violently you would consider us guilty by association."

"I don't believe in guilty by association," Radien commented as he took a drink.

"I'm glad I was right to send that message. As soon as the news that Firatyne was defended reached our ears, we knew we had to make the choice of whether to stay in hiding on this world, or try to do more in this fight that we're on the same side of."

Radien then remembered something.

"You never saw the post-victory broadcast, did you?" Radien asked. To this, Aldarezzix shook his head after taking another drink. To this, Radien grabbed the comm-link he kept with him in his left pocket, and called up the video that had gone about as viral as could be within the intergalactic community. Aldarezzix watched the commendations intently, enjoying watching the scum of his kinsmen getting their asses handed to them by Firatyne's defenders.

The video cut to the view from within one of the taverns, where one of the Death Worlders had called out *"The Rogues are real! We have allies in the Burning Hells! Toriyah!"* That was followed by the entire city chanting the Death Worlder call.

Aldarezzix was speechless. His expression was frozen in shock that the entire city had begun to resonate with the people of Raon-Arashal declaring with that one word, repeated over and over again, that they were eager to meet their new brothers and sisters in battle.

"I know that feeling, too," Radien said after the video ended. Aldarezzix poured himself another drink, slamming it down his gullet and then replacing it, deciding that the second one was the one to pace himself with. "There's no word to describe it that I know of, but you can't tell if it's elation, confusion, or terror that people are ready to believe you, that anyone is telling you 'yes.'"

"It is indeed a strangeness, very new for me as it will be for everyone else here, that they are not being shunned and dismissed..."

Radien's comm-link pinged. The reply from Arch-Militant Jor'Galn

JALTAI-VUUL IT IS.

Having heard the word they were waiting for, Radien and Aldarezzix began preparing Molthlagulia, and its residents for the journey to Raon-Arashal. The Demons were eager to get off of Selio-Vaqueri, considering how much risk they were running in sharing a planet with a still-developing species.

"Every part of this settlement can be easily refit into the colony ship that it was built from, and we'll have engines running before sundown," Aldarezzix informed as he hefted a chunk of plating into place on the vessel's hull. "Once we arrive in Jaltai-Vuul, it will be a trivial matter to disassemble the ship back into a settlement. It's what they were designed to do, but admittedly this model was meant more to quickly establish a forward base for an invasion."

"Well, good thing you're not invading, then," Radien commented, welding the piece that Aldarezzix had just placed onto the hull with a jet of Psionic energy that was funneling through his left index finger. "How long do you anticipate the trip will take?"

"Raon-Arashal is but a day's travel in the Warp Channel from here, though it will likely take us a week, as we will intend to travel more slowly within, so as not to stress this old rust bucket too much…”

Radien nodded, understanding well the desire to get things done right over quick.

“Today was a day that history would be cruel to forget,” Aldarezzix commented, coursing dark red power through his right arm that began to form a gem in his palm. “Though this planet’s species is still in its infancy, and though the desire to not interfere is a worthy one, this was still the first time that we have collaborated alongside Cynar’s warriors, and it should not be left uncommemorated.”

Radien looked at the cloudy, dark red gem that had just formed in Aldarezzix’s hand, and watched the Rogue Darkstar drop it on the ground. It seemed to anchor itself to the sand, to ensure that no storm or wind would blow it away.

“Whenever something noteworthy takes place in a Demon’s life, they will typically create a Fate Stone to place on the ground of where it happened. I cannot think of a worthier reason to place one than this.”

“Death Worlders have something like that, too,” Radien commented, coursing the azure energy of The Aura through his left hand and drawing a symbol in the air with it, before thrusting his palm at the symbol to ‘break’ it, though what had actually taken place was the imparting of the energy into the planet itself at this location. “Fate Markers, to be made and placed whenever a decision is made that begins a new chapter of one’s life, splitting the path of fate. They act as reminders of our drive to make our destinies our own.”

Aldarezzix nodded, and Radien looked out into

the desert, staring into the distance like he was trying to peer across continents to observe the Tanandar Gael on the other side of the planet.

"Much as I know that the rest of the universe would disprove of us leaving traces behind like we just have... I cannot bring myself to let today be invisible to this world. We've left proof that the Tanandar Gael aren't alone in the universe, and when the day comes that they find this proof, it may serve to inspire them to search for whoever it was that left those clues behind. A message that we're looking forward to meeting them when they're ready."

Radien then slowly breathed in and out as Aldarezzix joined him in pondering the horizon.

"It's a message I could've used back on Earth, all that time ago."

"Eons have passed since you last set foot on that world, and yet you still allow the evil that planet stood for to weigh in on your decisions and actions?"

"I have to remember the evil that planet stood for, so that I can choose to do my part to make sure no one has to suffer a planet like Earth again. If that means violating cosmic law, so be it, because it's the decent thing to do. And if decency be treasonous, then a rebel I shall always be."

Aldarezzix nodded. "If decency be treason, let us aim to misbehave."

Chapter the Tenth
Traitor of the Old Guard

"Zealots, thralls, minions, devotees, acolytes, pawns, cultists... why do I know so many words for enemies, yet not a single one to mean more than friend or ally?"
—*Miles Radien*

Radien twiddled his thumbs within his duty office at Torvaltyne Bastion. He wasn't used to having an office for duties, but apparently the Raon-Arashal Defensive Militarium insisted that the base commander must have an office. And so Radien had an office. However, this was not the most typical kind of office, given that it had a kickboxing ring within it. One certainly could describe Radien as 'addicted to training,' but then again, one could describe almost every Death World Vulpian thusly. He had initially thought about just making a section he frequented his 'office,' but the RADM's administration insisted that he have a dedicated office that he would be expected to use for office-related duties. Radien found this most annoying, as he preferred to be out and about, rather than in an office. Granted, he was not expected to do much office time, just a non-zero amount per month to affirm that there was indeed an office, and he did indeed occupy it.

On the desk was a fist-sized orb made of Carnelian. Radien grabbed it from its stand and held it, pondering his orb. It certainly was a ponderable orb. Radien definitely was getting some solid pondering done with this orb. However, the acquisition of the Carnelian Orb was a surprisingly involved ordeal, mainly centered around the fact that for some unknown reason, nobody bothered to shape Carnelian into orbs, they were always lumps. Palm-sized lumps of the stone at best, but never a nice, spherical orb for pondering. It was most annoying, because pondering a Carnelian Lump just isn't the same. What does one say when Orb becomes Lump? 'Oh, let me go ponder my lump on this one' or something? At risk of 'pondering my lump' being slang for some regard of naughtiness? Ridiculous. One must ponder an orb rather than a lump. Thankfully, however, Radien did possess an Orb of Carnelian.

The orb-pondering was broken up by a ping on the computer screen on Radien's desk. A message from Turazin, specifically from Xenidar Ralkas, Keeper of The Hideout, and a well-connected Pondering Orb dealer.

"We've managed to figure out who's in charge of the SWEEPS base here on Turazin," Xenidar began. "It wasn't easy, though. Guy's good at covering his tracks."

"Go ahead."

"His name is Adam Stratfordshire, and records seem to indicate he's from Old Earth, mainly since there's no birth records from any of the other Human worlds on file. It's believed that he was recruited to

SWEEPS while still on Earth, not long after the death of Avanchenvaldr. Despite the fact that SWEEPS personnel these days must give up their free wills to the Dark Six, Adam appears to have been 'grandfathered' out of having to do so, as it looks like the Demons recognize that he's more valuable to them with his consciousness intact."

As soon as the picture flashed onscreen, Radien's eyes widened with equal parts shock, confusion, and disgust. He recognized that face.

"Xenidar, I'm on my way. There's more to this guy you need to know. Grab Ellan and meet me in the main commons."

Xenidar nodded, and the communication terminated as Radien quickly stood up from his desk and began running towards the Transit Nexus, where a Way Gate to The Hideout was present. Radien also grabbed from his desk one of his Waypoint Stones, so he could drop it in a corner somewhere there.

Once he arrived at The Hideout, Ellan and Xenidar were waiting for him.

"His birth name is Jacob Valence," Radien explained. "It now makes sense that he thought about booby-trapping the server racks we grabbed in our last cavalry raid."

"You know this guy?" Ellan asked. "Old enemy of yours?"

Radien shook his head. "No, old friend... but friend no longer, it would seem."

A moment passed. Xenidar and Ellan both knew that Radien did not choose his allies lightly, and just what kind of retribution he'd be more than happy to administer to traitors. "What do we need to know?" Xenidar asked calmly.

"He's a lot like me. Vigilant, clever, calculating, logical... all these things that you've known me to be, he's got those traits too. It's why we became childhood friends back on Earth. We shared a disdain for Earth's bullshit, and that feeling like it was just us against the world. Why he changed his name is beyond me, Jake Valence has a better ring to it, in my opinion."

"Adam Stratfordshire... what is he, British?" Ellan remarked.

"No, but he *is* descended directly from the first British colonists to arrive in what later became the U.S., so... close enough?"

Ellan shrugged. Xenidar had no clue what the two were on about, so he just waited for more information.

"It makes sense that Adam thought about booby-trapping those server racks, it's on par with the level of vigilance we practiced back on Earth. He's not completely incompetent as a fighter, but we can expect him to not be present during any real fighting. He's better as a planner and overseer, anyway," Radien explained, remaining as calm as possible despite the anger welling up within him, the sheer rage that comes from learning of this kind of betrayal.

"I know how carefully you choose your allies, Radien. Is it possible that Adam is playing a long game to infiltrate SWEEPS and siphon information to us?" Xenidar postulated.

To this, Radien shook his head. "If Adam were planning to siphon information to us, we'd know all of

SWEEPS's dirty secrets already. Besides, he *did* detonate the server racks. If he were infiltrating, he would've let us get away with them."

"So, what's next?" Ellan asked.

"I'll make contact with Adam," Radien said. "Though he's switched sides since last I saw him, I know for a fact he'll have at least one last conversation with me before we fully commit to killing each other."

Suddenly, something slammed against the doors of The Hideout. Everyone stopped in place as they realized that someone was mounting an attack.

Radien threw out his left hand and coursed The Aura's power through it, and an azure barrier formed around the door, that was still taking impacts from some kind of battering ram, or perhaps a very large sledgehammer. Xenidar quickly slammed a button on the wall that shifted the main common area into its defensive configuration, complete with walls full of racks of various weapons, melee and ranged alike, as well as chest-high stone walls rising from the floor to take cover behind.

"Everyone who wants out before the fighting starts, now's your chance to evac!" Xenidar said into the intercom, ensuring everyone heard him. "Everyone else, grab your favorite and get ready to defend! SWEEPS is at our doorstep, and I'll be damned before I let those bastards have whatever they're after *this* time! Radien, how long can you hold that shield?"

"As long as you need me to!" Radien answered. "It's an all-Human squad, so that would explain why they can barely dent it..."

"Anything else?"

"There's one non-Human lifesign," Radien responded, as his eyes switched to the amber glow of the Second Sight. "Demonic! I think he's the leader—"

That one Demonic lifesign had just slammed its weapon against the door, pounding on the shield much harder than the Humans could muster with their weapons, and Radien *felt* it. He did not falter, but he knew he could no longer hold the shield indefinitely.

"A minute, at best!"

"Can you give me ninety seconds?"

"Ninety seconds, coming right up!"

Radien thrust forward his right palm now, coursing the power of The Aura through both hands, reinforcing the barrier he was stopping the enemy advance with. The Demon at the door swung again. And again. Then it suddenly stopped, slightly confusing Radien.

"Law of three, two of the same, change the third," Radien reminded himself, before bracing for an even bigger impact than either of the two before. Sure enough, this Demon slammed its weapon into the door again with a much harder strike, and out of time with the preceding two. Had Radien not been ready, the barrier could've shattered on the spot. He then heard some angered muttering from the other side. Something along the lines of the Demonic tongue for *'you've gotta be fucking kidding me...'* but it had come from one of the Humans behind the door.

The thralls of SWEEPS were Dark Six servants. Though it was known that any higher-ranking personnel had to surrender their will with an Oath of Dark Alliance, it was something else to see it on the spot. The only cure for them was death, now.

"*Our enemy knows the Law of Three. Do not underestimate him,*" another voice muttered as Xenidar signaled that everyone was in place, and the barrier could be dropped now.

Radien nodded back to Xenidar, and sent a bright red spark along the trail of energy that coursed from his hands to the door, disconnecting his end of the line as soon as the spark hit the shield around it. The barrier shattered on either side in the form of a wave of throwing knives, piercing through several of the Humans and killing them on the spot. The Demon, however, seemed to have anticipated this, and was able to block or avoid the projectiles.

Xenidar hit the button to let the door slide up and open, as replacing it was not a quick task anyway. The Frontliner of the Dark Six walked through the open archway, looked upon The Hideout, and then locked eyes with Radien once he located the warrior who was able to equal him, and pointed his sword at the Death Worlder.

"Fight whom you wish, but the *Greígoth* is mine!"

Gunshots and shouts soon followed as The Hideout's defenders engaged the SWEEPS thralls. Though not unskilled, the grunts of the Dark Six were proving to be little match for Cynar's warriors, all eager to show them the training they had undergone in preparation for this.

The Frontliner approached Radien with sword at the ready, and Radien was prepared to meet him with the Borfblade. The Frontliner leaped into the air with a thrust meant to pierce through the top of Radien's head, but the Death Worlder qresponded by suddenly moving forward with a spinning side kick that landed right into the ribs of his enemy. The forward aerial momentum of The Frontliner stopped, and the Demon groaned once he hit the ground, though he was still prepared to begin his attack, slashing at Radien with his unique 'one-handed Flamberge,' as that would be the best way to describe it. The jet-black sword met with Radien's trusted cutlass again and again in a series of strikes, parries, and ripostes from both sides, neither yet gaining a meaningful edge on the other.

Meanwhile, Ellan and Xenidar began engaging the Human enemies that were trying to storm The Hideout, as the Talvas Vulpian used his environment to lethal advantage, slamming the heads of SWEEPS soldiers into bookshelves and hidden panels, some specifically built to be ready to slam into an enemy's legs in the event of an attack. No less than six soon fell to a combination of getting their shins shattered by the metal plate, followed by a vicious, skull-crushing kick to the face from Xenidar.

Elsewhere in The Hideout, other fighters were keeping other key areas under their protection. In one of the Data Cores, Kieran Ebensen and the Felinian Nico prepared to meet their enemies, seemingly getting ready for a knife-throwing contest.

"I'm just saying, why not have a little flair to your throws?" Nico asked, grabbing two throwing knives from a table they had been staged on and throwing them one after the other, into the chest and then head of an approaching thrall of the Dark Six.

"Nothing against flair, but why use two on one

enemy if you're that accurate, when you can just knock off two enemies?" Kieran answered, grabbing two knives and throwing each into the neck of a foe.

"Well, you gotta have a little fun with you, you know? A touch of *je ne sais quoi?*" Nico then threw a knife at one SWEEPS soldier's thigh, then another into their abdomen, and then one more into their face.

Kieran scoffed before tossing a knife into the chest of the soldier behind the one Nico just turned into a pincushion, before a jumping spinning side kick knocked the Human over the edge of the railing, and into one of The Hideout's power turbines. Fortunately, they were of durable enough material spinning fast enough that the amount of damage throwing someone into the turbines would inflict was none at all, but the red mist in the air would need to be filtered. Naturally, it was fortunate that The Hideout had such filters in place just in case someone had decided to impressively kick one of their enemies into the turbine. "Don't accuse me of not being able to have fun with it!"

The duel between The Frontliner and Radien continued viciously, both fighters landing every now and again landing lacerating cuts on the other, that had to be healed with their powers lest they risk being overwhelmed, but neither could seem to really get a decisive hit on the other. The fight around them turned towards the tide of the defenders of The Hideout, as SWEEPS thralls were cut down by the skill of the warriors who defended it. Neither Radien nor The Frontliner seemed to notice outwardly as they continued to fight each other, save for when one of the Human shells tried to land an attack against Radien from behind, and in response, The Frontliner grabbed the head of this coward who dared interfere in their duel and crushed it, to Radien's surprise, but not his protest. Radien similarly saw a pantherine Hajitorr attempt the same against The Frontliner, only to be blasted back by a bolt of The Aura from Radien. Nobody was stepping in. This was their fight, and there was now a crowd gathered for it in the wake of the Human attackers being completely destroyed.

Back at the SWEEPS base, a Human stood with his arms folded behind his back, a Deceiver Demon next to him. A wall of monitors offered a plethora of views of motionless body-mounted cameras and static.

"We got what we came for, pull him out," Adam instructed the Demon aside him.

"Are you mad?! He is engaging the enemy!"

"Even if he beats Miles, he won't make it out those doors without getting pounced on by the guys who just trashed our attack squad. Pull him out, or he is going to die!"

If Demons could sweat, the Deceiver next to Adam would be doing just that.

"Don't worry, just be sure to explain yourself thoroughly, I'm sure he'll understand," Adam said halfheartedly, but not sarcastically. That he knew whoever pulled The Frontliner away from his fight would be torn to shreds eluded this Demonic subordinate, and so too did he fail to notice Adam excusing himself from the room as he hit the buttons on the console to make the warp-out happen.

Back at The Hideout itself, both Radien and The Frontliner noticed that one of them was being pulled away from the fray without their council. The Frontliner yelled in rage as he attempted one last swing before dematerializing entirely.

"I do not envy whoever was given the order to do *that*," *Radien* commented, as everyone who had gathered around to watch the duel between him and The Frontliner awaited his next word. That word was 'Toriyah!'

The crowd cheered in the victory they had just won against SWEEPS, against the Demons, against the Dark Six. Another one for the history books, another battle where the defenders of the universe had proven their skill and their courage once again, their *Kelvaltor* in the face of their foes.

The Hideout was defended.

Back at the SWEEPS base, Adam heard from outside the room he had just exited, the roar of an enraged lord of Hell, and curses that could set the minds of some men on fire as The Frontliner expressed his vehement disapproval of being pulled away from the fight, followed by the sounds of a Deceiver Demon being torn in half. It was at this point Adam excused himself to coincidentally remain on opposite ends of the SWEEPS base from The Frontliner until he had calmed down, and thankfully, the only one who knew that he had given that order was currently in pieces.

Revelry at The Hideout lasted through the night, in celebration of the victory won. It was tradition for there to be an open bar following a successful defense at The Hideout. By the time morning came for Turazin, everyone was back to business, with Xenidar's specific business being to add names to the memorial wall that commemorated all those who had fallen defending the known universe's biggest library. Xenidar's demeanor certainly couldn't be considered somber, as nobody who died defending The Hideout could be considered to have died emptily. A more casual air of respect and acknowledgment was more the tone as Radien approached.

"What could they have been after?" Radien wondered aloud. "There's no way they *didn't* know they couldn't take this place. Not with so small a force."

"Those Humans were basically being piloted by Demons remotely, so as far as they're concerned, they lost a bunch of empty shells. Expendable," Xenidar stated as he affixed a plaque and attached a hand-held router to etch a name, date, and species. "We also know the names of every SWEEPS grunt, soldier, officer... they sure can't infiltrate us."

"So they were looking for information. What else do you find in a place like this?"

Xenidar processed for a moment, before typing three lines into the device's built-in keyboard to initiate the engraving process. He then pressed a button on a nearby communications console. "Ellan, Nico, if you're still here, can you access the search logs and find out what information was viewed during the fight?"

"On it," came the reply from Ellan.

"All of the Human soldiers had bodycams, transmitting directly to the SWEEPS base," Xenidar continued to process and piece things together. "They could've easily pointed those cameras at a reading console, and as long as there was at least one frame's worth of clear footage, they could effectively make copies of whatever info they were looking for without having to take the time to download anything, and leave the kinds of traces downloading does."

A reply soon came through. It was Kieran.

"A bunch of stuff on Matter Compression Modules, but what pages were looked at are seemingly scattered and random. One terminal was viewing a paper on the incident at Oskallion Bay, another was viewing research logs from a satellite in orbit of a black hole with a Ringularity in the Ethylcloud Maze."

Xenidar thought for a moment, then shrugged his shoulders. "Anybody got a theory?"

Radien's arms were folded across his chest as he pondered intensely. "Black hole stuff? I might, I just hope I'm wrong."

"We could ask this prisoner I manage to take," Nico's voice came over the comms next. "Room of Silence Epsilon-Four."

Xenidar nodded to Radien to head to that area, and he'd catch up once he was done with the wall's additions. Once Radien arrived, Nico and Ellan were both waiting.

"Now, before you ask why I bothered taking a prisoner, it's because I've got an experimental techpiece on loan from a friend of mine in the Order of the Iron-Tipped Tail who's hoping I can find an opportunity to see if it works."

"The Iron-Tipped Tails are of honorable repute," Radien informed Ellan, who nodded. "Let's see what we can learn."

Xenidar then entered the room, ready to observe and moderate. Nico placed a small circular silver device with a glowing blue gem in its center onto the side of the Human's head. Or rather, 'placed' in this sense to mean that he slammed it against the Human's jaw with a quick snapping motion, landing the device right on the joint and cracking it. The Human restrained to the chair groaned in pain, before his arms began to convulse in the restraints, spasming violently like every hair along them had been yanked up simultaneously. Soon, the Human's yells gave way to catatonic chuckling.

"Are we speaking to the Human or the Demon?" Radien asked. The Human simply chortled quietly, offering no answer to which part of this equation was in control at the moment, thanks to Nico's device. Radien's eyes flashed amber as he looked over the prisoner with his Second Sight. "Well, if you insist, Nameless."

The prisoner snapped to attention with a look of pure anger. Demons that had not yet earned their names never cared too much about being called Nameless, but for those who had, it was a capital insult.

"It's the Demon," Radien informed the others, to which Xenidar nodded in a 'makes sense' manner.

"Are you sure we need to bother with this?" Ellan asked. "It's a remote-controlled flesh vessel, there's not really much we can threaten or do to it."

"I'm just testing the techpiece, man," Nico replied.

The prisoner convulsed for a few moments, before coughing and groaning, and muttering a comment that he didn't realize that Radien could hear, being a Death World Vulpian with particularly good ears and all that. "How the fuck am I back here..."

"And now it's the Human," Radien commented.

"Did your device just separate the Demon from the servant?"

Nico shook his head. "No, it's still in there, the device has just made it possible to communicate with the body's original owner. Human... you said that you're 'back' here, what happened when you surrendered your free will?"

The Human sighed and rolled his shoulders, seemingly disappointed that he was back in his own body. "It's like lucid dreaming, just my body's doing whatever the Ideal Masters want, and it's not like I knew how to be a soldier anyway... seems they're good at making me one."

He then looked at his arms and legs. "Holy shit, I've lost weight! Who knew that fealty to them could get you *built?*"

Radien looked over to Nico, who was intently jotting down notes. Radien had been hoping someone had been. The Human then struggled in the chair for another few moments before the Demon reasserted itself.

"You fight a war you cannot possibly win, why remain in the realm that we will dominate? You know now that the servants live in their dreams that they control, all while we control what matters—"

"You waste your taunts on me, *Sallakka! Bootlicker!*" Radien cursed as he used his power to grip every nerve ending in this prisoner's body and make *all* of them fire pain signals to the brain. The Demon in control roared in the kind of pain it didn't even know it was capable of feeling. "You may be controlling that Human remotely, but I consider it *very* fortunate that you can still feel pain in that vessel!"

"We were warned of a *Greígoth* among the protectors of The Hideout…" The Demon panted, still in shock that it had just endured more pain in a few seconds than some do in years at a time. "The Frontliner pledged himself to your defeat."

"I'm honored, but I still have no idea what that word even means, despite how many times that I've heard it by now."

"'One from the many,' translated," Xenidar mentioned, leaning against one of the walls. "In this context, it means someone who has proven to be a particularly nasty thorn in the Dark Six's side."

Radien nodded. "High praise indeed."

The blue gem in the center of the device on the prisoner's neck glowed again as he struggled in the chair for a moment, the Human temporarily back in control.

"He has a point, you know." The Human chuckled. "I live in a dreamscape under my complete control, taking a backseat to whatever the Ideal Masters need my body for. Hoo boy, the fantasies I have been *living!*"

Radien grasped every nerve in the Human's body once again with The Aura. "*Dulfuirsin Mokh! Duul zhern Nutorval'e pir shal-nah deyl akar fuurvikja-ej! Mockery of Opinion! You kill decency itself by continuing to live, and I intend to fix this!*"

The title that Radien had just bestowed on this vile Human, *Dulfuirsin Mokh,* was a Death Worlder insult for someone who made having opinions look bad by being such a wretched soul, that any point they may genuinely have is rendered moot by the sheer lack of decency they had in their character.

The Demon seized control once again, clearly quite fed up with Radien deep-frying his nerves. "You cannot stop what is coming! You cannot harm myself or my flesh-vessel in any way that will matter! So go ahead and execute him in whatever manner you see fit, Project Schwarzchild will ensure the victory of the masters, and will engulf every world you hold so dear in flames!"

Radien tilted his head at the name the Demon had just dropped. "So *that's* what they're planning... Nico, we're finished here."

Nico nodded, then removed the device from the prisoner's neck. Suddenly, both consciousnesses were simultaneously vying for active control of the Human's body, but the laws of physics knew well that two entities could not occupy the same space, and Psionic matters were hardly different to this end. The convulsions became more and more violent, and the bulging of what looked like air bubbles across his flesh promised that a messy end to this ordeal was inevitable.

Though the walls and floor would need to be deep-cleaned, nobody was actually hit by the flying blood and chunks of this Human's explosive demise, thanks to Radien summoning shields around each of the room's occupants.

"Pop goes the bootlicker," Ellan commented.

"Radien..." Xenidar said. "Is there a reason you couldn't just put the bubble shield around *him?*"

"Hey, at least it's not a carpet floor."

"You said that you knew what they were planning?" Nico asked.

"The information on matter compression they

grabbed, the schematics and blueprints they screenshotted, the fact that they're calling it Project Schwarzchild... they're making black hole bombs to destroy planets."

Xenidar's ears shot up as he suddenly went alert. "Are you sure they're making Planet Killers?"

To this, Radien turned to Xenidar and nodded. The Talvas Vulpian cursed profusely as he urgently made his way towards a control console. "With me, Radien! And tell me everything you can!"

Radien followed Xenidar, explaining himself along the way. "Schwarzchild refers to a Human term, Schwarzchild Radius, their name for the amount to which a mass must be condensed in order to form a black hole. With the blueprints they were able to take stills of, they'd be looking at a five-by-five-by-five foot Osmium cube, compressed to its Schwarzchild Radius. Of course, this black hole would immediately evaporate due to Hawking Radiation, and the explosion would be enough to tear a planet to pieces."

Xenidar hastily slammed his fist on a button that blared an alarm, before speaking into the microphone on the console panel.

"This is Keeper Xenidar Ralkas! Turazin will be entering a planet-wide quarantine until further notice, effective immediately, to contain the threat of planet-killer weapons being produced at the SWEEPS base on this world! No one enters or leaves without my personal authorization, starting now!"

A containment shield immediately began projecting itself around the planet, sealing it off from warp-outs or warp-ins, and once a few hours had passed, any ship that tries to pass through would crash upon the barrier.

"Radien, get the *Aura Runner* over here and monitor that SWEEPS base until the barrier has stabilized physically! I don't want any of those bombs escaping Turazin!"

Radien nodded before reaching out to Techbooth aboard the vessel telepathically. *<Techbooth, hear me. Urgent. Travel to Turazin and monitor the SWEEPS base from orbit. Destroy anything that tries to escape this planet!>*

Aboard the *Aura Runner,* Techbooth displayed a message on its console that Radien was able to see thanks to his connection to his ship, as the engines spun up.

ACKNOWLEDGED. I'D SAY YOU'D BETTER HAVE A GOOD REASON, BUT I GET THE FEELING I'LL KNOW IT WHEN I GET THERE.

<The Humans are building planet-killer bombs at the SWEEPS base, we gotta make sure none escape before the quarantine force field fully stabilizes!>

ON MY WAY AT MAX SPEED. ARRIVING IMMINENTLY.

"Xenidar!" Radien called out to the Talvas Vulpian one more time. "I can no longer stand idle as the entrenchment of our foes remains at our doorstep!"

"Give 'em hell, Radien!"

IN ORBIT NOW.

"Techbooth, Emergency Dimensional Recall!"

Radien was now at the helm of the *Aura Runner,* itself in hot pursuit of the Human ships trying to flee Turazin while the quarantine shield was still forming and stabilizing.

"I'm assuming manual maneuvering control now, start locking weapons onto the enemy craft!"

The manual yoke of the craft shunted out from one of the panels, and Radien took it, guiding his ship to dodge the shots being fired from the escort craft that were as desperate to see the Schwarzchild Bombs leave Turazin to wreak havoc as the Demonic masters of Hell endorsed their deployment. But this was not a weapon designed by Demons. No, only a Human could dream up such a honorless and morally destitute weapon. Only a Human was capable of such contemptuously senseless evil.

"Why haven't they jumped into the Warp Channel yet?" Radien wondered aloud.

THE HIDEOUT HAS EXTENDED THE RANGE OF ITS VORTEX EMULATORS TO A RADIUS OF ZERO POINT EIGHTY-SEVEN ASTRONOMICAL UNITS, PREVENTING THEIR FLIGHT.

"That means we've got that much distance to take them out! Start firing at the escort craft, shoot to kill!"

As Radien steered the vessel, Techbooth made the finer adjustments to the *Aura Runner's* pitch and yaw to line up the main kinetic weapon of The Ship of Myth itself: A pair of twin-linked cannons nicknamed the Tungsten Fangs, for the fact that they would fire a tungsten spear at hypersonic speed, and needed only the sheer force of its impact to tear most ships to shreds, or put sizable holes into larger ones. Between these two cannons was a co-axial machine gun of similar purpose, but it was a weapon meant more for combat near planetary atmosphere conditions, where the bullets were small enough to harmlessly burn up in an atmosphere before becoming a danger to anything on the ground. The Tungsten Fangs, however, were only safe for deep space combat. The only reason Radien was using them here so close to Turazin was because the weapons were pointed *away* from the planet below. Internal relative distance trackers embedded in the Fangs themselves would activate when fired, and once one of the Fangs had detected that it had traveled over ten thousand kilometers, a Shredder Module would tear it to atoms to ensure that there weren't giant tungsten darts wantonly sailing through space after every engagement. After all, if your shot had traveled that much distance before hitting something, you missed.

The first of the Fangs fired at one of the escort craft, and if it weren't for the vacuum of space, the sound it would have unleashed could make eardrums explode. The enemy vessel had no time to react before being obliterated by the impact. The next shot took out the ship it had been escorting, safely destroying the Schwarzchild bomb aboard it.

Radien pressed a few buttons on one of the consoles to begin scanning the ships for Osmium, the element of choice for the Schwarzchild Bomb's matter compressors to crush down to that radius. Sure enough, several ships were carrying staggering amounts of it, marking themselves as the priority targets.

"Remind me to send Micah that tip about detecting the bombs and Osmium and such," Radien quickly stated, hardly having the time to word things out more cleverly.

Another round of missiles were fired from the

escort craft, and though the *Aura Runner's* shields were able to shrug the impacts and explosions off, it was a closer shave than Human weapons had gotten before.

SHIELDS AT THIRTY PERCENT INTEGRITY.

"They've been practicing!" Radien noted. "But so have I!"

The *Aura Runner* skillfully maneuvered around the shots and pulses coming from the enemy ships, gunning them down with swift surety. None of the Schwarzchild Bombs escaped him, and it was now the case that they were all confined to Turazin, and the SWEEPS base upon it.

"Xenidar! I think the time has long since passed for you guys to flatten that damn base!"

There was a momentary delay, but a reply did come through. However, it was not Xenidar's voice. It was Ellan's.

"I couldn't agree with you more, Radien! I'm opening up a brief window in the shield for you to warp down, we need to get a counteroffensive ready *immediately!* They hit us again while we were distracted with knocking down those ships and putting up the shield, Xenidar's MIA!"

"*Nezhval Zhath Kiivoleth nejtoulth! Honorless cowards of strategy, these foes!*" Radien cursed, quickly warping back down to The Hideout when said window opened, instructing the *Aura Runner* to return to Raon-Arashal and deliver the report on this incident to Arch-Militants Jor'Galn and Wöllschlager. He had certainly fired one hell of an insult to SWEEPS, whose literal translation really didn't do it justice as to just what he had called them. The term itself *Zhath Kiivoleth,* denoted the kind of coward who would punch someone in the back of the head and then strut around like they had won the fight, rather than just mailed it in as they had.

As Radien and Ellan prepared their weapons and enlisted the help of Nico and Kieran 'Five Rings' Ebensen, Xenidar Ralkas entered The Hideout through the front door.

"Whatever you're thinking, gentlemen, rethink it!" The Talvas Vulpian ordered.

"What the hell for?!" Radien questioned. "This is more than enough of an excuse to wipe them off the map!"

"And we will, Radien!" Xenidar reassured. "But you're walking into a trap if you do! Also, glad to be back, good to see everyone here, too!"

"Explain yourself, Xenidar!" Radien ordered.

Xenidar raised an eyebrow at Radien presuming to command him. At that moment, the Death Worlder's eyes flashed amber as he scanned The Hideout's Keeper, just in case... but no trace of the Dark Six's vile power was detected. Xenidar had not been converted, so there was indeed a reason for this change of plan. But Radien still wanted to know it. That base had planet killers and gods know what else, it had to be dealt with.

"Fair enough," Xenidar conceded as soon as he saw Radien checking him over with the Second Sight. "You're right. That damn base has been a stain on Turazin ever since it was constructed, and now the fact that they've built those bombs means they've got to go up in flames. But they've got another weapon, one that means we *cannot* risk a direct assault, and that we *must* not allow *anyone* off of this planet, save for by way of the direct Quickgate to Torvaltyne Bastion. Even then, that thing is under lock and key, and nobody uses it without my personal authorization first."

"Accepted, but what kind of new weapon?" Kieran chimed in. "Something worse than the Schwarzchild Bombs?"

Xenidar mulled it over for a moment, and then nodded. "Honestly? Yeah, I'd say so. It's why I had to beat a hasty retreat out of their base, and couldn't risk trying anything fancy in my escape. Also, will someone activate our Defense Grid?! Maximum power, too!"

Nico and Ellan both sprinted off to do just that, as Xenidar informed Radien and Kieran of what dire devilry had been concocted behind those concrete walls. He looked over each shoulder, before producing a vial of swirling purple-black liquid that exuded an aura of sheer dread, pure vileness, and unfathomable abyss.

"This serum means they don't have to convince people to join, now," he said quietly to the pair, who looked to each other with equal disgust and horror at this new weapon. "Fortunately, like the Schwarzchild Bombs, it's contained here on Turazin. But it means anyone who gets within shooting range of that base risks getting turned. They're dipping their bullets in this poison, putting it on their knives and even coating the knuckles of their gloves with it. A mind poison, that directly assimilates consciousness, and turns it over to *them.* That's why we can't risk a direct assault right now. And right now? This needs to stay between us. I can't afford the kind of panic this crap will cause if word gets out. It represents the essence of the end of this war, and in all the worst ways that can mean."

"Deyl alnd huulekh-nah Nel Jalfjaa nudormej... My eyes vomit, my soul aches... Truly, SWEEPS knows no honor!" Radien commented.

"I'll say..." Kieran added. "How do we keep it on the down-low?"

"Leave that to me," Xenidar assured. "If I can trust you two to not blab about it, I can make sure that things stay cool here."

"People are going to get impatiently eager to take the fight to them, Xenidar," Radien pointed out.

"I've been the Keeper of this place for how many tens of thousands of ASC, now? I know how to do holdouts, I know how to keep people like that in line, and satisfied."

"Works for me," Kieran concurred. "I can't imagine these are the worst odds you've been stacked against."

"Far from it." Xenidar chuckled, placing the vial into a delivery chute to take it to the Talvas Vulpian's personal laboratory for further study. If there was an antidote, it needed to be found. If nothing else, if there was a way to target the Dark Serum with some specific weapon to neutralize every vial of it within the SWEEPS base, that also needed to be found. Though there was no fondness in developing such obnoxious weapons meant specifically to render others inert, SWEEPS had drawn first blood on this, not The Hideout. And now that blood demanded repayment in full. "Radien, you said you could make contact with Adam Stratfordshire?"

Radien shrugged. "All I know is that if he's half the person I remember, he'll be willing to have one last chat with me before we fully commit to killing each other."

Xenidar nodded. "See what you can do. If he's half the person you claim you knew, something tells me that the bombs and the serum weren't his idea. Booby-trapping server racks to deny intelligence is cleverness. But shit like this... it's a whole new breed of evil."

The two Vulpians went their separate ways to enact their plans. Radien's involved drawing a symbol into the skies of Turazin above the Red Rock Plains with The Aura, a symbol that Adam would recognize from when he and Miles Radien used to be allies on Old Earth. The symbol that had been with Radien for longer than he had been Radien burned in the air, a signal to the commander of the SWEEPS base that was in his interest to answer.

Slipping off into the night was a trivial task for someone with Adam's cleverness and vigilance, even though he probably could order the men under his command to allow him the time off for personal business, though it was likely that he'd be followed if that were the case. And Radien was not the kind of person to double-cross by bringing armed guards to an unarmed and alone-style meeting. Even then, both men brought their battlegear, just in case one or the other decided that the time for words was to prematurely end. On Radien's right hip was the Borfblade, and on his left was an axe he had been working on. A blade of Hunderfold Novasteel, and a haft of Voidtouched Ebony brought practicality and durability along with the aesthetic. The axe's blade itself had been carbon-plated to appear jet black like the Borfblade, given that Novasteel's natural color looks as though a rainbow puked on it. Some liked that aesthetic. Radien was not among them, though he comprehended the appeal. Red Dust lined the edge like it did the Borfblade, and at the end of the haft was affixed a pommel containing three gemstones from the Crystal Planet of Korvideyl, arranged in a triangular formation equidistant from each other. Adam's armament consisted of a pair of Archonium revolvers on each hip, as well as a single-edged straightsword on his right. Even though Adam was right-handed, it seemed as though the design of the sheath permitted a straight draw from the side it was resting on.

"Nice cape," Radien commented. It was a nice cape, after all. "You always did say you wanted capes to make a comeback."

"In some places, they already have," Adam replied. "You always did say you wanted out of that Human body."

"Seems we've both done pretty well for ourselves, despite the efforts of our planets of birth."

"Good gods, Miles, can't you just say *homeworld* like everyone else?"

Radien shook his head. "Not since Earth was never a home."

"Fair enough."

Radien breathed in and out, maintaining his composure. "What the hell happened, Adam? What brought you to become the enemy that we swore we would destroy when we were honored with the chance?"

"The Six have plans, Miles. Plans that not even the Defender can stop."

"Don't tell me this is envy for my accomplishments! I gave the Humans their chance to show the stars what good they could do when I left!"

"That you have. There is no jealousy between us, because like you said, we've done pretty well despite the efforts of our homeworlds."

"So what's the difference between us that made this so?" Radien asked. "What made you stray from the Path?!"

"I still follow the Path, Miles! Do not mistake this! I wouldn't have a pair of Archonium revolvers and a kick-ass cape if I strayed from the Path! But the Six, or as their more devoted thralls call them, the Ideal Masters, what they've got in store for the universe isn't something you can stand stoically against forever! They are a flood to carve a mountain in half! I choose to be the water of that flood!"

"You are a fool, Adam!" Radien finally yelled. "Do you think the Dark Six will spare you for aiding them? Do you think your collaboration and submission will save you?! It won't! You are not a Demon, you're a Human! They will rend your consciousness from your mind as soon as your use is through! You will stand under blackened suns and bloodshot skies, beholding a universe aflame, and it will be the last thing you ever see before you are thanked for your loyalty and then executed for not being born into their ranks!"

Adam stood defiant of Radien's words, though they were the truth. The Dark Six were indeed desperate enough to allow Adam his consciousness and the cleverness that came with it, but he wasn't one of them. He wasn't part of the club, and for it, the Demons saw him as nothing more than a tool to be used, a pawn to be taken advantage of to get what someone else wanted.

"You know me well enough, Miles. What's my plan when that day comes?"

"What, to fight as you always have?!" Radien scoffed. "Just like I have against them, since the day I took upon my powers?! Why did you not just fight them from the start, instead?!"

Adam was silent, and Radien soon processed the rest of his plan.

"*Duul akar Javalvius anzor-kyr, Nezhval! You are loyal to opportunity alone, honorless one!*" Radien insulted as he pieced it together in his head. Adam's plan was to be on the winning side, whatever it took. He knew of the Rogues well before the rest of Cynar did, and was sure to seek sanctuary with them in the event that the Dark Six took hold of reality, being as experienced as they are at hiding from an entire plane of existence that hunted them. Adam was also in a high enough position within the enemy ranks, and retaining his consciousness, that if Cynar began to turn the tide, he could defect safely, bartering with his sheer knowledge of Demons and their plans.

But Cynar was pushing back, the universe was turning the tide. So why had he not defected already? Why, in the wake of the Dark Six facing defeat after defeat by Radien's hands, and that of countless other heroes being forged in the fires of the crucible of the Second War for Reality, did he take up arms on the side of the enemy?

What were they planning, that Adam knew and

Radien did not, that made the difference in Adam's choice of allegiance, if only for the time being?

Radien drew the Borfblade and swiped it at Adam's neck with one motion immediately after he spat his insult, but it passed through harmlessly. "Of course, I already knew you'd never risk facing me alone, Adam."

"I'm not stupid, Miles," Adam responded, standing in his office within the SWEEPS base, his motions being matched by the hologram projected to the Red Rock Plains. "I know well your conviction."

"Then why side with *them?!*" Radien reiterated. "You have set yourself up to fail, Adam! Because even if every star in every galaxy forgives you, *I will never!* You're going to have to kill me just to stop me from coming for you!"

Adam processed this for a second, his head turning away and down from Radien, his arms folded behind his back. He then looked back to the Death World Vulpian standing before him. "Then I had best win this war for the Ideal Masters, because no death they will give me will involve more pain than the ones I know you can dream up."

Radien's eyes rested in a narrow gaze, devoid of emotion on the surface. But just behind them, his mind was already dreaming up the pain he'd make Adam feel for this betrayal. Not just of the friendship of old, but of all the stars in the universe for the side he had chosen.

"Miles!" Adam called out just after Radien turned away. The Death Worlder stopped, but did not look back. "Neither the Schwarzchild Bombs nor the Dark Serum were my idea. The name of their architect is a one Iramenas Enuz, and I hate the bastard and want to see his work fail more than I value my own life. That is why I will tell you that precisely three of the bombs escaped Turazin, but the schematics remain here, cutting off their design from the rest of the universe. Now you know what you're looking for, and how many you have to find."

Radien still did not turn around, but he knew that Adam was telling the truth. A traitor he may have become, but he was no liar. He knew how bad of an idea it was to lie to Miles Radien.

The hologram glitched out, and faded away. The die was cast, and the battle lines were drawn. There would be no going back for either of them, and they both knew it. They wouldn't have it any other way.

Chapter the Eleventh
The Era of Darkening Stars

"It is neither gods nor kings who decide the fate of worlds. That role falls to the Lone Zealot, a warrior with the wind at their back, they who are more than eager to demonstrate why gods and kings alike wish them dead, and why they have tried and failed to fulfill such a wish."
—Redarian proverb

Radien sat at the Torvaltyne Mead Hall, brooding mysteriously in the darkness. He was very good at it. It also helped that the architecture of the Mead Hall itself lent towards the art of brooding mysteriously in the darkness. Not even brooding in a depressed or glum sense, but in a mysterious wanderer sense. It was a fun pastime, brooding mysteriously in the darkness over a pint of mead, and Radien was indeed *very* good at it. So much so, that one of the art galleries on Raon-Arashal, which had an exhibit entirely consisting of moody pictures of Death Worlders brooding mysteriously in dark corners of taverns featured a photo of Radien brooding mysteriously in the darkness at this specific corner within the Torvaltyne Mead Hall. Quite the compliment, considering that every tavern on the planet had a designated Mysterious Brooding Corner, making Death World Vulpians somewhat of experts on the matter of doing so.

Arakai soon joined in on the mysterious brooding in the darkness. He was also quite good at it.

"Am grumpfox," Radien stated.

"That is fair. I too, have been grumpfox on occasions such as this," Arakai responded.

Radien sighed with an annoyed 'peff' noise, and Arakai motioned for another round. "I've always been prepared to find out that a friend has switched sides, Arakai. I trained myself for many years for it, and so did he. We both knew we always had to be ready."

"Well, I also know you better than to think you *didn't* prepare for you and Adam specifically to be on opposing sides of the battle line."

Radien scoffed as freshly filled pint glasses were placed in front of him and Arakai. "That's the thing, Arakai. We both *did* prepare for the day we may have to stand against each other. We just hoped that old age or a valorous death would get us before then. Somehow, though... we both knew that if we lived long enough, we'd see the day we stopped being allies, and became foes."

Radien then looked around while taking a sip of his glass. "Also, it's *way* quieter in here than normal... usually there's a couple guys using the sparring ring..."

"Word travels fast, Major. Though you may not discuss these things, it tends to be noticed when the old friend of the base commander is found out to be among the enemy. The eyes of the universe watch closely its protectors, whether to celebrate their victories beside them, or stand in solidarity to their tragedies."

"Tragedy is a strong word to be using," Radien commented.

"For anyone else, it wouldn't be. There are very few people out there who train as hard as you do, for as many different things. Who else would think about making sure they're prepared to find out that they are now enemies with *any* of their friends, let alone their closest ones from long ago?" Arakai continued.

"I train so that they are *not* tragedies," Radien affirmed. "Adam has made his choice, and I will not rest until the consequences are wrought upon him, for straying from the Path." He then stood up from the table, bringing his half-empty pint glass with him to set it on a countertop affixed to one of the support pillars that was near the open sparring space. Arakai soon joined him, grabbing two pairs of sticks, handing one pair off to Radien for them to practice.

Radien gave the *Saludo Maestro*, and Arakai responded with the traditional salute of the Crimsonian Fencers, as Arakai was half Crimsonian Vulpian. This involved striking his two weapons together twice, once right on top of the other, and then using that momentum to spin the bottom weapon around once to strike the first weapon in the same manner, before entering guard.

The spar began immediately after, and the two were quite evenly matched, though only going about half speed, for the sake of training, and also for the sake of not accidentally smashing one of their skulls in, or any of the nearby furniture. Whenever someone was using the sparring area of the Torvaltyne Mead Hall, it was always the main thing to watch. Sometimes, members of the peanut gallery would comment advice from the sidelines, and there would always be an 'ooh!' or 'oh, nice!' whenever someone landed an impressive hit, or dodged in similarly impressive manner, or sometimes even when someone merely threw an impressive technique, regardless of whether or not it landed, because despite the controversy that always surrounds spinning or aerial moves in martial arts, wheel kicks still look pretty cool, and when they hit, they are *devastating*. Hence the practice of them in this training space, that when the time came for a good coup de grace in the field, it would not miss.

However, both of these fighters were skilled enough to evade each other when their heels lashed out in this manner. It really wasn't clear who had the upper hand in this fight, not least of all because it was sparring, not an actual fight.

Inevitably, a timer beeped, marking five minutes since their spar began. They decided to keep going, as a display of endurance. Five minutes later, another timer beeped. Ten minutes of constant sparring had passed, and neither had broken a sweat yet. These two were endurance incarnate, they had trained to be.

As the two put their pairs of sticks back onto the rack of loaner sparring weapons to use in the ring, Radien suddenly was flung into a vision, another one of the Dreads of the Defender. But this time, something was... different? Perhaps that was the wrong word, but somehow, Radien understood that he was feeling two of them at the same time, the whirlwind of dark thoughts and a non-vision of evil for the fact of the sheer overload... The Tactician knew that the Defender could feel the Dreads, and know where the Dark Six were, so two at once was sending Radien's mind into a frenzy just trying to process and distinguish it all.

"*Djalsej!! FUCK!!*" Radien cursed loudly in the middle of the Torvaltyne Mead Hall, gripping his head as it throbbed worse than a white wine hangover, and Arakai immediately knew what was happening.

"Which one?!" He quickly asked, though no panic was in his voice, only surety.

"Two of them! I can't tell them apart, there's so much happening at once, I can't distinguish them!" Radien groaned as nearby patrons of the Mead Hall scrambled to get ahold of energy scanners and finding any way to help if they could. One Death Worlder even started channeling his power into Radien to transfer some of the raw headache to himself to try to alleviate some of the strain by taking it upon himself, so that Radien might get a clear enough head to figure this out.

"What do you see?!" Arakai asked instead.

Radien focused hard, no longer on trying to figure out which Dread it was, but where in the universe this Dread was being projected from.

A Rogue Planet, separated from its solar system by cosmic chance, whether another star or black hole passing by and ejecting it from orbit, shrouded in the eternal darkness of the space between stars. Upon it, a Demonic base where no other life dared live.

"It's a Rogue Planet, no telling which!"

"What's the nearest Stellar Formation nearby?!"

"Wait... I recognize those seven stars! The planet must have been ejected from the Pleiades! There can't be that many in the area, I've got a fix! *Get out of my head, Dark Ones!!*"

Arakai motioned to the Death Worlder who was taking on some of the psychic stress to tell him to let go, and he did. Radien then let out a furious yell as a wave of azure energy burst from him, resonating off the walls of the Torvaltyne Mead Hall, and the empty glassware across the bar shattered as the full bottles and sparring weapons were shaken on their shelves, threatening to fall from where they were placed. Radien's eyes crackled with blue lightning as his fury was awakening, the fury that came whenever someone dared to try to worm their way into his mind. He warped away from the Mead Hall promptly, aboard the *Aura Runner*.

"*Techbooth, engage Punch Drive, set course for the Pleiades Cluster!!*"

With speed to match Radien's furious urgency, his ship catapulted through space and into the Warp Channel at maximum speed, and were it not for Techbooth's mechanical precision, he may have risked slamming straight into one of the stars of the seven sisters.

His eyes still ablaze with the fury of The Aura, Radien searched for light-years around with the Second Sight, trying to vent the power that was driving him to such rage, knowing he needed a cooler head to prevail against the combined efforts of two of the Dark Six at once. Though his power demanded to be let loose with the kind of sheer destructive rage that could vaporize planets, he still was trying to reign it in, just in case.

When the planet was found, the *Aura Runner* sped towards it as Radien's arms began arcing blue lightning across the muscles, and the Death Worlder still couldn't help but feel as though he was being manipulated from the shadows into this rage state, that meant he needed to *not* be in it. This fury was too much and too quickly for what triggered it. This was the kind of hatred that one would feel towards the murderer of their allies, and even though the Dark Six were the greatest enemies of Cynar, they still had yet to strike a properly personal blow against Radien. Adam siding with them was his choice, and though pure hatred seethed from him, Radien knew that he needed to demand discipline from himself if he was going to be victorious today.

"*Un suul pirakar vel Fjar-Arvaiaathreyn gen fjarka deyl'e Nel Jalfjaa, tais nej Arsuul! A day will come when the Flames of Retribution must burn so bright in my very soul, but it is not today! Techbooth, open the airlock!*"

The door opened, with an oxygen shield covering the open cavity into space, though it was not a solid barrier, it could be walked through. Or in this case, something could be thrown into space from inside, which Radien did, charging an azure sphere of pure Psionic energy in his hands before hurling it into space, letting it detonate in an impressive explosion that saw this literal venting of his fury out of his body, and into the void between stars.

Radien breathed in and out slowly, watching the nebula-like explosion dissipate in space, still confused as to how this had happened. The Dreads were one thing, that two were simultaneous was another, but it just didn't make sense that it instilled such a destructive rage and haste within him... What he did know, however, was that he had just avoided letting that haste spell his doom. Though he awaited confirmation of that notion, and though he didn't know why events so nearly panned out in this manner, he just *knew* that ensuring his cooler head likely ensured that whatever plan the Dark Six had for him had failed.

The *Aura Runner's* communication line pinged. Whoever was on the planet below was hailing him, and desperately.

"Aura Runner, hold your fire! I am Darkstar Aentdoroth, The Void-Touched Legionnaire! I, and the other Demons on this abandoned planet are Rogues! Do not open fire, please acknowledge!"

Radien took another deep breath in and out as he approached the console at the helm, and pressed a button to reply.

"Aentdoroth, this is Major Miles Radien of the Raon-Arashal Defensive Militarium piloting the *Aura Runner*. Message acknowledged, but I come on the trail of a psychic attack from two of the Dark Six who just entered Cynar."

As Aentdoroth sent her reply, Radien powered up the *Aura Runner's* Interstellar Sound Channel Transmitter to contact Aldarezzix in Jaltai-Vuul, where the Rogue Demon settlement of Molthlagulia-Vex had been established. *"That would explain why we just had a high-level telepathic signature bounce off of us! Only The Tactician could think of a plan like that, but it would be The Deceiver with the Psionic skill to pull it off! Perhaps those are the two who have entered?"*

"Aentdoroth, hold that thought for a moment," Radien replied as he muted that channel, switching to the connection with Aldarezzix. "Aldarezzix, does the name Aentdoroth ring any bells?"

"Aentdoroth lives?!" Aldarezzix responded, seemingly as surprised as he was excited to hear this news. *"Radien, if The Void-Touched Legionnaire has made contact, you must aid her! She has vital information on the workings of The Dream-Taker!"*

"Thanks for the confirmation, Aldarezzix. Indeed she does live, I'm sending you the coordinates now." As he delivered this news to the Ruler of the Midnight Air, Radien sent the coordinates for the rogue planet that these Rogue Demons were based on. "Aentdoroth, I'll be heading down shortly, you didn't happen to trace where that telepathic bounce came from, did you?"

"Way ahead of you, Major. Warp down at your earliest convenience."

Radien soon found himself in a town seemingly built from the cannibalized parts of the major cities that used to exist on this world before it was ejected into interstellar space, and subsequently had its entire atmosphere freeze. The ship that these Rogues had arrived in, as well as the most salvageable metals and technology from the frozen world had been consolidated to create this one pocket of habitable space on an otherwise utterly inhospitable world. Aentdoroth was waiting for him, a datapad in hand.

"This is where that psychic bounce came from, imparting itself on this planet heavily before reaching you, wherever you were at the time."

Radien took the datapad and looked over it,

before letting out a groan. "Oh, fuck's sake... *Ultharn.* Of course they'd go to Ultharn, why wouldn't they?!"

"You know this planet?"

"It's a long story. Fortunately, the end of that story means I know the route to the core-vault that they've set themselves up at. The geothermal power of the planet's core, along with the remote location, and the fact that Ultharn is a damn fortress of an artificial planet means it's the perfect place for a Demonic Riftgate that could accommodate the Dark Six, especially if two at once."

"Wait, two at once?! You're going to have to explain—"

"Whenever one of the Dark Six enters Cynar, I can sense it. I've tried to hone this ability into being able to track their location, but with no success. When one of them arrives, a unique Dread hits me, and what exactly that Dread feels like tells me which one has arrived. However, it seems they are just as familiar with the Dreads as myself, and even found a way to spike them with... whatever the hell they just did there, that not only sent me on the warpath that I barely managed to cool down from before it was too late, but also disguised which ones even entered."

Radien's comm-link pinged, Techbooth was informing him that another ship had just exited the Warp Channel in orbit. Another Darkstar Demon then materialized in the city, having hastily arrived following the news that his oldest and most trusted ally still lived, and had even escaped to Cynar.

"Aentdoroth!" Aldarezzix called out once he saw his fellow Darkstar, and sister in battle. "Today is indeed a good day!"

"Aldarezzix? You still live?!"

"Do you two need a moment?" Radien asked. The two Darkstars looked to each other, then back to the Death World Vulpian, before shaking their heads simultaneously.

"It can wait," they both said, simultaneously.

"Uncanny," Radien deadpanned. "Either way, much as this smells like the plans of The Tactician, I seriously doubt he's crossed over into Cynar. Much as I'm sure he's not incompetent as a fighter, he probably knows he's best placed in whatever moldy corner of the Burning Hells he's holed up in."

"Speaking of moldy corners where the Lords of Evil like to hide," Aentdoroth remembered, grabbing another datapad. "This is a layout of the Dream-Taker's Citadel, the Nightmare Garden."

Radien thought for a moment. "Okay, the way you said *Citadel* makes me think that there's more to it, like I could hear you capitalizing a proper name."

"Each of the Six has a Citadel," Aldarezzix explained. "A particular moldy corner of the Burning Hells where they rub their hands together and plot evilly. The Dream-Taker's is the Nightmare Garden, and having a map of it that also dissects each segment and how to circumvent its deterrence measures will be vital in the event that the fight is taken there."

"Indeed. Even if the Dream-Taker is dealt with after entering Cynar and it doesn't come to that, I get the feeling it'll still be invaluable information," Radien concurred. "Also, Aentdoroth, you said that only The Deceiver possessed the Psionic know-how to actually weaponize the Dreads in this manner? By way of essentially sending my senses into overdrive, and encouraging rash and hasty action?"

Aentdoroth nodded.

"The Deceiver must be one of the two who entered, then. But that was such a damned whirlwind, I couldn't tell *which* Dreads I was feeling, I'm afraid I have no idea who the other one is, aside from the fact it's definitely neither The Frontliner or The Tactician, since one's already in Cynar, and I already explained why with the other."

"Indeed. But you are already familiar with their hideout, Ultharn," Aentdoroth hinted.

"I guess I'd better just go over there and see for myself who's arrived," Radien concluded. It still barely makes sense, what just happened... or rather, what *nearly* happened. I know myself well enough to know that I don't just get *set off* like that..."

"Such is the nature of psychic trickery," Aldarezzix reassured. "Driving people to actions they would never otherwise do is certainly a trick of both The Deceiver and The Seducer."

"Ten says that The Seducer is the second one, then," Radien commented. "Those two's efforts combined could very well represent the kind of trickery needed to pull a stunt like that. Had it succeeded, it would have likely been a disastrous defeat for us."

"Not only would the information on the Nightmare Garden I just gave you be destroyed, it would also fully cover their footsteps, leaving you with neither of the identities of which of the Six entered this realm," Aentdoroth continued. Both Radien and Aldarezzix nodded at this, silently acknowledging how fortunate it was that vigilance prevailed today, and ensured that such a disastrous defeat was not the fate that came to pass. But there was no further time to waste, and Radien took his leave, warping back aboard the *Aura Runner* and setting course for Ultharn.

"Yeah, that damn planet again..." Radien grumbled.

TECHNICALLY, YOU HAVEN'T EVEN VISITED IT YET. The displayed message from Techbooth read onscreen.

"Oh, shut up."

The series of electronic beeps from the console that followed were basically Techbooth's way of cheekily giggling as the *Aura Runner* tore through the Warp Channel.

Upon arrival, Radien grumbled again at the sight of the citadel-like planet. "Techbooth, Wide-Field Scan-Pulse. I want to see just how much of a base camp they've established in the core-vault.

The readout showed not only Demons, but a cluster of other lifeforms within the camp as well, too clustered together to be collaborators.

"Oh, fuck's sake," Radien grumbled further. "They took some prisoners just to make sure nobody blows it up from orbit without a huge guilt factor about it. Probably a merchant freighter's crew that just happened to be in the wrong place at the wrong time... *ugh, fine.* I'm going in."

A stable connection for communications between Cynar and the Burning Hells was already difficult enough to establish, let alone a temporary portal to send soldiers and supplies through, let alone a portal stable enough for one of the Lords of Evil to pass through. One could be forgiven for saying that it seemed like reality itself had a will to resist the Demons and the Dark Six from entering, because this was the case. Such was the nature of the barriers that the Aura Prism maintained.

A portal capable of allowing this universe's greatest enemies to pass through it despite reality's wishes was no small task. However, Ultharn and its remoteness, as well as the maze that surrounded the planet's artificial core had given enough time for a force less than a hundred in number to assemble the massive gateway that could achieve this feat, and do so repeatedly. And so, The Seducer and The Deciever of the Dark Six were now placing their footsteps upon Cynar for the first time in billions of years, and the very air around them seemed to revile at this fact.

A single Darkstar Demon bowed before his masters, welcoming them to Cynar. "Exalted greetings to the Ideal Masters," He began. "I am Folvashterox, He Who Brings Fear of the Night. Per your instructions, our humble force of ninety-two have painstakingly prepared this portal for your arrival."

"As you have, Folvashterox, as you have..." the Deceiver acknowledged. "For less than a hundred, you and your crew have done well, beyond all expectations. This cannot go unrewarded, no doubt. But the time for celebrations and formalities is short, for our presence in this universe will not go unnoticed."

"The Defender, yes," Folvashterox growled. "We are preparing—"

"It is already prepared for," the Seducer quickly

stated, four different tones emanating from one throat. An impatient snap, a calm reminder, an exasperated repeating, a cunning assurance. "Tactician devised a plan that would allow our covert entry, despite Cynar's will to warn him of our presence, and Deceiver has carried it out... at least, that is what you told me."

"Tactician's precaution was far from trivial to implement, but I had time, and it was done. By now, the Defender will have already incinerated the planet he believes we walk upon, and with it, so too does an entire colony of Rogues go up in flames."

The Deceiver's speech was slow and deliberate, but not so slow that it seemed to drag on. Her voice was enunciated as perfectly as possible, no word could be mistaken for a different one. Truly, her craft of lies was not in something as petty and unambitious as the misconstruing of speech, nor even was her preference in turning lifelong battle brothers against each other. No, The Deceiver was more subtle than that, more likely found pushing unstable minds over the edge of madness with sweet lies and affirmations, or instilling crippling doubt into otherwise unbreakable warriors. Of all the Dark Six, The Deceiver was the single most skilled wielder of Psionic power.

By contrast, The Seducer's words were more quick and articulated, bordering on impatience. When she spoke, the very words seemed to take on a demand to be obeyed. It was as though the words had life of their own, and The Seducer needed not make demands on her own, for her words would adopt whatever tone was necessary to make those who heard it bend their knee, where one person may hear the shout of a drill sergeant, another may hear the allure of a siren, and another still may hear the plea of a friend in need, or the reasonable tone of a diplomat. How she achieved this, none knew. The Seducer's voice was a chorus of tones, and only the tone that would get her what she wanted would be heard by whoever she was talking to.

"You will go no further!!" Those commanding voices suddenly yelled at a Demon that was approaching the structure that contained the fourteen prisoners that shared this space in Ultharn's core-vault with two of the Dark Six, and their lackeys. A strict command, a raging threat, a stoic warning, a confident statement of fact. The Seducer was clearly fully aware of the intent of this Trooper who was not actually planning to simply check in on the prisoners. "Those prisoners that you were instructed to take serve a *very* specific purpose, and that is to ensure that no one simply blows this planet back to whence we came from orbit! Defile a *single* one of them, and that asset is gone! Need I remind you that the Defender hails from Raon-Arashal, a planet upon which rape carries a mandatory death penalty?! He and many others wouldn't think twice about atomizing this world as an act of euthanasia for the broken!!"

The Deceiver began to weave raw power into the air, imparting it upon the portal and preparing to establish a communications line back to its source, per the instructions of one who did not intend to make his presence in Cynar just yet, all while The Seducer continued to explain why the wayward Trooper's plan was a *terminally* bad idea.

"If you are so desperate to satisfy yourself, I would rather see you renounce your title and become among the Rogues, to then flee to the planet of Haven Hall to spend the rest of your days among their carnal culture! I should tear you asunder right now..."

And so the subordinate was torn asunder. After all, The Seducer did say that she *should*, and thus it was done.

"Well, whatever else they may be, it seems there are still *some* matters we agree on," Radien muttered to himself from the shadows. They clearly had expected him to allow the unnatural rage The Deceiver imparted to him to have worked as it was intended, and they certainly didn't expect him to already be on Ultharn. After all, as far as they knew, he didn't even know about this planet. The destruction of the Time Ender that had been enthralled by The Unmaker had reset the memories of the universe such that as far as the universe believed, Radien had never been to Ultharn. And in a way, he hadn't. And yet, he had.

Shaking off the annoying nature of temporal mechanics, Radien forged onward, sneaking into the improvised structure that the prisoners were being held within. As soon as he entered, a knife nearly jammed into his throat, held by a Hajivakk who was waiting for some unfortunate Demon to try to enter. However, Radien's reflexes were fast enough that he was able to parry the hand that held it with the back of his own hand, and trap the arm. The two fighters then looked at each other and realized who each of them were.

"Jesus fucking shit, man, don't sneak up on me like that when Demons are about! I could've killed you!" Synval-Kolderan commented. Her tone was stern, but not loud.

"Synval-Kolderan?!" Radien quietly exclaimed, so as not to alert nearby Demonic guards. "Well, given that you're decidedly not bound by any of the contraptions in here, I can only wonder why *you're* the bunch they've taken hostage."

"As if," Synval scoffed, but only mocking her alleged captors. "We picked up anomalous energies in this system, so we took a rustbucket of a merchant freighter and let trouble find us. It's parked behind the moon of the neighboring planet by now, since we couldn't convince Velsarn to play along with the capture. He just hid on the ship and waited so he could get it in position to pull us out when it's time."

"Can't say I blame him," Radien followed up, releasing Synval's hand from his grip. "I don't think I could be convinced to feign capture, either."

"To each their own tactics, eh? You certainly look a lot better than when I last saw you."

"I've been keeping myself healthy. It looks like the war has been keeping the Chorgon Nehr busy."

"We've been finding stuff to do, aye. The rest of us have taken positions around the camp, plan's to ransack and assassinate."

"Works for me. I'd say just like old times, but Hulae was not exactly a stealthy affair."

"The number of old times is only one, anyway!"

"My point stands."

A Demonic trooper who was missing an arm stumbled into the prison, clearly a token of The Seducer's punishment. His horror only lasted for a brief moment before being cut short by Synval's knife into his skull.

"They really thought we were going to just sit around and wait for them to do whatever they were planning with us, huh?" Synval remarked as she wiped the blood off on the Demon's armor. "I, for one, am glad that I know no such cowardice and submission."

"Feeling's mutual. Let's wreck these bastards."

The Seducer and The Deceiver continued to converse with the being beyond the dark portal, who could only be The Tactician.

"Though the cogs of this artificial planet are nearly rusted beyond recognition, repair and repurposing should be a relatively trivial matter," the Deceiver noted. "Its remote location and status as a cursed relic of an ancient war will only make coversion easier."

"What of the Defender? A Death Worlder is not to be underestimated."

"It is unlikely he will find this world for a very long time," the Seducer explained. A tactful analysis, a dismissive wave-off, an educated hypothesis, a quick reminder of the plan. "With the induced rage that you tasked Deceiver with, his only lead is dust in the astral winds."

A few hundred feet away from the conversation, a Whiplance Demon was dragged off into the shadows and sliced to ribbons.

"Regardless, his presence has already spelled multiple setbacks for our campaign. The slaughter of our forces at Hulae was his doing, after all," the Tactician reminded.

"The Butcher of the Bulwark?! That was a Human, not a Death Worlder!" the Seducer corrected. A snarky reminder, a speculative reexamination, a pointed 'um actually,' an annoyance at inaccurate recollection.

"They are one and the same, the Human of Earth who became *Zhernrel-Vuljar*, now the Defender, is proving to be quite the thorn in our side, and Frontliner has even sworn him as his personal *Greígoth*, claiming the right to destroy him alone."

"Frontliner and his so-called warrior's oaths!" the Deceiver spat. An annoyed comment, a frustrated critique, a groaning remark, a sarcastic jab. "He is a relic of a bygone era whose relevance dwindles by the day! He only lives now for his sheer martial skill..."

"Martial skill alone he may have, Deceiver, but if there were any Demon in all of the Hells who could win a war of attrition by combat alone, it would be Zoln'Slan Thiild, The Frontliner," the Tactician reminded.

Near a storage tent, Synval-Kolderan and one of her compatriots began attaching recall beacons to crates of equipment, warping them back to their ship while Radien kept watch. They had no idea what they were stealing, but they figured there had to be *something* of value in this camp, if two of the Dark Six were here. It did seem like they were placing a lot of stock in their bet on Ultharn. All the while, Radien similarly waited for the chance to attack the two most valuable assets of Hell that were present. If he could get the drop on them, he could strike the mightiest blow against Hell ever struck in the history of time.

"It remains unwise to provoke him thusly," the Tactician continued. "Seek an opportunity to destroy the Defender at your leisure, but make sure you do so in a manner that does not intrude upon Frontliner's

Greígoth-Vantureil."

The Seducer gruffed with annoyance as she kicked a stone.

Synval-Kolderan nodded to Radien, the Chorgon Nehr's work was done. Radien signaled them to warp out, and let him take it from here, so they did. From the shadows, Radien prepared himself, charging a concentrated bolt of The Aura in his left hand, getting ready to snipe one of the Dark Six here and now.

Once the fist-sized azure concentration of energy was strong enough to make his hand vibrate just trying to contain it, Radien let it loose, flinging it right at the head of The Deceiver, and right through the head of The Deceiver. However, Radien suddenly realized that neither of the Dark Six were actually there, as the bolt harmlessly passed through the head of one of the Lords of Evil.

The two simulacrums crumbled to dust, and Radien heard the unmistakably evil chuckle of The Tactician from beyond the crimson gate.

"Credit where it is due, that *would* have worked," the Tactician commented, only slightly mockingly, but his tone ensured that there was no true commendation. "They and their vessel are safe within the void between galaxies, do you *really* think they would risk standing on something as immobile as a planet? Let alone upon the same one?"

Radien knew that The Tactician referred to the *Gadrigaridox.* This also meant that The Seducer and The Deceiver were clued in to the fact that their induced rage on him did not succeed. With the jig up, he stepped out from the shadows to meet The Tactician. Or at least, the image of him that was visible from this side of the portal.

"Miles Sorvenjar Radien, the steel and doom, skill and stone..." the Tactician slowly announced, to Radien's confusion.

"So, you got my message," he calmly stated.

"Indeed, the mantra that acted as your totem of defiance on Earth may have seen so little use in Cynar, now that you have escaped the former in favor of the latter... but not all that is forgotten, is lost."

Radien remained resolute, remembering that there was more to the Dark Six's influence over Earth than met the eye, or scanner. It was a mystery he had yet to solve.

"But know this, Defender: Steel rusts, and stone erodes. How long do you think you can stand against us? Do you truly believe that you can outlast us?"

"I will count the seconds, if that is what it takes. Every breath I take despite your efforts will give me the strength to draw the next. Six of you there may be to lead the dark legions, but in my sword I trust, and that is why you will all fail to defeat me."

"Then I shall look forward to facing a worthy opponent."

The gateway rippled and red lightning cracked around the ring that kept it open, and with the equilibrium of powers put out of balance, the portal soon violently crushed itself shut, as the barriers that the Aura Prism maintained asserted themselves back into this place on Ultharn.

But the red lightning soon struck a relatively small and seemingly insignificant part of the gateway's assembly, causing the very ground to shake, and Ultharn groaned under some unknown, yet potent energy spike.

Radien's eyes glowed amber as he looked over the portal again. The entire frame was laced with Osmium, specifically to increase its density and make this entire Way Gate far heavier than necessary... and then he realized to what end this served.

"Djalsej! Techbooth, hear me! Emergency Dimensional Recall!"

Radien was quickly warped out back aboard his ship. Normally, this would have been nearly impossible for most transmat relays aboard ships, but not only was the *Aura Runner* a ship of mythic technological capacity, it also knew well its pilot, and could distinguish their specific signature from an entire planet's population if need be. And with the population being none, thanks to Radien's efforts alongside the Chorgon Nehr, locking onto him was not only possible, but trivial.

Despite the fact that Ultharn was already in its death throes, Radien pressed a few buttons on the console to arm one of his Pulsar Missiles at the doomed world.

"Djalar fjaar sehlrel-vaikulreth!! Fuck this planet in particular!!" Radien yelled before slamming his fist on the red button, firing the modified planet-killer payload that he was already planning to use when the mission was finished, allowing the *Aura Runner's* automatic systems to ensure that both his ship, and the Chorgon Nehr's were at a safe distance before allowing the process to continue. Since the Chorgon Nehr were already out of the solar system, the missile fired as soon as Radien's hand caused the button to shatter on

impact. It wasn't the first time that his ship's fabrication matrix had to repair buttons that he hit so hard, they broke.

It was not clear whether the Pulsar Missile or Schwarzchild Bomb was what destroyed Ultharn, but destroyed it was.

"Techbooth, inform the following parties that there are now only two Schwarzchild Bombs unaccounted for..." Radien instructed, before listing off the names of the people who needed to know, Xenidar Ralkas on the top of that list.

Not long after, the first reply, from The Hideout's Keeper himself.

"Radien, I got your message. Do you want me to have the record say that the bomb destroyed Ultharn, or that your Pulsar Missile did? I remember you talking a lot of smack about that planet, so let me know who you want credited for its destruction. Also, get over here as soon as possible. There is an urgent matter to discuss."

Chapter the Twelfth
Blood on the Stars

"The Spirit of the Stone understands that good men and women don't need rules to tell them to be decent, and though warfare is warfare, and combat is combat, opponents are to be treated like opponents, and not insects to be stomped and swept aside."
—Excerpt from the Universal Treaty of Banning Obnoxious Weapons Technology

Personal log of Major Miles Radien, UDM 8-317,392,518-9-19. Less than ten minutes after learning of the Schwarzchild Bombs that were smuggled from Turazin before Xenidar was able to engage the Warp Lock, I had informed Micah Jorvask of this imminent threat. Micah has since personally taken it upon herself to get to the bottom of the matter, and has sworn to tear the abominable weapons to pieces herself once she finds them, of which there were three, but now there are two, that one of them was used to destroy Ultharn. The Eyes of the Daggers, the Shadow House of Nathineyl in which Micah is a high-ranking member, have designated this as her Test of

Proving. This means that upon the completion of this mission, she will be eligible to test for the rank of Master of Shadows. Two planet-level explosions waiting to happen are wandering the stars as we speak, and I know no words that can do justice to the sheer direness of the situation, and no curse in any language I know is good enough for their architect, a Human named Iramenas Enuz, according to intelligence reports courtesy of his embittered superior who would rather SWEEPS be destroyed than Iramenas be successful. Similarly to Adam Stratfordshire, Iramenas has been permitted by the Lords of Evil to retain his consciousness while in their service, due to the sheer value that it presents the Demon Lords, considering that Dr. Enuz also created the Dark Serum that has The Hideout on lockdown, nobody getting in or out, at risk of forced corruption. If nothing else, this proves that we have been striking decisive blows against them, that they are desperate enough to risk their servants being more than mindless puppets.

Speaking of The Hideout, Keeper Xenidar Ralkas has requested my presence, in one of the Rooms of Silence, in which no recording devices exist. They are called by this name for this fact, that they are tailor-made for discussing secrets. The urgency of his tone instills a great instinctual dread within me, though admittedly not one of the Dreads of the Dark Six. The difference between those and this, is that the Dreads of the Dark Six are specific, and what mortal peril they place me under the impression of is known. However, I instead dread what I do not know of why Xenidar has asked me to meet him with such expediency.

As soon as the door to the Room of Silence

closed and sealed, Xenidar sighed, bracing a hand on the empty table within.

"I knew that it was folly to hope it could be circumvented somehow. But even then, it still angers me as much as it pains me, what you must now know," Xenidar explained. The then placed a device on the table that showed a holographic model of the syringe-bullet that he had warned Radien and others of SWEEPS's possession.

"I know what these things do, and it's because I didn't escape from that base unscathed."

Radien's eyes flashed the amber glow of the Second Sight, and Radien looked over Xenidar again. His mind was still his own, but he could see that there was a dark growth wrestling with the consciousness of Xenidar Ralkas.

"I've spent the whole time since fighting it, trying to find a way to purge it from me. But just like how there's no cure for an Oath of Dark Alliance, there seems to be no cure for this."

"No wonder you needed everyone to stay put so badly..." Radien mentioned. "I mean, bad enough that they even have this stuff, but that there's no cure?"

"Maybe there is one, I don't know. But I also don't have long enough to find out," Xenidar continued. "At the rate it's gaining power, I have at most, enough time to blow that SWEEPS base to hell myself, and take those honorless rot-brained *Zhath Kiivoleths* with me. I know you understand the need to not die with a clean sword."

"I do, yes." Radien nodded.

Xenidar placed another device onto the table,

and put his right hand onto it. It scanned Xenidar's palm, and the Talvas Vulpian then turned it around towards Radien. "Place your dominant hand on there."

Radien placed his left hand on the device, and after it scanned his palm, it beeped with a confirmation.

"You're the Regent of The Hideout, now," Xenidar explained. "I've relinquished my leadership of this place as Keeper, and as Regent, it is now your responsibility to find the next Keeper of The Hideout. You must understand, this place isn't just the biggest library in the known universe, some of the knowledge contained here could make even the Perawls of Dor-Val-Der shudder! Fuck's sake, the secret of Planet One's location is within the Black Records! The Dark Six can *never* have that! They *must* never!"

Radien nodded understandingly. "Xenidar... *Skjeln thej duul'e Klatar. Skill guide your path.*"

Xenidar then removed a necklace from underneath his shirt that Radien had never noticed until now. At its center was a pendant, with the sigil of a tome in the center. Around the rim were words that translated as *Knowledge is the sword and shield against ignorance* from the old Kendrosian Dialect. After it all, it was the Kendrosians who first built The Hideout on Turazin, which used to be known as Kendrossos V. Xenidar then handed it to Radien.

"When I first became Keeper, I thought I wouldn't last long," Xenidar said, placing his hand on the wall of the Room of Silence. "Every one of us has shared an innate connection with The Hideout. No Keeper has ever broken that link while still alive."

Radien could hear a low hum in his mind, that

sounded like what it would if trees could groan in pain. The resonance made him feel as though his skull was vibrating in his head.

"Ow, fuck!" Radien exclaimed. "What am I *hearing* right now?!"

"That medallion represents the connection that each Keeper has to The Hideout. Places can remember, you know. You're feeling what The Hideout does right now. Confusion, pain, grief, despair... anger at how little it seems you can do, yet so ready to make everything right, and all those emotions are bathed in a lust for retribution. The Hideout seems to sense a kindred spirit in you, *Talgar Rhovaris.*"

Radien knew that word from the *Zhernrel-Vuljar* tongue, one's *Talgar* had no direct translation, but the closest one could get was to describe it as 'the flavor of the air' around a person. *Rhovaris* translated as *Lone Wanderer.*

"It's a feeling I once knew nothing other than, what The Hideout feels right now... So long ago, a different lifetime."

"Back when Miles Radien was a Human of Earth?"

"The very same."

"You were the first Human I met, you know."

"Shit, you're right! I was, wasn't I? Damn, that was a *while* back..."

Xenidar chuckled. "All the madness I had seen in my time as Keeper, and suddenly, a new species enters the wider universe from a corner no one even knew was basically a desert island in the middle of the cosmic ocean, and I remember *saying* 'oh boy, this should be *good.'* when you first hailed me for access to the Galus-Net."

"Are you sure you've got enough time for this?"

"Oh, yeah. It'll be a while yet before my mind's completely gone, I did say I had enough time to take SWEEPS with me," Xenidar assured. "Caltoran's end saw everyone scrambling to put the universe back together, barely enough time to grieve for Eluria and Kendrosium, and the dozens of other species that no longer walk among the stars... and yet, somehow, it turned out that there were worse places one could be stuck. Even the universe as it was when you first left Earth seemed like endless wonder to you, when to all those who grew up within it, it felt like the ashes of what once was, and never would be again."

Radien sighed. "Earth wasn't ashes, not even back then. It was more like... Like there wasn't even a fire to begin with. Inert. Dead before it had the chance to be alive. The Humans there made sure of it, that opportunity was as fictional as prosperity."

"The only way a tyrant species like *that* holds control is by convincing everyone that there's nothing else. And I suppose as far as anyone there could be concerned... there *was* nothing else. Or at least, there may as well have been nothing else. Avanchenvaldr did a number on that solar system, and really fucked with the heads of that species," Xenidar debated.

"They still had to choose to accept being evil. And accept it they did," Radien rebuked. "No tears for those without *Kelvaltor*. Not one drop, not one moment of sympathy and not one iota of pity."

Xenidar nodded in agreement with that

statement. "It takes a sheer lack of *Kelvaltor* to develop a weapon like what SWEEPS has... how did you survive among such a proudly honorless species?"

Radien shrugged. "By too many different ways that I never should've had to resort to in the first place."

A few more moments passed in silence before Xenidar spoke again. *"Skjeln thej duul'e klatar,* Radien. I will not return."

Radien simply nodded, and watched as Xenidar exited the room, making his way towards the main commons, his eyes taking in the sights of his home one last time, before he would liberate it from the shadow of SWEEPS.

"I always thought I'd die within these walls, only a few weeks into the job, trying to mount a hasty defense against some power-grabbing warlord," he muttered to himself, but quietly enough that no one could hear. But The Hideout itself could, if it were to listen. And somehow, Xenidar knew that The Hideout was listening. "I never thought I'd end up instead being the longest-serving Keeper in The Hideout's history..."

As he walked towards the front doors that he would exit for the last time, nobody seemed to notice Xenidar as he moved with purpose, as it seemed like just another day where the Keeper would wander the halls to everyone else. Whether others were reading, or lounging around and generally hanging out, or performing regular maintenance and checks, business, by all accounts, seemed as usual. Xenidar wouldn't want to leave The Hideout any other way. Not in ruins of a failed defense, or while basking in the glory of an incredible victory, but while the day looked like any other where the sun would rise and set without incident, because it showed him that the library that he spent his whole life protecting would stand, tall and proud, long after he was gone.

Xenidar Ralkas knew his place in The Hideout's history, and today, all doubt that this history would continue was extinguished. Countless ideas had been sparked within these halls, and countless more awaited their discovery. Ancient puzzles would be solved, new ones would be written, and The Hideout would remain to remember it all.

The doors shunted open as he walked towards them, and no one even saw him leave. His eyes forward, Xenidar's gaze locked upon his quarry: The crater-canyon in which the SWEEPS base had been built. It was never actually settled, which one it was. It might've actually been a lake before the planet dried up, and became mostly dry red rock. Perhaps the next Keeper would live to see the mystery solved.

The two guards at the main gate seemed to be waiting for him.

"About time!" One of the Humans said, but Xenidar knew that there was not a Human consciousness in that body. "We were wondering how long it would take for you to assert over your host! You have inhabited quite a remarkable vessel, you know."

Xenidar looked at one, and then the other. He then thrust out his palms, and blasted a hole in each of their chest with the cannons that were implanted in his palms, before summoning unnatural strength to force the gate open with a single shove. It took a few moments of confusion before alarms began blaring, but by then, Xenidar had already yanked an entrance door off of its hinges and tossed it at a charging guard, entering the base as the Human was crushed by the metal door.

"Commander! Xenidar Ralkas is here!" One of the senior scientists urgently informed Adam Stratfordshire as he burst into the base commander's office.

"Let me guess, he still hasn't succumbed to the Serum? Has some time left, I'd imagine? Is using that time to blow this place to kingdom come before his mind falls to the Ideal Masters?"

"Well..."

"I *warned* you about creating that serum, Doctor Enuz. I *told* you that creating a weapon like that was only going to *anger* the greater powers of the universe, and the Keeper of The Hideout can certainly be counted among those powers!"

"All right! Fine! Lesson learned! Now let's get out of here before he punches the reactor core!"

Adam stood up, and switched on a view of the security feed along the route to the main power core. Sure enough, Xenidar was making his way to it, plowing through guards and turrets like they may as well have been made of toothpicks and balsa wood. He then flipped a switch on a metallic assembly, a point-to-point Quickgate, and motioned for the doctor, the one whose brainchild was the serum that was getting this base destroyed, to stay put.

"Let me make sure the LZ's clear first," Adam explained. Iramenas nodded nervously. Adam stepped through the Quickgate, emerging safely on the other side of Turazin, in an old supply bunker that had been repurposed as a SWEEPS safehouse, and then looked back at the portal to the SWEEPS base that was due for demolition. After a few moments, he cursed the doctor.

"I hope the gods don't make the mistake of showing you mercy!" Adam spat as he drew one of his Archonium revolvers, and fired at the Quickgate assembly on his side, breaking the connection and stranding the architect of both the Dark Serum *and* the Schwarzchild Bomb in the doomed base.

To say that Iramenas Enuz was mortified was an understatement. To say that he was in disbelief that he was doomed to perish in the inferno of the place he created his doomsday weapons within just didn't do it justice, and it certainly would feel to an observer like justice was being served, as horror and fear seized and throttled the mind of one whose career had him with the nickname, the Armorer of Carnage. And now, the Armorer of Carnage's mind seemed to snap in his skull as his heart fell into his intestines, and he could only stand there, shocked and stunned in disbelief that his time was up, that fate had caught up to him.

His face inches from the reactor core of the SWEEPS base, Xenidar Ralkas stared at the beating heart of the bastion of evil that had burdened his world for so long, too long. He knew no fear, he knew no pain, and he knew no anguish. He knew only the serenity of certainty as his right hand began to glow from the charge of raw power coursing through it. Soon, all that would be left to do, was throw a single punch.

"For Turazin."

The ground shook all the way back at The

Hideout, and confused comments were abound. What was that tremor? It couldn't have been natural. This was confirmed by the sighting of a great mushroom cloud forming over the basin where the SWEEPS base once stood.

"The SWEEPS base! It's destroyed!" Someone yelled. "SWEEPS is defeated! Turazin is defended!!"

Celebration cheers filled the air, as the blight that had scarred this world's surface had finally been snuffed out. Though it had been useful for a time to know *where* they had set up shop, and though there was no denying this, everyone knew just as well that someday, that base would have to go down. Or in this case, up, considering the size of the explosion that had just occurred. Radien simply looked at the cloud forming in the wake of their reactor being destroyed, knowing full well what else it meant, and what price had been paid. It wouldn't be long before others began to realize that price as well, as the Keeper was strangely absent, and the lights of The Hideout seemed to be slightly dimmer than usual, as though the very structure understood what was missing from its halls.

As word of Xenidar's sacrifice began to spread, questions followed in their wake as surely as they were expected. Questions that Radien only had some of the answers to, as everyone gathered in the main commons to hear him address and debrief the events of today.

"A great victory was won today, there can be no doubt," Radien began. "The destruction of the SWEEPS base also means the destruction of the abominable weapons it created, and the creators of those weapons now burn forever for their sins against the principles of honor. But the cost of this victory... even I wonder if we have any right to claim this as a victory because of it."

Radien grabbed the medallion that Xenidar gave him, pulling it from his pants pocket and holding it in his left hand, studying its construction and intricate engravings as he continued to speak. "Xenidar denied our foes their victory from the moment their deplorable serum of darkness sealed his fate. He knew from that moment, his days were numbered, and so he chose defiance. SWEEPS, their plans, their scientists and their weapons, are dust in the winds of Turazin's red plains. Our enemy is denied their prize, they are denied The Hideout, and they are denied its Keeper, its Keeper who chose *Kelvaltor*. For these reasons, Xenidar Ralkas did not die in vain. He did not die with a clean sword, and so it can *never* be said he died emptily."

Whispered agreement and nods of affirmation fell across the crowd, there could be no denying what Radien had said of Xenidar's sacrifice.

"As Regent, it now falls to me to find the next Keeper. It may take until long after this war against the Dark Six ends. It may only be a few weeks from now. I don't know, I'm not an orcale. What I *do* know is that we *must* keep fighting, we *must* keep striking blow after blow against their ranks in order to see the day, that new dawn! The Lords of Evil have issued us a challenge in resorting to such deplorable methods! I for one, accept their challenge, and will see every Demon and loyalist burned to ashes around me!"

The crowd was roused with renewed spirits, Xenidar would be no martyr, but he would never be forgotten, and he would be avenged. So long as The

Hideout stood, it would be a bastion of resistance against the Dark Six.

"We will fight on, we will fight fiercely, and we will fight forever! For Xenidar!" He called out, as the glass roof in at the apex of The Hideout's ceiling began to open.

"For Xenidar!" The crowd repeated.

"For Turazin!"

"For Turazin!"

"FOR CYNAR!!"

"FOR CYNAR!!"

Radien's left hand drew itself up his center, and from the palm was fired a deep sapphire-blue beam of The Aura's power, through the opening that had just been made in the building's ceiling. Almost instantly, everyone present at The Hideout did the same, whether by their own power within, or by laser cannons in their arms, or drawing Ion weapons from their hips and firing a shot into the air. The prismatic beam of The Hideout's warriors lit up the night sky, and the plains below them. No SWEEPS base existed to cast its shadow over Turazin, and this beacon in the night was one of defiance, and the oath to never stop fighting.

Radien would order that the Warp Lock was to remain active until the base's ruins were searched, and that it was confirmed that no Schwarzchild Bombs remained on the planet, or a single drop of the Dark Serum. Once this was confirmed, and the Warp Lock was disengaged, a wake was held across The Hideout, as was tradition when a Keeper passed on. The rest of the week was to be spent in light spirits, and imbibing many spirits in celebration of his service as the leader of The Hideout, reflecting on his best moments and most valued contributions to the history of the universe's largest library. This was not a time for mourning the loss of Xenidar Ralkas, but celebrating that he was fulfilled his duty for so long, longer than anyone before him.

"What of Adam?" Ellan eventually asked Radien during the observance. "Do you think he went up in flames with the base?"

Radien shook his head. "I have no doubt that he escaped. He probably had a plan ever since Xenidar engaged the Warp Lock."

"What even *could* he plan?"

Radien thought for a moment. "The Warp Lock stops people from *leaving* Turazin. Point-to-point teleportation *on* Turazin was unaffected. The planet only has three buildings as far as anyone who cares is concerned, all of which are shielded independently from warp-ins. Which leaves the rest of the planet to establish a hiding spot. My guess? Quickgate to a supply bunker that he built himself and told no one of. It's what I would've done."

"It still appalls me that he turned to their service," Ellan grumbled. "A mind like his, valuable enough for the Dark Six to leave intact, and he uses it *for* them instead of *against* them? He will pay for what he has done."

Radien nodded as he raised his glass and drank from it. "I will personally see to it. He even told me that the Schwarzchild Bomb and the Dark Serum weren't his ideas, but instead the brainchild of one Iramenas Enus. But he was only the commander of the base, he could not order anyone to stop developing these weapons, only make sure the turrets worked and that everyone was doing their jobs. If I know him well enough, and quite honestly, I do... I bet you he stranded Iramenas at the base before it blew up, he hated the guy and everything he stood for."

Radien continued to ponder, still confused as to his former friend's choices. "Adam's plan is to be on the winning side of this war, whichever that is..." he pondered aloud. "He would've had to be convinced that the Dark Six would win, but I'm just not seeing it... what did he learn that told him to side with them?"

"Does it really matter?" Ellan scoffed, but more at the idea of Adam's continued existence rather than Radien's curiosity for his motives.

"Not particularly, but I would like to know before I put his head on a pike, for closure's sake."

Radien returned to his drink, glaring at his pint glass between sips, concocting just what he was going to do to Adam Stratfordshire, to the Dark Six, to every single foe on their side, no matter their rank or importance. Pawn or patron, cog or colonel, every single one of them. But despite the quiet rage that seethed in him at the circumstances of Xenidar's demise, Radien somehow knew that this was not the last major blow that would be struck against Cynar, courtesy of the ruinous powers.

Radien pondered his glass of mead. How easily could he have found himself in Adam's place? How easily could he have been the one betraying reason and justice? How close did he come, trapped on a world so wretched on Earth? He breathed in and out, wondering if he could even blame Adam for siding with the only power he could see. Power is power, and if it means control over one's own destiny, no one is immune from allegiance to even the darkest ones.

Even so, it was still undeniable that for his choice, by whichever name he called himself, whether Adam Stratfordshire or Jake Valence, the Human must die.

Elsewhere within The Hideout, a red-scaled Dragon, descendant of the First Defender, wandered the halls and wondered to himself.

"I always meant to visit this place, when I found the time and chance," Crimzin said to himself. "And yet, even though this is the first time I have seen these halls, I feel as though they are emptier than I remember... though I have nothing of these halls to remember?"

He continued to wander down a corridor, shelves filled with tomes and accounts of just about whatever one could think of. "This place cannot be *that* old... can it?"

When he said *that* old, he did not mean in the idea that this place was recently built. He remembered that he once shared the memories of his prior, Ahron Kasven, First of the Defenders, and the only Defender to ever sire offspring. He knew the name of the Darkstar at Tenbork Station, he even *spoke* with Kasven's voice, that the Demon recognized. The Hideout's history didn't span *that* far back... did it?

Crimzin then realized he was in the largest library in the known universe. If there were answers to the strangeness he experienced during the battle of Tenbork, they would be within these shelves.

Encyclopedia of Psionic Phenomena, Vol. 211:

Manifest of Raven's Eye, to Osterkaan's Delirium.

Not quite the one he was looking for.

Encyclopedia of Psionic Phenomena, Vol. 66: Esi X'Tohn (Hajikahl fertility deity), to Extracapability-Related

Maybe this was the one. Extracapability sure *sounded* like what Crimzin suddenly had. Knowledge or experience from beyond his time, that he didn't know, until the moment it was being spoken through his mouth.

"Let's see…" Crimzin processed aloud as he paged through the tome in his hands. "Extrapsionic Synergistic Feat… no, not that. Extramnemonic Hallucination, nope. Extrachronological Knowledge Incursion… that might be it."

He flipped the book to the page.

An Extrachronological Knowledge Incursion is when a Psionically-inclined individual suddenly gains factual information that they had at no point before then possessed, without the context of study or exchange. This can manifest in a number of ways, such as suddenly knowing the name of someone you have never met, or being able to recall a recipe you were never taught. Other names for this phenomena are known as well; to the Cynofrax Vulpians, it is called an Extrahistorical Feat. To the Elurians, it is called an Umbric Infusion. Regardless of the local colloquialism, the pattern remains similar: A person is suddenly imbued with knowledge that they did not previously possess, or had any means to possess, and no conventional method of learning had previously imparted it.

"Like remembering something that your ancestor knew, I wonder?" Crimzin wondered aloud.

"Hellfire, it seems like insanity when I say it aloud..."

"By the gods, do I know *that* feeling," Radien said from a few feet away as he paged through a different volume of the Encyclopedia of Psionic Phenomena. "Something seeming like insanity when said aloud, that is."

"And what do you make of what I find to be?" Crimzin asked, looking over to the Death Worlder.

"I have been to a supposedly cursed planet only to find that the undead warriors upon it were just putting on a show and laughing it up. I've spoken to a Kendrosian spirit aboard a derelict spaceship where a battle in intergalactic space was once fought. I led a resistance against a Primal Draconian who sought to replace the memories of everyone in Cynar... I get the feeling that remembering something that an ancestor once knew seems like a pretty silly place to draw the line," Radien recalled his past. All of it before he was a Death Worlder, the form he was proud to possess rather than that old and rusted Human flesh-prison from before.

"Then again, I remember living too many years in a place where all of that was fiction." Radien then sighed. "Felt like I was stuck in the timeline where all of the good ones weren't real and never would be, and that anything I dreamed up or imagined was banished to the realm of fiction, for the fact that I had thought of it. By making it manifest in my mind's eye, I condemned the fulfillment and decency I longed for to the annals of fantasy, never to break free of the immaterial."

"I've heard the legends of Elder Terra's evil," Crimzin said. "Makes Caltoran torching the stars seem kinda insignificant, now that I think of it. But that was before me. I grew up in a universe that believed itself lost, even though the immediate threat to Cynar was quelled."

"And I grew up unknowing of if there was a universe to speak of at all." Radien remembered that wretched planet as he put the book he held back onto its shelf. "Let alone any chance to be a part of it. I couldn't bring myself to dream, because I found myself believing that dreaming of something banished it to a different timeline, forbidding it from ever being a part of my future."

"I suppose suddenly gaining Ahron Kasven's knowledge of his enemies isn't too far-fetched, then... not to mention speaking in his voice when addressing Saarinthaal."

To this name, Radien's ear twitched as his eyebrows furrowed, he was clearly trying to piece something together from this. "One moment..." He then made his way to a lookup terminal, and began to search through The Hideout's historical accounts database. "Saarinthaal, Terror of the Acid Sea?"

"The very same! How—"

"I saw that name in an account from the First War for Reality. Apparently, Ahron and Saarinthaal were at nemesis levels of rivalry during the First War for Reality. They kept meeting and clashing, but neither could gain a true upper hand on the other... until the battle of Tenbork, apparently."

"Saarinthaal recognized the voice of Ahron as well, addressing me as Kasven, clad in new scales!" Crimzin added. "I guess this confirms that what happened was real, and that I'm not going nuts!"

"Always a good thing to learn, that you're not going nuts," Radien affirmed. "If Kasven's knowledge is yours, Crimzin... that could be invaluable. His knowledge of Demons is why we know that Hunderfold weapons destroy them permanently, and that's only scratching the surface."

"Not only that, but I slew a Darkstar from the First War for Reality. That's no small loss for the Lords of Evil!"

"Today seems to just be getting better... despite the current circumstances."

"It means all is not lost, Radien. Right now, that's all we need to know."

Chapter the Thirteenth
The Battle for Nathineyl

"I wish I could explain why it is a terrible omen, when Demons flee from battle."
—Arch-Militant Darek Jor'Galn, in his report following the battle of Tenbork Station

Explosions rippled across space as attack, counterattack, defense, and last stand all played out at once across the theatre of the void. Ships torn to shreds by cannons and missiles alike, and the defense of the Gravity Well that bound two worlds together was doing all in its power to hold.

Koros-Nathineyl was under attack, and Micah Jorvask of the Eyes of the Daggers was on the front lines, her sword carving through Demonic flesh as her parrying dagger ensured that none could put theirs in her back as she dispatched her foes, endless as they seemed today.

Suddenly, a bolt of azure energy punched a hole

clean through the skull of a Demonic Trooper that was trying to raise its weapon against her, and when her head whipped around to see who had come to her aid, she was glad to fight by his side again.

"When I said we should do this again, but in less dire circumstances, this is *not* what I meant!" Radien commented.

"Wasn't it *me* who said that?" Micah scoffed.

"Fucked if I can remember!"

The two began fighting side by side as they brought each other up to speed as to why there were so many enemies on what should otherwise be a pretty well-held world.

"I've been tracking those Schwarzchild Bombs that escaped Turazin, and was able to extract from a prisoner I took that they were planning to detonate them within the Velani Array! Not sure if they're planning to hit Redaria Prime, Omega, or Laksor, but they only get two since one of them blew up Ultharn!"

"Excuse you, *I* claim the kill on Ultharn with a Pulsar Missile!" Radien retorted. "I fired it *exclusively* so that the Schwarzchild Bomb in that Way Gate *couldn't* take that planet's life for me!"

"Either way, the two that remain are meant for Velani!" Micah reminded of the objective. "But there's no way in all the realms that the Demons can set one cursed foot on either planet without going through Koros-Nathineyl first! So they've got to try to take this one down the hard way, or nothing of theirs is getting within a dozen AU's of the Redarian Core Worlds!"

"How's Koros doing?"

"They're fine! It's Nathineyl they're hitting the

hardest! Here's where all of the Shadow Houses are based!"

"Even so, if the Shadow Houses have any sort of evacuation protocols for saving all of their stuff, I suggest you tell them to get to it, just in case of the worst!"

"I agree! I'll warn the Houses, you make some Demonic heads roll!" Micah ordered.

"I like this plan!" Radien said as he lopped off the head of a Demon with the Borfblade. It subsequently rolled across the ground, just as Micah had ordered Radien to ensure.

At the Citadel of the Sunless Sword, where the Shadow Houses of Nathineyl made their headquarters, several Darkstars were at the sealed gates, doing their best to break through. The defensive cannons that lined the outer structure, hidden in alcoves within the walls barely visible to the enemy were lighting the causeway with white-hot lead, but the Demons had enough bodies to throw at the problem to keep the gunners occupied while the true threat was at the gates.

Three Darkstars versus one Micah. The odds were not in favor of the Demons.

Micah threw the parrying dagger in her off hand to attract the attention of the Darkstars, retracting it back to her hand with the chain attached to the pommels when it was blocked by the quick instincts of one of them.

"Come and fight a Disciple of Shadow, vile scourge!" Micah challenged. "I will show you the meaning of darkness!"

Two of the Darkstars nodded to their comrade in

the middle, who scoffed as he twirled his staff, intending to duel the Redarian before him. Micah chuckled at the foolishness of facing her alone, but wasn't about to stop him from trying. After easily and skillfully evading a leaping attack from the Demon's staff, Micah then cleaved through the bolts of energy that followed with her longsword, before her parrying dagger caused another thrust from the staff to miss her face, which she took full advantage of, keeping her weapon binding the staff and closing the distance, until she finally had the change to plunge her sword into the chest of this Darkstar.

The footsteps of the staff-wielding Demon's comrades could be heard by Micah's trained ears rushing towards her. The first to reach her yelled curses as it swung its blade, but to the horror of Micah's foes, the blade passed cleanly through the Shadow Clone that had been left in place of the Redarian assassin, and subsequently, clean through the throat of the wounded Darkstar, sealing its fate.

As the corpse of the staff-wielder hit the floor, its head rolling down the steps of the Citadel of the Sunless Sword, A dozen Redarians bearing the exact same appearance all took up stances around the Demons at the gate.

"Fol'Zath! Which one of them is real?!" One of the Darkstars cursed.

"Tower of Arcane Might, forgive me..." the other begged of its fallen compatriot.

The blitz of blades that followed saw the remaining Darkstars in pieces.

Micah then sheathed her weapons, catching a

quick breather, before entering the Citadel via a hidden entrance in the wall thirty feet away from the gate itself, that itself was a deception. Nothing but solid stone and metal wall was behind it. The true entrance was hidden, but this place was Micah's home on Nathineyl, and she knew it well.

"Disciple of Shadow Jorvask!" One of the Masters of Shadow greeted as soon as he saw her. "Impressive use of the Shadow Simulacrums and Blade Blitz techniques!"

"I had a good teacher, Master Gerostus," Micah greeted her Sensei with levity. "Major Radien of the RADM recommends that preemptive evacuations begin, as well as the Preservation Protocols, just in case. With two Schwarzchild Bombs somewhere in the system, anything's possible."

"More than you might think, Disciple. Matriarch Vedens has already ordered it. Enemy sappers are hitting the Gravity Channel hard, and though Koros is seeing far less enemy activity by comparison, we may need to evacuate and consolidate for an attrition campaign."

Micah nodded as she approached a console. "Matriarch Vedens of the Jade Petrifiers has always possessed the gift of foresight."

"What are you looking for?" Gerostus asked as his pupil used the console to initiate a planet-wide scan.

"Osmium," Micah explained. "Radien briefed me on the construction of the Schwarzchild Bomb, it uses a sizable amount of it. If one of the bombs is anywhere on either planet, we can find out where. Neither Koros or Nathineyl have deposits of it enough to meet the demand of the bomb's construction."

Suddenly, the ground shook, both Micah and Gerostus knowing what it meant.

"Son of a bitch!" Micah cursed. "The bastards severed the Link!"

The Gravity Channel that kept the binary system of Koros-Nathineyl intertwined had been severed by dark means. Micah pressed another few buttons, and a holographic map of Nathineyl showed, surrounded by a barrier that was not put up by the planet's defenses.

"A Prismatic Shield!" Gerostus observed. "A thousand eternities of torment upon these foes!"

The comm-link in Micah's pocket buzzed, and a voice came through.

"Micah! They just put a Prismatic Shield around the whole planet, I'll see what I can do about breaching a segment of it to allow warp-outs, but as it stands, we're cut off except for stationary Way Gates! The upside is that almost every Demon committed to this takeover is on Nathineyl, and they're locked in here as well!" Radien informed.

"He's a quick one," Gerostus commented.

Micah nodded before speaking back into the comm-link. "We've already ordered Preservation Protocols, so right now your priority is getting everyone off the planet! I'm sending you the location of hidden Way Gates for evacuation, they'll be able to bypass the Prismatic Shield! Let planetside batteries worry about breaching it, focus on securing the Way Gates!"

"Aye! I've got the locations!"

"What else needs to be done here?" Micah asked Gerostus.

"The Litany of Shadow must be retrieved and

evacuated," Gerostus informed.

"I'm on it! Can you secure the Grand Record of Deeds?"

"It would be my privilege! Shadows fight beside you, Disciple Jorvask!"

"Shadows fight beside you, Master Gerostus!"

The two Redarians went their separate ways to secure two equally significant artifacts of the Shadow Houses. If the Litany of Shadow and the Grand Record of Deeds were secured, the Shadow Houses could be rebuilt, even if Nathineyl were to fall.

Even so, the Litany of Shadow was in danger. So too was the Grand Record of Deeds. Micah knew that the Redarian who taught her all she knew could secure the latter objective, and so it fell to her to ensure the preservation of the Shadow houses, and to this end, she would fell any enemy that stood in her way.

The shadows as her ally, Micah Jorvask's blades knew no falter, and the Demons who thought they stalked the night found themselves instead hunted by one who knew the darkness in ways they could never dream of.

But this did not mean Micah would restrain herself to merely hiding behind corners and sticking a knife in the ear of any Demon who passed by her, no, Micah was a *fighter* in the shade, and so she *fought*.

Squadrons of troopers were carved asunder by the blitz of blades, longsword and dagger in a symphony of parries and ripostes, and acrobatic tumbles by the Redarian Disciple of Shadow that meant no foe could keep track of her, let alone land a hit on her.

Between her and the Litany of Shadow was a

Darkstar, poised to claim the annals of the techniques and tactics of the Nathineyl Shadow Houses, and Micah would be damned before she would let the Demon wrap its claws around this dictionary of death that was everything her life among assassins taught her, and what she still had yet to learn.

Micah Jorvask would not duel merely for the possession of a book that was the center of a planet-wide martial order, she would duel for the future of Nathineyl's warriors, for Nathineyl's very identity.

"I am Darkstar Vazhnorvax, the Hatred of—"

"*I don't give a fuck who you are!!*" Micah interrupted with a leaping stab from her longsword, which the Demon barely was able to raise his shield to block in time. It immediately afterwards had to block a low swipe from Micah's dagger, followed by an additional slice at its legs again, as the Redarian tumbled and rolled across the ground, lashing out with cuts from her blades at the lower half of Darkstar Vazhnorvax, the Hatred of Kendrosium. This foul creature was on the front lines when Kendrossos fell, the walls that protected the once-proud species destroyed by a corrupted Ninth Defender.

This would not sway Micah in the slightest, as her assault continued on a Demon whose fame and skill would otherwise intimidate an entire battalion into quivering in their boots. Micah, however, knew no such intimidation. She was not one who could be intimidated, not by even the fiercest and most skilled of opponents.

Vazhnorvax soon went on the offensive once he noticed a pause in Micah's attack, and now the Redarian was on the defensive, her swords and kinesthetic maneuvering managing to avoid every jab from her foe's weapon, to his frustration. A spear in one hand and a shield in the other, Vazhnorvax conserved his energy as best he could, but there were only so many ways and angles that a spear can thrust. Then again, one only needed so many ways to win a battle, and the match was proving quite even between the two fighters, evinced by how Micah defended herself from Vazhnorax's Hundred-Thrust-Second technique.

Vazhnorvax's spear soon was caught in a trap from Micah's longsword and parrying dagger, and merely yanking back on the weapon wasn't going to set it free, as Micah began closing the distance. In desperation, the Darkstar she fought dropped its spear and pushed forward with its shield, trying to surprise rush his opponent. Though the bronze-colored disc slammed against Micah's face, the gambit was not without its trade. Micah stumbled back, recovering her footing and stance, and flicking the blood off her nose. But her dagger was covered in Demon's blood, that had managed to sneak its strike in during the sudden offensive.

Micah struck a new stance. Vazhnorvax did the same. The two moved in on each other again, the Darkstar retrieving its weapon to begin the assault anew. But the thrust that was aimed for Micah's chest hit nothing but air as she dropped to her knees and slid across the tile floor, her back nearly to it with the acrobatic bend, past Vazhnorvax's shield, and her sword that was held out, though it did not completely carve cleanly her foe's leg. Instead, the longsword embedded itself into the shin plates that armored Vazhnorvax, digging deep through the metal and halfway into the Demon's shin bone.

Vazhnorvax yelled out in anger and pain, trying to kick his foot out to throw the Redarian and her sword off of him. Micah held on, and as the Hatred of Kendrosium's leg retracted, she hit the other one with her dagger, sliding between his legs and a few feet away. Digging her claws into the ground, Micah then righted herself.

Vazhnorvax cursed as his legs started to lose function with the sheer damage caused, that he would now need to use Psionic power to heal, lest he risk losing them entirely. But the wound in his side from earlier was taking its toll, he could not simultaneously retreat from the encroaching Redarian, whilst healing his wounds, and staving off her attack.

He didn't have time to even decide which to attempt first as the side of Micah's foot slammed into the invader's chest, denting the cuirass well into its sternum with the strength of a Redarian scorned. Vazhnorvax could not hold onto his armaments from the sheer force of the blow, and dropped his spear and shield.

Micah ducked under the desperate haymaker that followed, yanking her sword out from Vazhnorvax's leg, to the Demon's yell.

"*This* belongs to me!" Micah yelled back once the blade was forcibly pulled from the wound it caused. She then grabbed the dagger, and yanked it out too. "*This* belongs to my uncle!"

With Vazhnorvax on his knees, Micah then jammed the blades into his shoulders, through the plating that could not stand the pierce of Redarian Gigasteel. Micah then grabbed the Litany of Shadow from its pedestal, and held it before her defeated foe.

"*This* belongs to the Shadow Houses of Nathineyl!"

She then smacked Vazhnorvax across the face with the book, before placing it back on its pedestal. The two blades embedded in the Demon were yanked out once again. Micah then produced a blade from the strap on her thigh that sheathed it.

"*This,* however, I'll let you keep."

The hundred-folded blade then sank into Vazhnorvax's skull, and the Darkstar slumped over, before vanishing in a disintegration of red sparks. The weapon vaporized as well.

With the Litany of Shadow in hand, Micah made her way towards one of the Way Gates that was slowly but surely progressing evacuation efforts. With a Prismatic Shield locking off the planet from warp-outs, and the Gravity Funnel that connected the sister worlds of Koros and Nathineyl disabled, it was a necessary measure. The planet could not be considered lost by any means, but it was likely that Koros-Nathineyl would inevitably cease to be a binary system with the Gravity Funnel severed.

"Master Gerostus!" Micah called out once she saw her mentor. "You have the Grand Record of Deeds, too. I assume the Demons didn't give you too much trouble?"

"Nothing I couldn't handle!"

"Same here. Can I entrust you to take the Litany of Shadow through the gate with the Grand Record?"

"That you can, so long as you save some foes for me when I return!"

Micah handed the book to Gerostus, who soon went through the Way Gate to Laksor. The books were under his protection, but Micah trusted no one more than Gerostus to keep them safe until a new place for them could be found, or reclaimed.

"Micah, Jarrek's got the Spear of Velani working on punching a hole through the Prismatic Shield so they can do warp-outs, but I think—"

Radien was suddenly interrupted by the ground shaking most violently, both where he stood, and Micah felt the tremor as well.

"Was that a planet-wide tremor?"

"How many of the bombs originally escaped Turazin, was it?" Micah realized aloud.

"Three! One of them is already gone after Ultharn, but why would they use one of their remaining two here?!"

"Because they're starting to lose here, damn it!" Micah cursed. "Tell Jarrek to drill that shield with everything his ship's got, and start mass warp-outs! Tear chunks out of the ground if he has to!"

"On it! Hey, you two! Stop beating that corpse and get the fuck off the planet!!"

The ground shook again. Nathineyl's time was running out. Micah seethed as she knew why the Schwarzchild Bomb was being activated here. With two bombs, they could target Redaria Prime and Redaria Omega. Or Redaria Omega and Laksor. Targets far more valuable that such a weapon should be used for, but someone, somewhere along the enemy's chain of command had decided that Nathineyl wasn't allowed to get the victory it was poised to earn. A scorched earth tactic so literal, there wouldn't be much of this earth left to speak of.

The tremors were getting stronger and stronger as another loud noise was heard outside of the Transit Nexus people were evacuating through. The Prismatic Beam of the *Spear of Velani* had pierced through the shield that was locking Nathineyl in on itself, and could start warping people out en masse. It wouldn't be enough, though. There wasn't enough time to get everyone out.

The ground began to crack beneath Micah's feet as she ran outside, throwing a knife at one of the Demons who was just standing there, awaiting its fate, with no care of being sacrificed to spite the Redarians of Nathineyl. She barely had enough time to watch the blade embed itself in the Demon's head before being warped off of the planet, and onto the Redarian flagship.

From orbit, Micah could only bear witness as the planet below cracked and blew apart from south to north, chunks flying off bit by bit into space as Koros's Planetary Defense Grid bore the brunt of the debris, slowly being ejected from the binary orbit it once shared with its sister world.

Radien was soon aboard the *Spear of Velani* as well, with a group of survivors he had managed to take with him, but Nathineyl's fate was sealed from the moment the Schwarzchild Bomb finished arming itself.

The very core of the world seemed to detonate once the explosion's wave reached the equator of Nathineyl, tearing the entire world and all of its history asunder.

To say that Micah was enraged could not do it justice. There were no words in any tongue to describe the hatred that coursed through her as she screamed curses and tore a practice dummy to shreds with her claws.

"They *knew* they couldn't have it! So they fucking blow it up, the *Glaeth-va Pollthast Rhinivath Keene!!*"

There was barely a translation for the curses she spewed as her claws made quick work of the dummy that she was tearing to pieces like she would the architect of such a dishonorable end to the battle. Two different words for paramount cowardice, a word that meant 'a brat when compared to brats,' and a fiery insult at the expense of its recipient's honor, or lack thereof, rather.

With little left of the dummy, Micah stormed off and ordered one of the nearby Redarians to find her a bottle of *Sathentha,* a potent brandy from Laksor.

The survivors that Radien had warped aboard the *Spear of Velani* with, grateful as they were to have survived the battle, knew that the cost was too high.

Too high for both sides, perhaps. The Demons had just wasted one of their planet-killers on a move of spite. Perhaps they didn't know that the number of bombs they had was known, and were trying to bluff the amount, willing to use an entire one on the planet that acted as a buffer between the three major planets of the inner Velani Array and the rest of the universe. Perhaps they had grown so tired of losing battle after battle, that they just wanted *some* form of victory, even if so wasteful of manpower and resources.

Nobody won Nathineyl. The Demons wanted to, but couldn't, and so they chose to make sure nobody could. Honor itself had died today.

Epilogue

How many oaths of vengeance have been sworn today?

As Micah placed her arm into the machine to hold it still, she prepared for the freezing cold that would soon be pressed onto her bare shoulder.

My home is dust, because my enemies are sore losers.

Her other arm rested at her side as she braced herself for the responsibility she was about to take.

Of the Nathineyl Redarians, which once numbered billions, I am one of less than nine thousand that remain.

The Freeze-Burn tattoo machine first used its programmed precision to shave a small patch of fur on her shoulder in the shape of a symbol. Or at least, half of a symbol. The first half of it, that would be bestowed upon her now.

Though the essence of my people is preserved in the Litany of Shadow, the Grand Record of Deeds, and the digitized model of the Citadel of the Sunless Sword... too much was lost, lost forever to the contempt of the Dark Six.

The freezing cold of the machine pressed against the now-exposed skin, though Micah did not groan. She made no pained noise at all, her emotions as cold as the machine that pressed the first half of the symbol upon her.

What little of Nathineyl remains, however, we have agreed that this formal burden is mine.

The machine then sprayed a mixture of chemicals onto the shaven patch to rapidly regrow the fur that was on it, so that Micah wouldn't have to wait for long to see if the process worked.

I suppose the advantage to there being so few of us, is that it takes a lot less time for us all to decide something.

There wasn't any real doubt of the process being successful, it was a trivial one. The white, discolored fur that regrew on Micah's right shoulder was in the shape of an incomplete symbol. But this was the custom of a Redarian Oath of Retribution. One half when the Oath is sworn, the second when it is complete.

Until the murderer of Nathineyl is dead, until the architect of this genocide draws his last breath at the point of my blades, I will never stop hunting.

How she knew that the one who armed the bomb after placing it was still alive, she wished she could explain. Somehow, though, intuition told her that the Demon with Nathineyl's blood on its hands found some way to flee the planet after arming the Schwarzchild Bomb. Intuition, that when paired with one's own wielding of the cosmic powers that be, had yet to be wrong.

This, I vow, a Redarian Oath of Retribution.

Once she had put her shirt back on, Micah exited the chamber, returning to the bridge of the *Spear of Velani.*

"Eight thousand twenty-six," Jarrek informed. Micah nodded. "The Demons have made a mistake today."

"Don't I know it," Micah responded.

"They didn't just disgrace themselves and ignite countless vengeful fires," Jarrek explained. "They wasted one of only two Schwarzchild Bombs they have left. Redaria Prime, Redaria Omega, Laksor. All three of them are way more valuable as targets of planetary destruction. Not to decry Nathineyl…"

"I understand what you mean. Go on."

"Now they have to choose only one to go after. They no longer get to destroy both Redarian core worlds, or one of them and the Laksorian homeworld. They have to choose only one."

"Which one will they go for?"

"Redaria Omega," Jarrek said. "If I were The Tactician, I'd want to destroy the highest-value planet I could with that last bomb. Redaria Prime may be the capitol, but Redaria Omega has the Harrows of the Red Sun."

"How could they do it, though?" Radien asked as he made his way over. "The entire solar system is on maximum alert, the callous use of the bomb on Nathineyl is going to galvanize entire galaxies against the Demons… they can't try to land a small force on the planet, it'll get caught in a second. They can't try to overwhelm Redaria Omega's defenses… can they?"

Jarrek shrugged. "Today showed they have the bodies to spare, even if not the weapons. They probably can afford to send billions of Demons to Redaria Omega to eventually break through, seize the planet, and then destroy it with the Bomb. And I hope they do, honestly."

"Because you have a plan for that?" Micah asked.

"Because I have a plan for that, yes," Jarrek responded. "Gradually evacuate all non-combatants, quietly move all the important stuff so that they can't figure out we know they're coming... let as many onto the planet as they can cram... and then, Shakuras Maneuver."

Radien's ears perked up with alarm. "The universe has just lost a whole planet of the Velani Array, and you speak of planning to make that number two?!"

"If Redaria Omega is the target, the planet is dead already, Radien! So if that world's going up in flames whether we like it or not, *I'm* going to make its death on *my* terms, and I'm going to make the Demons *pay* for every inch they take, and it won't even be worth it for them in the end! Planet for planet, spite for spite! I will *bleed* the Dark Six on that world, and I will bleed them more blood than they can spare!"

Radien knew that Jarrek was right. If The Tactician truly planned to destroy Redaria Omega in order to see the Harrows of the Red Sun destroyed, it would happen. This way, they could at least control the circumstances. They could get everyone who wanted off, off. They could get everything that needed to be preserved off as well.

"We've got to evacuate the planet quietly, though," Jarrek said as his ears flattened. "Too quick, and the Demons know we know their plans. Micah?"

"Yes?"

"If you can, I'd like you to verify that this *is* The

Tactician's plan, going for Redaria Omega."

"I... need a few days before I can begin, but if you give me that time, I can do it."

Jarrek nodded. "I'll see what can be done in the meantime. As likely as it is that this *is* his game, it's still possible they may back off of the Velani Array to try to plant the bomb on Caren'Das or something."

A few moments later, Jarrek reconsidered his order.

"Actually... Disciple of Shadow?"

"Yes, Arch-Militant?"

"Your orders have changed. Find the son of a bitch who armed that bomb. Make him suffer. Fulfill that Oath of Retribution I know you've taken."

Micah nodded. *"That,* I can do. I recommend Master of Shadows Gerostus be assigned to verify that Redaria Omega is the next target."

Jarrek nodded. It was most likely that the target was still in the Velani Array, even if not Redaria Omega. Koros-Nathineyl had been effectively neutralized, with all efforts being focused upon stabilizing Koros's orbit with Gravity Satellites, and Nathineyl having nothing left of it, the buffer worlds that acted as the first line of defense for the solar system were gone.

"Vice-Admiral Enzhok, get the Dyson Swarm activated in Shield Configuration," Jarrek ordered, to a respondent aye. "Much as I know the bastards are just gonna open rifts, I still don't want one of those Battle Barges they have hiding in intergalactic space to back-punch us while we're this vulnerable."

"How many Battle Barges are left, anyway?"

"Four hundred seventy-two is the number from

the end of the First War, and of that, about half were destroyed between then and now, plus one at Fortem Terra Nova some time back."

What more could be done in the face of such a vile display from the enemy, but plan for their next? There would be time to mourn Nathineyl, but it was not now, while the greater threat still loomed. The sapper of Nathineyl had to be found, and justice exacted. Redaria Omega needed to begin its shadowy evacuations, in preparation to try to bleed the Dark Six with every inch of the planet's land before its demise. There were still countless battles to be fought, countless objectives to be completed and every skirmish they all entailed.

As they sharpened their weapons and tightened the straps on their armors, seven warriors understood in their very souls that they would be more than vengeance.

They would be doom.

ABOUT THE AUTHOR

GREGOR FJELLREV is an author, musician, actor, martial artist, woodworker, strategy game enthusiast and black hole of carbonated, fermented and distilled beverages alike from Auburn, Washington. Among the greatest compliments he ever received was when a US Air Force recruit told him his beard at the time made him look like a Cavalry Officer from the American Civil War (Union, obviously).